The Christmas Tree and Other Christmas Stories

Tales for a Christmas Evening

Paul John Hausleben

Cover design and concept by Paul John Hausleben
All photographs by Paul John Hausleben
Interior illustrations by Jan Gillespie

ISBN: 978-0-9886336-4-3

DEDICATIONS

The Christmas Tree

To the old man and everyone that ever owned, or who rode in a 1964 Putter Classic model 200

The Collector

To Heather Claire who always wanted to read my serious side

The Watchman

To those poor souls who may have forgotten the magic of hearing the ringing of church bells on Christmas morning

Cats Do Not Have Calendars

To Pussface the cat wherever you are now

A Simple Gift

To everyone who has ever received that one special Christmas gift that lasted a lifetime

This is a work of fiction. Names, characters, businesses, places, events and incidents either are the product of the author's eccentric, strange and unusual imagination or used in a fictitious manner. Any resemblance to actual persons, living or dead or actual events is purely coincidental, and was not the intention of the author.

CONTENTS

The Christmas Tree

Featuring the old man and other characters from the Adventures of Harry and Paul

The Collector

Featuring Paul John Henson and Binky Hobnobber Henson from the Adventures of Harry and Paul

The Watchman

Featuring Walter P. Thrump

Cats Do Not Have Calendars

A short story featuring the old man, Pussface the cat and other characters from the Adventures of Harry and Paul

A Simple Gift

A short story featuring Paul John Henson and Binky Hobnobber Henson
from the Adventures of Harry and Paul

"Dreams, especially at Christmas time, do not cost anything. So, dream as big as you can, for as long as you want, whenever you want."

Paul John Hausleben

24 December 2012

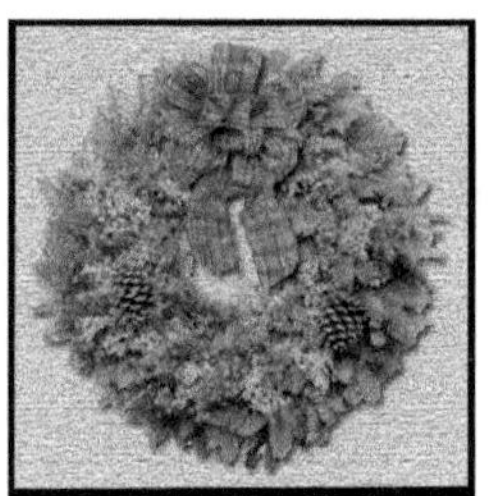

ACKNOWLEDGMENTS

Thank you to the old man who taught us all to keep Christmas in our mind and hearts forever. I need to extend a special thank you to Mr. Steven Michael McMillan, Harry M. Rogers Jr., Lydia A. LaGalla, Jan Gillespie, the giant guy who sold Christmas trees on Chamberlain Avenue in Paterson, New Jersey, and all the other folks who provided endless inspiration towards this book. I would also like to say, TNX K2ORS DE WA2ASQ. You wrote the ultimate story for Christmas, which inspires all of us who dabble in humor and memories to try in vain and hapless attempts to equal, or even in our wildest dreams and efforts to attempt to surpass. 73, Shep. DI DI DI DAH DI DAH.

Foreword

By

Steven Michael McMillan

I am sure that you have had many memories over the years about happenings or big events that revolve around that time frame from ohhhh sayyy . . . October 1st through January. Yep! The holiday season!

I know I do!

My story is also about a large sled, my sister, what looked to have been the side of a mountain and a large body of water! My name is Steve Creakster in certain circles, and my good friend Paul asked me to write this foreword for him.

It is my honor to do so. . ..

Anyway, enough about me.

Paul and I have only known each other for a handful of years. My wife introduced me to him. They work together at taking over the world day by day. We quickly formed a bond. Not sure what kind of bond, but a bond nonetheless. I am a musician and play many instruments, even doing a bit of recording here at the house, and Paul listens to music and plays with a large radio. We have much in common.

One does not need to know Paul long to be swept into one or many of his life's stories and feel as if you grew up with him on that same city block. Truth be told, I don't think I have personally met a better storyteller than this man.

Paul knows that I am a sucker for the holidays. I love this time of year. I don't know why, I just do. Maybe it is because of all the craziness that entangles us throughout this time of year.

Who doesn't like to sit down and watch one of those old classic movies or listen to the greatest holiday music (yes . . . Elvis) of all time?

If you don't, I assure you that by the time you have finished reading this book, you will. Paul has captured the true essence of what this time of year really means, whether it is funny, loving, warm, serious, or even sad.

You, the reader, will be shooting a warm thank you to Paul for opening this opportunity for you to travel down your own holiday memory lane. You, like me, will be amazed at what stories you can conjure up from holidays past!

This matters! It really does!

It's important to keep a hold on those good old times and new ones and allow ourselves to really be in the holiday magic.

This time of the year, it becomes so easy to be swept up in what the talking heads (not the band) suggest we feel and do, that's just not real. Take a little while and sink back into what is real to that feeling of connection and love, humbled with gratitude.

Enjoy,

Steven Michael McMillan

Friend

Preface

Christmas is without any doubt a special time of the year. Whether you agree with the celebration of the holiday, or the origins, one can never doubt the overall impact of Christmas on all of our lives.

For different people, it has a varied and diverse impact these days. For some, it invokes strong religious overtones, and is a time for worship and church services. For other people, it is all about holiday merry making, families gathering for a once-a-year meeting and celebration, spending money that they do not have, giving gifts that are soon forgotten, and taking days off from work to just relax, eat, enjoy sports on the television, and drink too much.

Nowadays, for me, Christmas is about quiet times, fires at midnight on Christmas Eve, music, and memories. In my heart that is what the holiday brings to me most of all. I tend these days to keep Christmas in an introspective place within my heart and mind and not go overboard with the celebration.

I do, however, enjoy the holiday, and I thought that I would enjoy putting together some Christmas stories for another seasonal compilation.

Of the many stories that I have written, one of my personal favorites is, "*The Time Bomb in The Cupboard*." That particular story has a Christmas setting, and some special meanings to me, but I felt there might be just a few more Christmas stories stashed away in the deep recesses of my own cupboards.

Keeping that in mind, I decided to resurrect two old stories that I actually wrote in the early to mid-1970s and to include them within this anthology.

"*The Christmas Tree*" was actually the first story that I ever wrote, and "*The Collector*" was the second one that I ever put an actual pen to.

Yes, I used a real pen back then!

I thought it would be a fun project to update them, add some new characters, keep some old ones, and bring them back to life in a very roundabout manner. I then added a new story or two (or more) at the end of this compilation to round out the mix.

One of the newer stories, I actually wrote on a blazing hot and humid summer day; not exactly the ideal time to compose Christmas stories! I am continually amazed at the strange times when inspiration decides to pay a visit to me. The other novelette, I wrote on a Christmas Eve, and finished it before the stroke of midnight on Christmas Day. Now that makes much more sense!

I hope that whatever time of the season that you are reading these stories, be it during the Christmas season, or just any old time of the year that you enjoy them. Perhaps, they will invoke your own memories, and it is my humble wish that you have a wonderful time, full of joy, as you continue on life's journey at Christmas time or at any time. I pray that your own memories are merry, and they are yours to keep not only at Christmas time but also close to your heart at all times.

I hope you enjoy reading these stories as much as I have enjoyed putting this collection together.

Thank you for reading them.

Paul John Hausleben

04 November 2013

Prologue

Christmas, wonderful, exhausting, glorious, Christmas.

It may be that one time of the year, when you stop and take a deep breath to see exactly where you are. Sometimes, when you do stop, it is an overwhelming situation, and you feel as if you should run and hide until the holiday passes!

It might be that you find yourself tangled up in wrapping paper, dealing with bills to pay, staring at a tray of burnt Christmas cookies, planning visits to annoying relatives that you wish you did not have to see, and fretting over some deadlines that you cannot possibly meet.

Oh no! Only three weeks left to prepare until Christmas!

The preparation is underway. Let the madness begin! The endless Christmas music piped in the stores makes your ears ache! One more, jingly bell and you may lose your mind! Do we really have to go to that company party this year? The boss tells the same old jokes and besides; he has really bad breath, always becomes drunk and sloppy, and wears a cheap hairpiece.

Hidden underneath all of this hustle and bustle, is one undeniable fact about Christmas; of all the times of the year, not any other holiday invokes the memories, emotions, and attention, as does Christmas.

It wraps them all up in one tidy, wonderfully, wrapped Christmas present that includes, money we do not have, reunions, memories, loved ones, laughter, wonder, hope, peace, joy, loneliness, sorrow, the promise of a savior for all of mankind, the dreams and wishes of children and older folks too.

Be sure that you wrap all the good things and some more in your own Christmas present and place it under your tree. Indeed, it is a magical time. All of this wrapped up in one tidy, wonderfully wrapped present that thankfully arrives only once a year.

Christmas, wonderful, exhausting, glorious, Christmas.

The Christmas Tree

Chapter One

A Traditional Christmas

A few days before Christmas, I pulled my old wreck of a jeep into the Foodworld shopping center. I swear that I have had this old jeep forever, I really have.

Someday, I will finally sell it or just junk it, but when I do, it will feel as if a part of my soul will go with it. I am, in many ways, not unlike my own father, who held on forever to a 1964 Putter Classic model 200 automobile, until the floorboards rusted out, the wheels rolled off, and the fenders fell off. Only then did he finally concede that after thirty years, it was time for something new.

I think it is a Henson family tradition to hold on to these old wrecks until the bitter end.

I stop quite often at this same shopping center. In fact, in all honesty, it seems as if I am here every day. My wife sends me on missions quite often to pick up food supplies from Foodworld for whatever culinary delight she happens to be working on at the moment.

Today, my dear wife, Binky, had given me a list of items to pick up for one of her famous cooking exploits that she whips up at this time of year. Since she is such a fantastic cook, I would be smart not to argue, and I happily agreed to picking up a few supplies that she had requested.

I waited before shutting the ignition off on the jeep until the song that had been playing on the radio ended. It was a good song, and I wanted to enjoy it from the beginning to the end. This was a tune from the golden age of Christmas music in the 1950s named, "The Christmas Tree," by an English songwriter and bandleader. It was a song always featured on the old A.M., "easy listening" radio station in my home City of Paterson, which played Christmas music in the weeks before Christmas.

I always enjoyed hearing it at this time of year because it reminded me of my old man because it was a Christmas song that he particularly enjoyed. A flashback popped into my mind, as I could hear him whistling the melody once again in the old house at 182 Belmont Avenue in Haledon, New Jersey.

The tune turned out to be a perfect prelude for an afternoon of holiday shopping, only a few weeks before Christmas. The song ended, and I turned the key to the off position. I reached for my hat, opened the car door, and stepped out into the parking lot.

I really made every effort these days to not go out on a shopping mission, wearing my traditional pastor's collar and suit, but since I was stopping here on my way home from work, I had no real choice. It was just that sometimes, wearing the "uniform" of my profession in public caused too many questions and stares.

Please do not misinterpret this apprehension, to be a display of my unwillingness to assist strangers with pastoral questions; it is just that sometimes, I needed to make haste, as my English mum would say.

I zipped my overcoat up so someone could not see my pastor's collar and suit, and with my long hair, mustache, beard, and hippie appearance, the last profession that folks would guess my employment to be would be a Lutheran clergyman. My intention was to jump into the Foodworld here, pick up a few things, and then quickly head straight home.

I was planning not to linger.

It had become quite a bit colder now, as it was later in the afternoon, and the hustle and bustle of the season was in full flight. While I turned to walk to the front doors of the stores, my eyes caught a section of the parking lot where real, cut Christmas trees were on sale. It was a typical display, with trees lined up along temporary wooden frames and light bulbs strung by old wires for when darkness came. It was a scene repeated all over town at this time of year. Even from where I was standing, I could read the sign next to the display, "Annual Bears Club Christmas tree sale."

It must have been the combination of the song on the radio and seeing the display of trees for sale, but I found my mind wandering back in time. Back to a time, when my sister and I decided that, a real Christmas tree was the ultimate goal for our yearly celebration, and the adventures and pain in which we put our father through, as he pursued the perfect tree to fulfill our request.

At the same time, the old man also found the special Christmas spirit that he had lost so long ago.

In life, sometimes, the simplest things are the hardest to obtain.

The old man loved Christmas. It was by far his favorite of all the holidays. The old man would go on and on, telling my sister and me about how Christmas was years ago, in his house when he was around our age. My sister was about thirteen years old and I was around ten or so, when the old man really started preaching to us about how, "All this money and commercialism," has destroyed and ruined the traditional Christmas celebrations that he used to have when he was a kid.

"Christmas nowadays, is nothing like when I was a kid," the old man would preach fervently as soon as December arrived on the calendar. "It is all about money, money, money, and selling you more junk made in some foreign land that you use one day and stick in a box somewhere. The only reason, the person gave you the crummy gift in the first place, was just to say they gave you something! It is stupid. You have to be careful about preserving traditions and not become conned into buying this and buying that. It is all about ripping you off and selling you stuff you do not need or want."

You could feel the passion of the old man when he spoke. He certainly was very convincing!

It was a common lament from the old man this time of the year, and the closer that Christmas came, the more intense the old man would harp on it. The true spirit of Christmas had been lost long ago, according to the old man. The old man would tell us about the wonderful holidays they had right after the Great Depression. According to the old man, despite the hard times and not having any money, those Christmas celebrations were the best because it was all about families and traditions. People made do with what they had, he carefully and patiently explained to us.

My sister and I would listen to his stories intently. The old man was a very passionate speaker and he could captivate you with his stories and speeches. His arms would wave over his head like a madman, and his eyes would dart back and forth in his head as he studied the body language of us dopey, little kids for any slight movement that we did not believe his words.

He then would move, or change the story on a dime, and the changes in his voice inflections alone, had you convinced that the old man had come face-to-face with Santa Claus many times on Christmas Eve!

One of the main elements of the old man and the key to his Christmas season celebrations were these incredible, intricate rules and regulations that he strictly attached to the season for all of us to follow.

Our dad was very fervent in his defense of these rules and he would easily frighten us into following them by warning, "You will ruin Christmas, and have to wait a whole year for another Christmas to come around," whenever one of us tried to circumvent one of his many rules.

It was so powerful a message that you sometimes felt as if you should hide in terror under your bed in fear of ruining the entire Christmas season.

The number one rule to follow, and the one rule that he strictly enforced above all the others, was that the Christmas season could not begin until after Thanksgiving. In fact, the old man really did not kick into full Christmas mode until about two weeks before the big day. This was hard for us as little kids, because we would go to the stores in early November, and see that all the Christmas trees were already on display, and the sign at the Santa Claus display would report; "Santa will be here soon. He is feeding his reindeer."

The old man's sad tale of woe always included a long diatribe that detailed the woes and pitfalls of the early Christmas celebrations, and the outright breaking or ignoring, of his Thanksgiving rule.

On and on, he would rant, about how we bypass Thanksgiving now, and the day after Thanksgiving sales whip people into a frenzy of spending money they do not have.

He would sit in his favorite living room chair and complain as he read the latest sales flyer in the newspaper a week before Thanksgiving, which was advertising, "Day after Thanksgiving sales." There was no such thing as "Black Friday" back then. He would say, "Whoever heard of such a thing, what a bunch of whooey that is! Thanksgiving is not even here yet."

He would then ramble on with evidence and testimonies of how people dash out with their bellies full of turkey and stuffing, in order to grab up more junk they do not actually need.

He really took the "holiday creep" very seriously!

The other thing that set him off was when stores or radio stations started playing Christmas music in September. Now, the old man loved music, and he was very fond of Christmas music, but when the music played early in the season, it fired him up!

"Geez . . . it is only Labor Day," the old man would complain, as we walked in the department store and we were subjected to canned Christmas music being piped over the store's sound system.

"There are not that many Christmas songs, and by the time the big day actually comes, you want to rip your ears off your head, if you hear one more Christmas song!"

I had to agree with him on that one. By the time Christmas came, I was very sick of the music as well.

The old man would follow the same general route when he continued on a tirade about the upside-down retail world, "I swear these people have all lost their calendars! You cannot buy a winter coat in January, and you cannot buy a bathing suit in July! The stores are all backwards. To make matters worse, ten seconds after Christmas ends, all the Christmas items, cards, and any other thing that has to do with Christmas, is removed from the store shelves and the Valentine's Day stuff is put out!"

Once more, the old man was indeed correct. It was very hard to argue with the facts surrounding his long-winded, continual Christmas speeches.

For the old man, Christmas centered upon the Christmas tree, Christmas music, and his famous Christmas village. In constructing his famous miniature Christmas village, he carried on a tradition started by my grandfather of assembling by hand; a miniature Christmas village, long before the villages became popular seasonal displays.

This particular year, which the best I can remember would land in, or around 1968 or so, wayward Christmas celebrations really fired up the old man and got under his skin. He proudly proclaimed that despite the best efforts of the commercial media and other outside influences, he was going to make his best effort for us to all experience a traditional Christmas, just like when he was a kid.

Oh, oh, even though I was a ten-year-old runny-nosed kid, I could sense that this could have some serious ramifications.

One night after work, much to the chagrin and horror of our dear Mum, the old man went down into our basement and made a ton of noise. You could hear that he was moving things around and you knew this was going to be an adventure.

He then dragged and bumped up the stairs, a four foot by eight-foot-long old board from the basement, which was what the Christmas village was set up upon and displayed. He moved a lot of the furniture out of our living room while Mum watched and asked what he was doing.

"Starting, our traditional Christmas," was his answer. I got the strange impression that our dear Mum was completely happy with our regular, old, Christmas celebrations, and she suspected that this traditional celebration was trouble on the Henson family horizon. Our father worked like a madman clearing out the sofa, extra chairs, and the coffee table, much to the vexation of our mother, who protested the loss of her living room.

The old man continued undaunted with his mission because he had now focused on a one-man mission to save Christmas. He was not going to allow a little thing such as furniture, get in his way this Christmas season. He was piling all the living room furniture into the spare bedroom.

"But where will our company and guests sit for the holidays when they come to visit?" Dear Mum asked, as she watched the old man move pieces of furniture out of the living room.

"On their tookuses . . . where the hell else would they sit?" The old man was on a bit of a roll as he answered rather smartly to Mum. My old man had a custom language of his own. It was a mixture of Paterson, New Jersey street slang, military jargon, and some other unknown gibberish. Despite the obscurity, we all knew the location of the human body to which he was referring.

He worked on the village feverishly, with his eyes bugging out, and a wild look in his eyes. Single-handedly, he turned the house into a full out Christmas billboard. While he worked, he still would ramble on and on about a traditional holiday, while our mother just wrung her hands, asking when she could count on this all being over.

The sweat ran down the old man's face mixed with blobs of gold tinsel and artificial spray snow as he explained to dear Mum, "I promise, honey. You and the kids are going to love Christmas this year."

Mum just stood there and shook her head. I had the feeling that she felt as if it was a vain promise.

"We are going all-out to celebrate a Henson family Christmas just like it was when I was a kid," the old man promised, while he dragged the last chair out of the living room and moved it towards the spare bedroom.

Have you ever noticed that in the midst of these happy times in your life that there is always a little interruption? Yes, an interruption, it is a sudden bump in the road, a thorn that sticks into your backside while you merrily dance through the golden fields of happiness singing cheerful songs, or maybe it is just some unexpected lumps, which appear in your mashed potatoes.

This joyful event was to be no exception to the rule.

You see, then, it happened, in the midst of celebrating,

and elevating us all up into joyous traditional Christmas celebrations; my sister made the fatal mistake of asking a simple, logical question.

"Since we are having a traditional Christmas this year, Dad, does this mean we can have a real Christmas tree instead of that horrible, artificial thing?" My sister asked.

Right in mid-move, the old man stopped, and dropped the chair he was moving into the spare bedroom. His jaw dropped, and his eyeballs popped out of his head. If there was one thing the old man recently and firmly placed as number one on his rule list, (We had thought it was the Thanksgiving thingy, but the old man had not yet printed a scorecard to follow all of these rules) it was that you had to have a fake tree.

He refused to use the word artificial. The old man called it exactly what it was; a fake Christmas tree!

His reasoning was actually very simple, and in his opinion, very factual, as to why you could not ever have a real cut tree in your home for your Christmas celebration. The pure, simple fact of the matter is that real trees are never fresh, they cut them down months before the holiday, and they always dry out before Christmas.

The final nail in the real Christmas tree coffin was the most dramatic, as his stance always included that you cannot enjoy the season because, "You have to sleep with one eye open since you worry if the house will burn down or not. Those trees on the Christmas tree lots are all dried up, old relics of Christmas trees."

Sure enough, once my unsuspecting sister had asked the fatal question, the old man fired back with guns blazing, "So you want to ruin Christmas already, by having a real Christmas tree in the house? You will have us all worried every day if the house will burn down!"

My poor sister quickly retreated from her question. She was truly sorry that she had ever brought it up; after all, the last thing we wanted was to burn our house down, even if it meant having a wonderful, happy, traditional Christmas celebration!

"But Dad, the signs always say fresh Christmas trees," my sister gallantly gave it another try.

"Ha! Fresh my Christmas tree ass! Fresh, maybe in July, but certainly not at Christmas time. Those Christmas tree stands are all run by thieves, crooks, and charlatans," the scoffing old man struck at the very heart of the matter.

Since we were actually very stupid kids, we were, of course, scared stiff. Visions of infernos and incinerated Christmas trees danced through our heads. I had a horrible thought of Santa Claus himself, dropping his pipe in our Christmas tree and then running for his life as the flames licked his red suited backside!

This was some serious stuff. After all, I respected the old man; he was a very smart man. He knew an awful lot about the world, and the cruel and unpredictable pitfalls that lurked around virtually every corner. He read all about the latest in conspiracies, plots, theories, and tragedies every month in his *Dark Secrets* magazine.

Therefore, I went along with it, as did my sister, just as we had for many years in the past. When this had come up previously, I had asked my buddies at school, if they had heard of the inferno Christmas tree theory, but none of my buddies had ever heard of it. I also checked the newspaper around Christmas time and I diligently searched for any articles on houses burning down to the ground, in which the cause of the fire was dried up, old, relics of Christmas trees that were cut down in July, and sold by charlatans, but it seemed to be to no avail.

Despite the lack of proof to substantiate the dried up, flaming, Christmas tree theory, this year seemed to be the same old stance. In spite of the potential opening presented by this year's traditional Christmas caveat, the old man had already dug in on the issue of the real tree. We were doomed forever to having a fake tree for our yearly

Christmas celebration.

All the rest of the time while he worked on setting up the miniature village, he ranted and scolded us for even bringing up the idea of burning our house down with some dried up, old relic of a tree.

He even told us for the one-millionth time the story of how our grandfather had shown him as a kid how Christmas trees dry up and ignite. The old man brought up once more the tale of how our grandfather had taken a match to their old tree after Christmas and lit it on fire in their driveway.

"Within seconds it was gone! Poof! A blazing inferno, I never forgot that!" The old man testified in a very fervent and emphatic manner, waving his arms and hands over his head to demonstrate how the tree had burned to a mere twig and then ashes within a matter of seconds. My sister and I clung to one another, shaking and trembling at the mere thought of the blazing Christmas tree.

Oh, the pain and the shock of it all!

Thwarted once more by the old man and his dramatic and frightening testimony of blazing Christmas trees! Regardless of the proclamation of this being a new and profound, traditional Christmas year, the cold, stark reality remained that the old man was not going to let up on his stance of ever allowing a real Christmas tree anywhere near our home.

He even added for the proverbial icing on the Christmas cake, a simple fact. He stated that you never fully enjoy a real tree. The reason is that even if you by some remote chance, make it through the holiday without your house becoming a pile of smoldering ashes, then you cannot enjoy it long, because the tree is so dried up that you have to throw it out the day after Christmas, rather than risk leaving it up until after New Year's Day.

This was, of course, a major violation of his famous, "end of Christmas rule." You see, another rule, in the old man's endless holiday regulation book, was that according to him, the Christmas season actually ended on New Year's Day. Then you were finally cleared and authorized to take down the tree and put away the decorations.

The Hebrews had nothing on the old man with their books of laws; the old man had them all beat.

The entire rest of the night, as he worked and set up his Christmas wonderland, he continued to state his position. The old man was determined to knock any remaining foolish whims out of our heads as to having a real tree for this year's holiday.

Generally, kids are relatively evil in nature when they do not get what they want.

My sister and I were no different.

Over the next few days, we dug in and relentlessly bombed the old man with every angle we could muster up over this real tree situation. Therefore, it began what would become an all-out verbal warfare and conflict, as we campaigned for a real tree, and the old man fought back to preserve the family home, as well as to save his traditional Christmas!

My sister, being three years older than I was, had a unique and certain flair for how to work the angles. She was a more seasoned antagonist than I was at this point; after all, she had a lot more experience!

"Well, Daddy . . . all my friends have real trees," my sister would randomly report during the week at the dinner table.

She would then announce a list of about twenty or thirty kids in school, who she was sure had real trees. I would then swoop in for an attack with my testimony of Harry, Jeff, Ray, and ten other kids who have real trees.

It was a well-prepared, tag-team match of the real Christmas tree promotion, which was in reality a well-concealed, verbal assault on the old man.

During this endless provocation, the old man would do

his best to ignore us, and he would make his best effort at trying to enjoy his dinner. We were annoying, and every kid knows that you can eventually wear your parents down by bugging the living stuffing out of them until they want to squeeze their own eyeballs out of their head. Our father was no ordinary parent though. He was tough, and he hung in there. When we saw that our initial efforts were a hopeless failure, then we shifted gears, and we tried to drag our mother into the debate, but she remained wisely neutral and stayed on the sidelines.

Our mum, as we called her, was of English descent, and she had her own particular nuances of the holiday that she would bring up occasionally, but for the most part, she conceded that the old man was the household king of Christmas. Venturing into the dangerous waters of his endless rules and regulations of Christmas was just not worth it to her. Looking back, I think behind the scenes, our mother would also advocate for a real tree, but she carefully plotted her attack, not willing to risk upsetting the old man too much.

After the old man clearly won the first rounds, my sister and I were a bit glum, but not yet willing to give up the fight! However, the horizon was not to remain morose for very long, as the first slight crack in the proverbial, fake Christmas tree armor came from an unlikely source, which was our old Christmas lights!

We did not realize it at first, but eventually when we looked back at the steps that led us on this adventure, the lights were the first glimmers of hope that we had.

Every year, as a prelude to the big decorating celebration day, we would drag out the big, giant strings of gaudy, ugly Christmas light bulbs, and the old man would test them to see if any were in need of repairs.

The lights were very old, and most of the time, they required maintenance, such as rewiring socket repairs, other various inspections, and work, in order for them to last for one more year. The old man would pull out his special electrical repair kit that he bought from Substantial Industries a few years earlier and set the tools and lights up on the workbench to check them out before decorating.

He rubbed his hands together and licked his lips in a fervor at the prospect of sparks, fried ozone, and December fireworks. A repair and an excuse to utilize one of his beloved tools from Substantial Industries were more than enough to stir up his soul.

The old man untangled the first string, reached over, and plugged it into an electrical socket, as my sister and I watched. Of course, not a single light bulb lit on the string, and we heard some electrical crackling noises, so the old man was off on a troubleshooting mission.

These were large bulbs, and around them went a shiny, metal reflector that you placed over the bulb socket. The reflectors, which we had, were only available in a few different colors, and my sister and I thought they were hideous. The bulbs were in standard colors, with reds, blues, and greens being the primary colors, and they were all so old now that the paint inside was chipping out. You could see a clear light shining through where the paint had chipped off, and they were old and ugly. In addition, the bulbs were like an inferno, and they burned really, really hot. In fact, it felt like you could heat the living room by turning on your Christmas tree!

As we watched the old man testing them one-by-one, we noticed that he suddenly was having very little success in repairing them. None of the lights would light.

Sparks popped in the air and we all jumped back as the old man pulled the plug from the wall socket on his workbench. There was the distinct smell of fried ozone in the air, and a heavy electrical odor surrounded us. After popping two fuses in our house's main fuse box, the old man was becoming frustrated. After replacing another fuse, he looked at the two of us, shook his head, put some of his tools away in his special kit, and turned off the light over the workbench.

He then strangely put the strings of lights aside and waved for us kids to head out of the basement and back upstairs. The old man did not say a word; he silently made his way behind us and up the basement stairs.

"Aren't you going to fix the lights, Dad?" I asked.

"Damn, shitty old lights. Don't worry about it, kid. I will get to them. I have an idea. You ask a lot of questions there, kid," the old man mumbled back to me.

Ah hah! An idea, but we did not know what it could be at this point. Of course, these bulbs because of the heat they generated, only favored the old man and his anti-real tree position, since they could cause a fire in the middle of a rainstorm, so we thought it did not make any sense when he pushed them aside.

What was the idea that the old man had up his sleeve? What would we do now?

It was only a few days away from our famous light stringing exercise, so if we did not have working lights, what was the plan?

We wrapped up in a Henson family Christmas celebration, many annoying and peculiar exercises. One of the main rules and regulations in the old man's step-by-step Christmas celebration manual was that we would put all the lights on the Christmas tree one day before the proclamation of "the official tree decorating party."

"No one likes to put the lights on. It is very tedious, and boring," was the old man's stance, so he created a separate event to put the lights on and preserve interest.

The old man, my sister, and I, would assemble the tree and then put the lights on. It was a strenuous operation as we helped the old man position the lights perfectly on the tree. He would wind them on, and we would hold the lights strings up and get them tangled around our feet and head. The old man would tug on them and yell at us to give him some slack, and for us to pay attention to what we were doing.

I had to admit, putting the lights on was a major operation, and it was not really very exciting. My sister or I would fall victim to daydreaming, or looking out the window, and sure enough, a bulb would fall on the floor and break, or a string would be stuck in my sister's hair, or some other pitfall would occur.

The old man would pop out of some small section of the tree, look around to see what had happened, and then reprimand us for being bums! We were inferior Christmas tree-light stringer-helpers!

After the horrible light stringing exercise that went on for hours, the tree would then be ready for the final decorating. The actual decorating event, unlike the bulb stringing operation, was a fun and enjoyable time. The decorating of the tree was a full blown-out party. In fact, it was an elaborate and enjoyable party, with drinks, snacks, music, and other fanfare.

Other than the horrible inferno lights, the other annoying element of our fake tree was that the old man insisted on using this artificial Christmas tree scent that came in a spray can. It came in a green can with Christmas lights and ornaments printed upon it, and once the tree was set up and the lights were on, he would reach for the can of artificial tree scent. The old man would grab it and unleash a bomb of this foul smelling, horrible spray all over the place.

It was supposed to smell just like a real Christmas tree, but all it did was cause our mother to have this atrocious headache.

He would spray it all over the place, while Mum would hold her head in anguish and complain, "My goodness, that stuff, gives me such a headache. It smells like cheap, awful perfume! Do you have to spray it all over the place?"

"Nah, nah, nah, this here is great stuff," the old man

would say. "It makes the tree smell just like a real tree."

Then Mum would read the instructions printed on the spray can and tell him the same thing she told him the year before. She knew that the directions on the can clearly state that you should never spray the scent on a lit tree, as it was a fire hazard.

Mum would then report, "You are not even supposed to be spraying this stuff with the tree lit as it can cause a fire. It is right here that the spray can cause immediate and spontaneous combustion of the Christmas tree."

"Don't pay any attention to that," the old man would fight back. "No one ever caught a fake tree on fire. Those real trees are the ones that cause all the fires you read about in the paper around Christmas."

Being stupid kids, and still working the "wear your parents down angles," we would bring up the horrible, fake tree spray, saying that Mum would not have to get a headache all Christmas season, if we had a real tree. Since the real tree smells great on its own, then you would not have to spray that fake scent around.

We would save, dear Mum!

I do not think it was that the old man did not care that his beloved wife would obtain a scent-induced headache due to his obnoxious spray, but I really had no explanation as to why he continued to use it.

Perhaps I should not dwell on that angle.

The tree scent angle was a hopeless and futile argument, as there was very little weakness in the old man's fake Christmas tree armor and he was not going to let little things like headaches, spontaneous combustion of the Christmas trees, or fake scents interrupt or get in the way of his plan.

The next day after work, the old man burst through the back door, carrying a bunch of shopping bags from Crumbley's Department Store in downtown Paterson, New Jersey.

"Come into the dining room. I need to show youse guys something!" He shouted as he carried all the bags into the dining room and set them on the table.

"These are the latest thing," the old man exclaimed as he pulled a box out of the bag. "Look! Are these lights amazing or what?"

In his hands, he held a number of brightly colored boxes. As we gathered around to check out his excitement, I could see that emblazoned across the boxes were the words, "Miniature Italian Lights" in big block letters. We could see that inside the boxes there were all kinds of little, different colored Christmas lights, formed into tiny, little bulbs. These sure were a stark contrast to our big, clunky, old fashioned light bulbs.

"I saw these out at the store by the shop, and since it was payday, I took a little dough and grabbed them. All the guys in the shop are buying these! You see, they will save a bundle on electricity."

He excitedly started to pull out the strings of the new lights from the box. My Mum, my sister, and I had now gathered in close to share in the excitement. We could now clearly see that they were a stringed collection of little tiny, beautiful, multicolored lights.

"They came over from Italy. I read all about them here on the box. See what the box says about the fact that they use very little electricity. They are the latest thing this year." The old man explained while his eyes were darting back and forth in his head. He was clearly enamored with his new Christmas lights.

Sure enough, the box did say, "Italian Christmas lights. Made in Italy" and there were a wider variety of colors in the new light strings than with our old-fashioned, boring, old clunky lights. There were yellows, purples, light greens, dark greens, light blues, pink, and on and on. The assortment of colors went.

The old man pulled the lights out of the box and

plugged them into a wall socket.

"I am going to get rid of those old lights with the big metal things. The bulbs are all chipped up, they are all shorted out, and they need major repairs now. Besides, these will save a lot of dough on electric costs," the old man explained as he turned out the dining room light. He scurried back and forth as he prepared the lights for display.

We cheered loudly when we saw the new lights come on, and we stood in admiration at the wonderful, twinkling of the tiny wonderland of the Italian lights. The old man looked back at us, smiling. He was very proud of himself for picking out such an immediate hit for the Christmas season.

Secretly, the old man had tried a covert plan to divert our attention from a real tree with his new, whiz-bang lights. He thought this would be the final blow, and due to the soft glow of merry, Italian Christmas lights in assorted colors, we would forget all about real trees and other such twaddle. He hoped that this would put a stop to the relentless battle that my sister and I had inflicted upon him.

The old man had indeed made a fatal mistake and miscalculation.

I was an annoying, geeky little kid, and I was lurking in the background ready to pounce on the error.

I picked up the box that the new lights came in, and I started to read aloud the sales pitch on the cover, "These lights burn safely, use only a quarter of the electricity of old-fashioned lights, and there are NO FIRE HAZARDS! There are fuse protectors, and if one bulb goes out, or there is a short circuit, the entire string shuts down to provide extra safety."

I was going on and on, reading the carton and relaying all of this technical safety, mumbo jumbo.

The old man detected that I had broken the secret anti-fake Christmas tree code, and he ripped the box out of my hands, while he instructed me to hand over the evidence, "Give me that box, Paulie! I have to pack the lights up in them before you kids step on them."

"But, Dad," I started back, "if the new lights are so safe, maybe we can get a real tree without worrying that it will burn the house down."

Ah hah! Suddenly, an opening and a little chink in the real Christmas tree defense shields of the old man. The old man realized that he may have made a major misstep, and he immediately downplayed the new light situation.

Our mother chimed in and said, "I like these new lights, maybe the kids are right, and we could get a real tree, it would really be a traditional Christmas this year."

Now, we knew that Mum had shown her hand, and she was secretly on our side in advocating for a real tree.

The old man sensed that perhaps the tide of the battle had turned a little in our favor now and he dug in.

Since the old man was always on his toes, he said, "Look, we are going with these new lights," and shifting gears a little away from the whole house, burning down argument, he continued with a previously unrevealed, anti-real tree angle, that he had kept close to the cuff for emergency back-up use. He laid the initial groundwork for his final deathblow.

"The biggest trouble with real trees is that they are never fresh. You can never get a fresh tree and what happens is that all the needles fall off. Christmas day comes, and you are left with a dried out, old, relic of a tree with no needles on it, and you cannot enjoy the day."

Then, the old man in a calculated and cunning strategy, turned to Mum and predicted, "The whole house will be full of old needles, you will be vacuuming all Christmas, and you will still be finding needles in the kitchen on the Fourth of July."

Mum's eyebrows lifted, and she clenched her fists, as soon as she heard the word, "vacuuming."

Our dear mother waged an eternal battle with dust, dirt, what she called fuds, bits, bobs, and other previously unidentified household annoyances. She was a fervent housekeeper, intent on defeating every dust bunny and sucking up dirt forever more into perpetuity.

There in our stupid, little kid minds flashed visions of Mum sucking up needles and tree trunk pieces with her vacuum hose from a real Christmas tree, forever until the end of time.

The old man stood there with a smirk of victory on his face, and he knew that he had won. He had pulled a magic bunny out of his hat at the last moment. We all had to hang our heads and admit that we did not want more work for Mum, and we all wanted to enjoy our Christmas.

Therefore, just when it looked as if he had committed a major error, and he went backwards into a real Christmas tree corner; the old man had rebounded and fought his way out with his guns blazing. Once more, the old man had won a victory, and clutched a real tree out of our eager little hands.

Chapter Two

Victory!

The day of torture arrived. It was time for the arduous task of putting the Christmas lights on and for us to assemble the fake tree. All of this was a prelude to the infamous official tree decorating party. At least this year, even though we were depressed over the lack of a real tree, we did have a slight element of interest with the new, miniature lights that had admittedly put a new twist to the season.

The old man summoned me to go with him for the yearly adventure of pulling the fake Christmas tree out of storage in the attic. You see, fake Christmas trees are a unique and strange item. When you first purchase it from the store that specializes in selling fake Christmas trees, this giant, seven-foot high, four-foot-wide fake Christmas tree is packed down into this small, almost tiny, cardboard box.

The sales pitch on the box always proudly proclaims, "Comes with a handy, dandy, storage container with a carrying handle, to preserve the quality of your tree for years to come," or some other type of propaganda similar to that.

The sad reality is that once the tree had been taken out of the box and been assembled, the tree transforms into a giant spring monster. That seven-foot high, plastic symbol of strategic marketing might as well be a giant Sequoia Redwood tree.

There is no way, no how, that you will ever compress or

flatten the tree to put it back into that handy, dandy, storage box. You could roll it over with a freight train, drop a twenty-ton safe on it, roll it over with an asphalt-paving steamroller, and it will not go back into the original container. It is one of the great-unsolved mysteries of the world, how they package these trees to fit in those boxes at the fake Christmas tree factory, located in some previously unheard-of country with a weird name, like the country of Zippyakistan or something similar to that.

After many futile efforts at repacking the tree, you then concede defeat, and use the handy, dandy, storage box to store window curtains and drapes in.

The size of the tree forces you to put the tree into some substitute box of enormous size, such as a refrigerator box, a washer machine, television box, or something of a similar size.

The Henson's fake Christmas tree storage box was a leftover from when the old man bought a new lawn mower. It was about a seven-foot long and two-foot-high box. We extracted the box down from an attic hatch, in our attic that a circus acrobat would shy away from, due to the difficulty in accessing the area. We then carefully lowered the box to helpers on the attic floor. Although, I was tall for my age, I was still the smallest of the family, and of course, very flexible, so it was my job to climb up in this wretched location, and tug at the box with all of my strength in an effort to move the box an inch or two at a time, towards the hatch.

Far be it from me, to inject some type of reason into the situation. I was a problem solver, and it would actually serve me well as my life went on and I grew older.

Those are stories that we will leave for another time and place down the road.

I decided to offer up a solution to this yearly adventure of holiday madness. "Why don't we find an easier place to keep the tree, Dad? We could put it in the back room of the basement. It would be a lot easier to get it out than this is!"

The old man, of course, had no rebuttal, so he just ignored me and when I persisted, he whispered for me to shut my trap and to pull the tree out.

Well, he did not exactly say it that way, but you understand the general gist of his instructions.

All the time we were performing the tree extraction process, Mum was simultaneously dusting the dust and dirt off the box. (Rather pesky dust, fuds, bits, and bobs covered the tree box from being stored in the attic loft all year.)

It was a dangerous and precarious operation.

Upon a successful extraction of the fake tree, we carried it into the living room for the final assembly and the light installation. My sister and I noticed that during this initial Christmas operation, Mum was supplying the old man with a steady flow of his favorite Big Boulder beer. Mum was working hard to ensure that he was remaining cool and calm. She knew the first time that one of us dopey kids stepped on one of the new Italian lights or the wires became stuck in one of our ears, then the old man would launch off to the moon without a rocket ship.

Ah hah! It seemed as if Mum might have had a secret plan of her own after all!

The old man was becoming happier and happier, as he consumed a steady input of the frosty, ice-cold, Big Boulder beers. Once one beer was empty, and the can tossed aside, then Mum came dashing in with a fresh replacement beer for the old man.

He was happily whistling the melody to "The Christmas Tree" as he pulled the first of the plastic branches and the metal trunk out of the mower box.

Now, the living room was already crowded with the old man's famous Christmas village. Therefore, we moved the tree assembly operation a bit into the dining room, as we pulled all the parts and pieces of the tree out of the box.

Our artificial (fake) tree was a veteran of many Christmas celebrations. It was old, worn, and it was not in the best of condition. Every year, when we pulled the branches and parts out of the mower box, more and more plastic needles had fallen off and accumulated in the bottom of the box.

This artificial (fake) tree was the type of tree that had color-coded paint colors on the end of the tree branches. To assemble the tree, you then matched the color of the paint on the end tip branch with the colored hole in the tree trunk.

The only trouble was that this tree was so old; a good majority of the colors had rubbed and worn off the tips. It had become increasingly difficult to tell exactly what the paint color was on the tip end of the branches since they had worn off so badly.

My sister, the old man, and I put the trunk in the base holder and then we attempted to sort the branches into piles, according to the colors on the ends of the tips. We all did the best we could, but we found ourselves holding the branches up to the lights in the room, checking for just a hint or remnant of a color that remained on the tip.

At one point, the old man went and pulled his Substantial Industries magnifier out of his special tool chest and he was examining the tips of one of the longest branches.

"Red! I see a little tip of red paint there on the end. Come over here, Dorothy and check it."

My sister peered into the magnifier glass and nodded her head in agreement, "Yes Dad, I think you are right, I do see a little blob of green on the end of it."

The old man screwed his mouth up like a corkscrew and said, "I said red . . . not green."

My sister shrugged her shoulders and the old man tossed the branch into the red pile of branches. We asked each other for opinions of what color was what, and we organized it to the best of our abilities. I had to admit that I was just really guessing on most of them, and threw them into the piles according to not only a guess but also according to the size and shape of the branches.

Once we had completed this exercise in futility, and we had the branches separated into piles, we began the actual assembly of the tree. I should clarify that fact and say that we were going to begin the attempted assembly of the tree.

Mum was watching from afar, and she ran into the kitchen, and she promptly returned with another Big Boulder beer for the old man to replace his empty one. She had sensed that this was going to get, as she would say, "a bit of a sticky wicket," type of operation.

We started the futile operation by pushing the first few of the misinterpreted colored tree branches into the holes. My sister and I knew right from the placement of the first few branches in the metal trunk that something had gone seriously wrong. We had a strong sense of doom and that we had enveloped ourselves in the world of fake Christmas tree confusion.

"I think this is a blue one," my sister said, holding up a Christmas tree branch end to the old man.

"Nah. That is clearly purple," was the answer.

"Where do the red branches go, Dad?"

"Long red, short red, or medium red?"

I looked down at the branch in my hand and shrugged my shoulders.

The old man looked at it and pointed, "That is a medium red."

"I cannot find medium red on the trunk."

The old man pointed at a hole in the top of the trunk and said, "I think all the medium reds went here. Yeah, yeah, yeah, this row is all medium red."

My sister and I were not sure if the old man was becoming half in the bag, or if he was just guessing, but we both knew a two-foot-long fake tree branch did not go in the top of the tree where the old man was pointing. The colors had all worn off so badly that it now was impossible to tell where anything went and putting this tree together was now becoming similar to picking out winning lottery ticket numbers.

After about a half an hour of this exercise in uselessness, we stood back and studied our fake tree. The top of the tree was wider than it should have been, the bottom was skinny, and the tree tilted to one side. The very tippy top of the tree seemed to point both north and south at the same time. The middle section had a combination of short and long branches sticking out of it at odd angles.

"This tree looks really bad, Dad," I said. Continuing my keen observation skills, I added, "I think we have it really messed up."

My sister went straight to the heart of the analysis and simply said, "This tree is a mess."

The old man was undaunted. He looked at the both of us and waved his hand at us.

He then sat down on the floor at the base of the tree and reported, "No, no, no, you two kids give up way too early. We just have the green and red branches mixed up here, right at the bottom of the tree. See . . . let me show you two what the problem is. It is simple to move them around here."

He then rearranged a few rows at the very base of the tree.

Our mother dashed in from the kitchen with a cold Big Boulder beer, looked at the tree and said, "Oh my."

Mum stood back in horror at the sight of the tree as she handed a new beer to the old man. Her words just about summed up the situation.

The old man stood up, took a few steps back from the tree, and sighed at the sight of the poor, old, fake tree. Switching the two rows had made the tree look even worse than it did before.

The sad reality was that our beloved, fake, Christmas tree had become some sort of sadistic jigsaw puzzle, whose secrets of successful assembly lie safely hidden away.

It now stood there in the corner of our living room; a sad, twisted relic of past Christmas celebrations.

My sister and I sank into chairs and just shook our heads.

"What are we going to do, Dad? Our tree is a disaster," my sister moaned and groaned.

The old man sipped the Big Boulder beer, stood in front of the object that formally used to be known as our beloved, fake, Christmas tree. He sipped his beer and stared at the sad display of twisted celebration.

It looked like some sort of hippie pop art.

Mum could sense the tension building in the air, and the rapid fading of our happy, traditional Christmas celebration. She attempted a defusing of the situation by suggesting a change of beer brands to something different. She was grasping at straws to change the mood. Happily, Mum made a desperate and valiant attempt.

"How about a Dingleberry beer, honey? Would you like to try one of those?" Mum smiled and batted her eyes at the old man as she presented the suggestion and diversionary tactic. The happy moment and suggestion did not work.

The old man looked at Mum and shook his head. "I hate those Dingleberries! They are way too sweet. I need another, Big Boulder beer. Why the hell do we even buy those stupid, Dingleberries? No one ever drinks them!"

We could see the side of his temples pounding like little drums as the anger percolated inside of him like a little steam kettle. I had encountered these types of moments, many times, while working around the house with the old man on various jobs. When things went bad, and the jobs went south, it was only a matter of time before that short fuse on the old man's patience dial blew and the relief valve popped.

After a long moment of pondering, while we all stood by, watching for his next move, the old man set his beer down on the end table. He then charged the tree in anger, seemingly determined to launch it into orbit, and we knew this was about to be the first beloved, fake Christmas tree to land on the moon. Mum stepped in with a beer can in hand, and in a perfectly timed moment, she appealed to the old man's only known weakness.

His own love of the holiday season proved to be the great neutralizer.

"Oh now, do not ruin your Christmas over this old crummy, worn out tree, dear," Mum said.

She continued her attempt to save the traditional Christmas. "You are the one pushing for this traditional Christmas, and we want a real tree this year, anyway. I do not mind cleaning up a few needles."

Mum stood in front of the object formerly known as a beloved fake Christmas tree, and pleaded her case, while defending what small amount of honor the fake tree had left.

"You can get a real tree for this Christmas, and then buy a new beloved, fake, tree in the after-Christmas sales for a quarter of the price. I am sure that you can get a fabulous deal in Crumbley's Department Store on a tree on the day after Boxing Day."

Mum, in a moment of incredible elegance, fantastic timing, and keen judgment, had won the battle!

The old man stopped in mid-lunge and he turned his head to us. The thought of him ruining his own traditional Christmas was too much for him, and he smiled. In addition, when Mum had uttered the keywords, "fabulous deal," he stopped in his tracks.

Being a legendary deal making, Paterson, New Jersey street guy, a deal, was something the old man could not resist. The beers had sufficiently softened up his defense forces. The thought of a bargain in the after-Christmas sales and moving ahead with his traditional celebration was too much for him to withstand.

He stopped in front of us, took his beer back from Mum, and took a long sip of it. He had a calm look on his face, and the tenseness of the previous situation had faded.

The old man folded like a cheap tourist camera.

"Yeah, yeah, yeah, you're right, honey," the old man answered back. "This old tree is a piece of junk, and we need a nice tree for our new lights. Besides, we can get a new storage box to store the new fake tree in when we buy a new one! We can get rid of the enormous mower box and you can store your curtains in it."

Success! At long last, we finally won the war! We all stood and cheered, and if we had been strong enough, my sister and I would have lifted our mother on our shoulders and carried her around the house in victory.

"Tomorrow is Saturday and we are going out tomorrow on a mission," the old man explained as he started to dismantle what used to be our beloved fake Christmas tree. "I have it all planned now! First, we are going sleigh riding, and then we will all head over to the shopping lot and pick out a real tree. We will find a really fresh tree and pick out a good one! It will be a fantastic day, a perfect kick off to our Henson family traditional celebration!"

Now technically, a sleigh is a larger version of a sled, you usually pull it along with a team of horses or with one horse, or in a unique case, reindeer; it has large runners and folks ride inside on seats.

I had seen pictures of them on Christmas cards; you know the scene. A sleigh pulled by a horse, gliding happily along on a snow-covered landscape, with a cut (fresh) Christmas tree stuffed in the rear of the sleigh. The riders all bundled up, singing Christmas tunes, smiling, and the drivers are always smoking a pipe.

We were going to zip down hills upon sleds, not sleighs.

No authentic, self-respecting northern New Jersey resident ever would say, "We are going to go sled riding." Nope, it is not going to happen. It is sleigh riding here in the land of youse guys, gals, Hot Texas Weiners prepared, "all the way," "whadda ya want," and all other things, New Jersey.

The old, beloved, fake Christmas tree ended up in a forlorn heap next to our trash bins. It sat there, sadly waiting for a trash pick up the next day.

I looked out my bedroom window and saw the pile of tree parts out next to the trash cans. I must admit that it was a little sad to see it out there in the cold sitting in the snow. I thought there should be a more dignified way to dispose of your old, beloved, fake Christmas tree. I thought in many ways that it should be similar to when you retire an old, tattered flag.

Maybe, we should have played some type of sad elegy for it, while the tree was disposed of and crushed inside the giant mouth of the trash truck. I secretly hoped that it came back to this world as something with purpose, maybe as a recycled milk jug or a soda bottle, or a new part for our family car, which was the infamous 1964 Putter Classic model 200 automobile.

As my sister and I went off to dreamland, we had the promised excitement of a great day out in the snow, riding our sleds down snowy hills and picking out the perfect tree circling around in our minds.

Little did we know that while this seemed like a great plan, we were about to experience that life is full of twists and tricky turns along the way.

This traditional Christmas stuff may not be all that we had thought it was going to be. Somehow, a very simple thing such as picking out a real Christmas tree for the Henson family was going to turn out to be quite the adventure.

Chapter Three

The Quest Begins

It had snowed earlier in the week and there are certain rules that govern everything, even sleigh riding. In northern New Jersey, sleigh riding is an art. It is a sport for sure, but it is also a blessed and sacred event! The first day or so, after the snow has fallen, sends a multitude of thrill seekers out in every direction, seeking out the slightest hill, bump, or mound to hurtle down the hills on top of a sled, trash can lid, snow disc, tire tube, or in extreme cases, a simple chunk of cardboard, or your mother's plastic dish pan.

Utilization, of virtually ever known item that a person could fit their backside on or into, has long been a tradition for sleigh riding in northern New Jersey.

As all experienced sleigh riders know, you never go out on the hill right after a snowstorm. That is the job of the hard-core, dedicated sleigh riders, who trudge out on the hill to groom the snow and smooth the snowpack out. The initial rides in a deep snow are slow and difficult, and until the snow packs down, it is hard work to groom a hill into good shape.

The real fun begins a few days after the snow is packed down, completely groomed, and the hill is ready to go. It is even better if the sun was out the day before and it then became bitterly cold at night. That perfect combination of conditions will turn the hill into an icy nightmare, sending kids and sleds careening and screaming down the side of the hill, heading for certain annihilation, out of control, and at incredible speeds.

A few hours after a heavy snowfall occurs in northern New Jersey, the local emergency room starts gearing up for a wide assortment of sled accident victims that will shortly arrive to be stitched, splinted, sewn up, and otherwise medically patched after a day of fun and excitement sleigh riding.

It is all part of the happy, traditional Christmas celebration, or so the old man told us.

In order to venture out into the icy and frozen wonderland, we required transportation or a reasonable facsimile of such. We had a car in our family, or what the old man proudly called a car. The sad fact of the matter was, it was slightly unreliable, and it caused even the simplest of trips to become all out adventures.

The Henson family automobile was a legendary, 1964 Putter Classic model 200, with a dashboard mounted push button, super deluxe, automatic transmission, a straight six-cylinder engine that produced about twelve horsepower and had a top speed of about thirty-five miles per hour with no one in the car, and a tailwind at the rear.

Any family outing or excursion was always without fail, going to be an adventure when we all climbed in the Putter. The old man loved the car, and he repaired it almost every weekend in our driveway with his Substantial Industries Whiz-Bang, Super Deluxe, tool set.

The car had at least three hundred thousand miles on it and had been painted a summer or two ago at one of those paint shops that painted cars for fifty bucks. The old man could never match the original paint color, so touching up any rust spot was a precarious task. He just picked any blue color that was close, so the Putter was actually about four or five different shades of blue.

Saturday morning came and the old man was slightly groggy from sucking down as he would say, "One, two, three . . . too many," Big Boulder beers in an effort to dull the pain of the demise of our beloved, fake, Christmas tree.

Nonetheless, we were up early for the promise of our fantastic sleigh riding and a real tree procurement adventure!

We packed the 1964 Putter Classic model 200 with our two Substantial Industries Flexie Flopper sleds. The old man stuck them in the trunk with the runners hanging out. He tied down the trunk lid and put an old red painter's rag on the end of one of the runners, to prevent some poor driver behind us from impalement on our sled runners. Mum gave us a thermos of hot chocolate and sent us on our way. She was going to stay at home, prepare meals, as well as the house, for the exciting arrival of the real tree.

The old man shook his head and just waved his hand back to her when she yelled out the side window, "Be careful out there. Those hills are so dangerous and there are a lot of trees! Make sure the kids do not lose or drop their gloves or mittens on the hill!"

My sister and I climbed in the back seat, armed with hats, coats, mittens, gloves, goofy looking, red and black boots with buckles on the front instead of laces, and other thermal gear for our excursion into the ice and cold. Equipping stupid kids our age with thermal gear was irrelevant. No matter how many gloves and mittens you came equipped with, within about fourteen seconds of sleigh riding, your hand gear is soaked to the skin, and your fingers turn a deep, purple color. Ice and snow coat your mittens or gloves and they freeze solidly in the cold air. I had twenty-seven pairs of socks on my feet to fill in my boots (the boots were too big; they originally were my sister's boots) and still my feet were already becoming numb from cold.

"Yeah, yeah, yeah, I hear you," the old man mumbled. "She knows that I am a sleigh riding expert, I know what I am doing, cuz, I have been riding these hills for forty damn years," he muttered as he turned the key in the ignition and the Putter coughed and choked to life. After fifty-two thousand adjustments of the manual choke, the engine finally started to smooth out and idle. He backed out of the driveway and turned the Putter out onto the main drag.

The roads were mostly clear now. There was some snow and ice cover here and there, but it was no big deal. It was cold, a little overcast, and the sky looked as if it could snow at any minute. It did not matter though; nothing deterred the old man and his Putter. He did not back down from the coldest day or the deepest snow. He had not missed a day of work in thirty years, and he was not going to let a little thing, such as ten inches of snow on the road, derail him in his quest for fun and tradition.

There were no excuses for not being able to make it to your destination or to work back then, due to a little foul weather. Now, in the more modern era, a drop of rain or snow comes down, and even though people are better equipped, panic sets in, and people cower in fear and hide under their kitchen tables at the sight of snow on a roadway. We now consider the play-by-play dramatic coverage of the weather on the television to be acceptable entertainment. The media whips people into a frightened frenzy on the television, putting the fear of pending doom and isolation into the minds of the viewers due to the approach of a snowstorm!

They have field reporters live and, on the scene, standing out in the cold in their parkas next to a highway, as the cameras zoom in on the first snowflake fluttering to the ground from the storm of the year, which they named, "Barney."

We now name all storms, not just tropical storms, but all storms, winter, spring, summer, and fall, now have names.

Years before SUVs, four-wheel drive, all-wheel drive, and front wheel drive, millions of Americans like our father, plowed and pinballed vehicles through giant snow drifts, and ice-covered roads to their destinations by strapping steel chains on tires, and loading trunks down for traction with sandbags, weights, huge toolboxes, and shovels. The click, clank, of steel tire chains going up and down the roads in the winter, was a common noise that we all grew up hearing. I could tell if it snowed overnight, even half-asleep in my bed, by just listening to the sound of the city traffic outside my window. Back then too, cars had real steel rams on the front called bumpers, not the fake, phony, frauds of a cheap, plastic bumper they have nowadays. A little collision with a snow bank or two was part of the ballgame, not the demise of your vehicle.

The Putter puttered along, choking and spitting a bit, while the old man still tinkered with the manual choke control on the dashboard. The engine protested due to the cold night, but as it gained some speed, it started to warm up and move along. We could hear the ice cracking and creaking underneath the vehicle as it moved along in the ice-cold morning.

My sister and I huddled in the back seat already slightly frozen to death, and the old man tuned in the radio station WPAT from downtown Paterson, New Jersey, on the A.M. radio dial. The station was now playing a merry little Christmas tune.

The dashboard speaker crackled with snow static and we heard, "Silver, and gold, and yackity-smackity and so forth on your Christmas tree," as some folk singer strummed his guitar and crooned out of the speaker to us. It was as if it was some kind of covert marketing plan for precious metal investments.

Station WPAT located at 930 on the A.M. dial, according to the old man, always played the best Christmas music. We thought it was a cornball radio station. The station had a playlist that was in the classification of easy listening, and we thought it was boring, but years later, I came to appreciate and understand, more of the type of a radio station that it actually was.

"This is going to be a great day, kids! We are heading over to Washington Park on the west side of Paterson! It is going to be a blast. I passed the park the other day heading home from the shop, and it looked like the hill had been groomed perfectly." The old man was starting his sales pitch for the day. We just nodded our heads in the back seat and both of us had stupid smiles frozen on our faces.

The Putter pulled into the parking lot at Washington Park, and we passed an ambulance stationed at the base of the hill, waiting to haul sleigh riding crash victims off to the emergency room.

This was New Jersey, so I am sure the ambulance driver made a commission on victim hauling. Therefore, the driver picked a strategic location that was sure to drum up some business today.

The hill leading into the park was snow and ice covered and the old car slid and clawed a bit at the surface, struggling to gain a little grip. The old man easily fought the steering wheel back and forth and expertly wiggled his way safely to the top of the hill.

We actually knew Washington Park in our neighborhood, as Monument Hill, due to the miniature facsimile of the real Washington Monument built at the top of the hill. It stood there, as some strange needle pointing forever to the sky, and it did not seem to have any real purpose. The monument had no inscription, no plaques, no identity; nothing but a phony monument sticking out of the ground. But hey, this was New Jersey, which is the headquarters of all things, which are weird.

The monument sat dead center at the top of the hill, and one side of the hill sloped away from the top in a gentle, flowing, low grade all the way down to the road, which seemed miles away. The other side was sheer torture for sleigh riders since it was about one hundred times steeper. The top of that side of the hill was in the clouds, it was shady, and therefore, more ice-covered, and just to add more odds for inevitable crashing, there was a huge stand of large, maple trees looming along the side of the trails.

Now, it was a known scientific fact that trees alongside a hill filled with sleigh riders had some type of magnetic force that pulled your sled in their direction. An expert sleigh rider could steer around them, but for a dreamer or clueless sleigh rider, the tree magnet could prove to be an insurmountable obstacle, and many a rider had met their fate with tree stands.

The old man parked the Putter; we popped out and started to pull the sleds out of the trunk. Huge masses of kids and parents gathered around the top of the hill. Puffs of smoke filled the air and circled around their heads. You could see clouds of warm breath hitting the cold air as everyone yelled, laughed, and conversed at the sled launching point. You could hear in the distance loud screams and yells of both joy and horror, as the sleds screamed down the side of the hill.

The old man untied our two sleds, and we grabbed the ropes and started to drag them behind us to the hill.

We had two Flexie Flopper sleds. One was a single rider, and the other sled was a double sled that two people could sit on. Old cotton ropes passed through two holes in each end of the wooden bar, and the ends were tied into a loop, which allowed you to not only drag the sled around, but you also could steer with the ropes by pulling on one end or the other, while you sat on the sled.

The old man pulled out an old wax candle from his pocket and picked up the sleds while barking out instructions.

"Here, hold them up while I wax the runners," he said as he rubbed the candle up and down on the runners of both sleds. "This will make them faster in the snow until the rust knocks off them."

The excitement was really building now, and being typical, stupid, pesky, kids who are never satisfied, we immediately attacked our poor father with, "We want to go down the big side, Dad! Not the little bunny trail! Can we please go over to the big side?"

"No way," was the loud and clear answer. "You kids are not able to steer well enough to manage the big side. We are going to go down the little side here. I will teach you how to sleigh ride."

Now, we both knew that this was as much an outing for our father as much as it was for us kids, because he absolutely loved sleigh riding. The first couple of runs were made by him because he had, "To test the hill out," and make sure the sleds were in good shape for us.

We stood at the top of the hill moaning, groaning to him, and impatient to ride ourselves. We then each took turns riding with the old man. He would be steering in front, and during the ride down the slope, he would instruct us on the ins and outs of sleigh riding. He would allow us to ride solo on the single sled, while he shouted instructions and coaching from the top of the hill. My sister and I would also go down on the double sled, with my sister in front steering.

On and on it went, down you would go, then drag your sled back up the hill and zip down again, over and over. It was an endless production line of sleds. Frozen feet, ice packed pants, legs, frozen fingers, frozen ears and hands were all common now, as we slowly were freezing solidly in our quest for fun and tradition.

During this entire experience, there was a constant background of yells and screams of horror coming over to us from the big side of the hill. As a sidebar interlude between screams, you would hear the occasional sound and wail of the ambulance siren as they hauled another victim off for medical treatment.

While over on the bunny side, we would go down the hill like little turtles puttering along at boring, safe speeds.

"Oh, come on, Dad. Can't we please go over to the big

side? This side is for the little kids, and we are too big for it now," was our joint complaint.

He shook his head back and forth. "No, no, no . . . those trees over there, you dopey kids cannot steer well enough, and you will crash right into them. Listen to me, just go down a few more times and we will head out and get our tree. You have not lost your mittens or gloves, have you? Mum will kill me if you lose them." We both looked down at the hand gear attached to our coat sleeves with little strings and nodded that we still had them.

Just to keep consistent and stick with our normal methods of operation, it did not stop there. We haunted him continually for the next half an hour, until it was obvious that it was nearing noontime, and we were winding down the operation in order to leave enough time to go pick out a tree.

"Please, Dad. Can't we go down the big side just one time before we leave? I promise to steer away from the trees," my sister pleaded with our father.

The old man looked at these two half-frozen, iced over kids of his with a suspicious frown, but he finally gave in, "All right one time, and one time only, then we have to get out of here. I will point the sled on the top of the hill and guide you. Youse guys are not just going off on your own. Grab the single sled." As he started to pull the double sled over to the other side, he leaned over his shoulder and added, "And don't tell your mother!"

Over on the large side of the hill, it was a stunning assortment of frozen humanity. Teenagers, fathers, mothers, large people, small people, old people, all half frozen to death, and all gathered at the top of the hill in their own individual quest for fun and tradition.

Some folks had sleds, while others had plastic garbage can lids, old tire tubes, huge inflatable rafts, and other assorted items that they dragged from their home. In fact, currently in use on this hill, it seemed as though there was one of every known item to mankind that a person could sit on to propel them down the side of this mountain. We watched in amazement as a giant tubby man with a large backside squeezed into a plastic dishpan and flew down the hill!

There was even the pure, scintillating adventure of riding the non-steerable wooden toboggan. I stood and watched as a group of brave teenagers all sat on an eight-foot wooden missile. They grabbed the rope handles on the side and slid over the side of the hill.

They shot like a rocket ship down the hill, and you could hear the screams of horror from the young girls onboard as the leader sitting in the front yelled, "Lean left!"

In unison, the group leaned left, and I watched the wooden sled steer away from obstacles.

"Lean right!"

The sled moved smoothly to the right, and it came to rest at what seemed as if it was about twenty miles down the hill.

"Wow, can we get one of those, Dad?"

"Forget it, kid, you will kill us all on that thing," was the answer from him, and looking back at that mobile wooden torture chamber, I knew that he was correct.

"Come over here, kids," the old man directed and pointed to a spot on the top of the hill. "This is a clear spot. Paulie, take your hat off and tuck all that long hair of yours into the back of your jacket. You will catch it on something for sure. I wish you would just cut it all off." I had long reddish-blonde hair that hung down past my shoulders, and the old man was always haunting me to get a haircut.

The old man had positioned the double sled on the side of the rest of the sleigh riders and on an opposite side from where the trees were.

"You will get in the front," he instructed while pointing to my sister. "Dorothy, you have to steer because your brother is too small and he will head straight for the trees."

My sister was three years older than I was, and she was without exception, always assigned the leadership position over me, because I was too little to be trusted at this point. We climbed into the sled, and I settled in behind my sister, who put her boots on the wooden steering bar, and grabbed the rope in her hands. She moved the rope anxiously back and forth, testing the steering.

"Yes, that is right, just like you steered on the little side, good, good," the old man continued with his last-minute instructions before launching us into the hands of fate. "See how clear it is on this end," he continued.

Even though I was just a dopey little kid, I immediately identified that there was a problem. All I saw in front of us was a migration of what seemed like hundreds of people, either riding down the hill or dragging something back up the hill. My sister nodded strangely in agreement, and since all I wanted to do was go down the big boy side, I just went along with the charade.

On and on he went; stay away from the trees, steer, hold on tight, watch out for people, steer away from the trees, the coaching was endless.

"Look, the way is clear now," he said, and with a strong push on my back . . . over the edge, we went into the wild throws of the hillside.

Off we went, like a missile, and the smile on my stupid face quickly turned into a face of horror. We both now realized that we were hundreds of feet above sea level, and we had gained speed so quickly that we were both scared out of our wits, and we were screaming at the top of our lungs.

It was the old adage of be careful of what you wish for!

We were about to realize that we were not properly mentally prepared for this rocket-propelled ride down the ice-covered hillside, because hundreds of trips down the bunny trail had lulled us into safety and comfort.

"Steer away from the trees!"

I could hear the old man bellow from far behind us. Down, and down, we went, faster and faster, while we were still gaining incredible speed. I noticed that this side was solid ice, as the surface snow had turned to ice from the friction of thousands of sled runners. The intense cold had now frozen this hillside into a treacherous slope of torment.

Despite the speed, my sister was doing a good job of stabilizing and steering the sled. Suddenly, there in front of us, was some kid with his head down, not paying attention to anything. He had his hat pulled over his eyes, dragging his sled behind him as he pulled it back up the hillside in his quest for fun and excitement.

The kid was a clueless dope, he was not aware of the danger all around him, and we both started yelling at the top of our lungs, "Move, kid!"

It was to no avail, as the kid was not paying any attention to his imminent demise, while our sled missile careened straight toward him at nearly supersonic speed.

Other people on the hill started yelling, "Pay attention, ya dopey kid! Look out for the sled!"

Everyone was yelling and waving their arms in a vain attempt to warn him. At the last second, the kid looked up and dove to the side, just as my sister had jammed the steering bar into a full right turn. We missed the kid by a whisker, and now the sled headed off in a completely opposite direction across the hill.

Of course, of all the directions that we could have turned towards, we were now heading straight for the trees.

"Steer it back!" I screamed at my sister and she had jammed her boots into the steering bar while pulling the rope with all of her might, in a vain attempt to steer the sled in the other direction.

It was now hopeless.

The tree magnet had captured us, sealing our fate forever more.

Our speed was so fast that all that the sled runners were doing was skidding along the surface. The ice was laughing at our feeble efforts to correct our direction.

"STEER AWAY FROM THE TREES!" We heard the old man bellowing behind us. I looked behind us and saw that the old man was trying to run down the hill in a valiant, yet futile, rescue attempt.

The entire hill now focused on our fate.

As if it was some strange scene from a science fiction movie, the entire hill of riders stopped and turned in unison as they all shouted together, "WATCH OUT FOR THE TREES, KID! STEER AWAY FROM THE TREES!"

I could see that the ambulance driver had turned his lights on and gave the siren a test wail in preparation for our injuries.

"I can't turn it! The sled won't turn!" My sister screamed.

The trees loomed closer and closer, and it seemed as if they were right in front of us now. A feeling of self-preservation took over, and we did what anyone else would have done in the same situation.

"Ditch the sled! Jump off!" My sister instructed me. "You go right, and I am going left," she said, and off the sides of the sled, we went. I hit the ice with a thud, and we both rolled repeatedly until we finally ran out of momentum. I recovered and sat on my backside as we watched our sled, which was now rider-less, blasting off on the ice towards the trees.

It hit a bump on the hill, bounced high in the air, and then came down with a thud. It then miraculously missed the first tree and jumped up on a smaller bump, only to impale itself into the next tree trunk like a spear.

We cried aloud as we watched our sled explode into a mass of wood and steel. All the riders on the hill shook their heads and went back to their own missions.

You could hear a quiet murmur of, "Wow, they were

lucky, they would have been killed in those trees."

The ambulance driver had flipped the lights and siren on, and he was preparing for the job at hand. Once the driver saw that we had somehow miraculously survived, he turned off the lights and siren, and went back to reading his newspaper, while waiting for the next victim.

The old man finally made it down to us. He was covered head to foot in snow and ice, as he had slipped and rolled most of the way down the hillside.

"I told you to steer away from the damn trees," the old man screamed.

"I tried to, Dad, but there was this stupid kid, and he would not move," my sister sobbed back. She was now crying and all upset.

"What kid? I didn't see any stupid kid," the old man retorted as he checked us for injuries and counted our limbs to make sure there were no parts of us missing. "You're both all right," he said as he picked us up. "Your mother is going to kill us. I will never hear the end of it. Stop your blubber gushing," he told my sister as he picked us up and dabbed at my sister's eyes with his handkerchief.

"Look at our sled, Dad," I said, pointing at what was left of our once proud, shiny sled. "And, I lost my gloves in the crash, Dad!" I was looking at my coat sleeve at the now empty strings hanging from the end of my sleeves.

The old man shook his head and said, "Put your mittens on."

I felt my pockets and realized that I had lost them too. I would strategically wait for a little better time to spring that tidbit on the old man. We all climbed down the hill, and the old man picked up some pieces of twisted metal, of what used to be runners and a few hunks of splintered wood.

"Not to worry, I can fix it," the old man testified, in what seemed as if it was an overly optimistic assessment. Wanting to believe that was in fact the case; we nodded our heads and then dragged our broken mess of a sled and ourselves back up the hillside.

"Let's go get our tree now," the old man said, as he put the intact sled and the remains of the other one down next to the trunk of the Putter. The sled incident had slightly derailed our quest for tradition and fun, but we had survived, and had now recovered. We were now right on track with the prospect of finally capturing the elusive real Christmas tree. My sister and I were now anxious and jumping up and down because we realized that a real live Christmas tree was finally at hand.

Well now, not so fast, as the traditional Christmas seeking gremlin had one more trick to place in our path. The ongoing quest for a real tree, and a fun, traditional Christmas would not come so easily.

The old man stood next to the car patting his coat and pants pockets as though he was looking for something.

"That's strange. Where are the car keys?" The old man mumbled while he was now pulling his pockets inside out and frantically patting his coat pockets and searching.

We stood there, frozen and staring at the old man, as we knew in our hearts that this quest for tradition and fun was really not going too swift.

"I must have dropped them here next to the car, don't just stand there! Look around," he waved, and we immediately started patrolling around the car for the lost keys.

We went around and around, up and down, and the search expanded to include the area where we were originally sledding over on the bunny side. There we all were, in a hopeless pursuit for the lost keys that could be anywhere on the entire hillside! Our mother did not drive and even if she did, we only had one car, so we would have to take a cab back to our house to pick up the spare car keys.

The situation was looking bleaker and bleaker, as we

were now hungry, tired, frozen solid, and close to frostbite. Just to add a little frosting on the disaster cake, it was now starting to snow heavily, which would cover up and conceal our car keys!

The hill was now beginning to empty out a little. A loud-mouthed, cigar chomping guy spotted us with our heads down like hound dogs and he made the mistake of asking the old man if he lost something. That conversation did not go over very well, and the verbal scolding that the old man gave the old cigar face did eventually make a vague reference to the fact that our father's idea of fun was not looking for lost keys on a hilltop.

I always picked up some colorful language from the old man in these types of discussions that were useful to me during hockey games later in my life.

The old man had successfully chased away the pesky cigar smoker and then he looked and pointed at us, "You did not hear that, and don't tell your mum that you heard that either." We both stood there nodding our heads up and down, and I stuck my frozen hands in my pants pockets.

"Paulie, where are your mittens? Why do you have your hands in your pockets?"

"I lost those too, Dad. And I am hungry."

He just shook his head and did not say a word, but I heard some faint mumbling, "stupid mittens."

Now it was really getting frustrating when my sister remembered the now famous rescue attempt by the old man. She suggested that perhaps the keys fell out of his pockets when he tumbled down next to us when we rolled off our sled.

"I am freezing, Dad. And Paulie and I are hungry," my sister mentioned to him, while continually pointing out the overly obvious facts, as we worked our way down the icy slope to the scene of the near-death incident. The old man pointed out that his keys were in a large black leather case so they would be easy to spot while lying on the snowy white background. We all fanned out and started to scan the area. Sure enough, after spreading out a bit, God had pity on us, and miraculously poked the keys up out of the snow and ice for someone to see. The old man spotted the keys lying in the snow and he eagerly scooped them up!

We cheered and hugged each other in victory. Redemption came quickly for my sister for her keen suggestion to look on the hillside in that nearly tragic location.

"That was a great idea and suggestion to look here, Dorothy!" Our father shouted at the thrill of finding the elusive keys. The old man was already spinning this adventure as to how much fun we had. I was searching for my textbook knowledge from school and remembering the definition of fun, but I was having a difficult time placing this day in that category.

Back up the hill we made our way, with the car keys now safely in our hands. I kept an eye out for my gloves and mittens, but it was hard to pick them out amongst the other twenty-five thousand lost pairs that we passed on the way. I also spotted frozen hats, a boot or two, seventeen pairs of broken eyeglasses, a hearing aid, and even a pair of false teeth stuck in the snow, all of which I pointed out to the old man and my sister.

Up to the Putter, we climbed, and I decided to put a positive spin on the accident. I pointed out that at least now, we did not have to tie that rag on the sled runners, since the tree collision and resulting explosion had created a much more portable version of a Flexie Flopper. It now all fit nice and neat in the trunk. Neither my sister nor the old man commented on my observation.

We all got in the car and, with a turn of the rediscovered keys, we waited for the lovely sound of the engine to sputter to life.

We waited, and we waited, and we . . . waited.

"CLICK, CLICK, CLICK," the Putter just weakly taunted back to us. Oftentimes, starting the Putter on a cold day can be an adventure in itself. The old man just put his head down and tapped his forehead on the top of the steering wheel numerous times. He was mumbling some more words that would be very useful in a hockey game in the near future.

"Wait here. It is that stupid, loose-ass battery cable."

The old man climbed out of the car, and my sister and I looked at each other, but we did not say a word. We heard him in the trunk of the car, and then I saw him carrying a hammer and a wrench as he lifted the hood of the car up. Due to the unreliable nature of our family car, the old man always carried his Substantial Industries toolkit in the trunk of the car to perform roadside repairs. There were some banging noises, then some other noise, and the old man closed the hood. He put his tools back in the trunk.

The old man got back in the car and turned the ignition key. This time, the old car had sympathy on our already awful plight, and it teased us just a little, but it finally turned over. We had been holding our breath during the car starting, but now that it had turned over, my sister begged for heat. The old man told us that it would have to warm up and he handed us the thermos of hot chocolate.

And now that the calamity had safely passed, the old man already put a happy spin on the day's activities. He was not deterred in the least by all the crazy and uneven events of the day.

"Well, kids, since we had such a great day here on the hill, we will need to head home and go out for the tree tomorrow. It is snowing pretty hard now and we are all hungry, so let's head back to home and regroup."

I was looking around as the old man was speaking. I needed to make sure that he was speaking to us and not to different kids when he mentioned the great day part. I then realized that he firmly refused to fold on his traditional

Christmas this year. We only moaned and groaned for a minute. To be honest, after all this Christmas fun and tradition, we were both ready to attend a nice Fourth of July picnic.

We were very willing at this point to forget Christmas together.

On the drive home, the old man coached us on how to "Best present this entire situation" to our mother. He remained in fantastic spirits, still talking up what a great Christmas season this has been so far. As we chugged along, the old radio crackled with station WPAT. The radio was now playing Christmas music about every three or four songs in the daily rotation. My sister and I gradually thawed out, and we stared out the windows. We were both too exhausted to speak very much. We were both very happy to be arriving home, still intact and not on a hospital stretcher.

We pulled into the driveway and Mum anxiously opened the back door. She was slightly surprised to see us not dragging in a Christmas tree.

"Did you lose your gloves and mittens?" She asked, while inspecting me for damages. Oh, boy . . . Mum nailed it already . . . after two lousy seconds into the house! I nodded. She looked at the old man, and then at me, while shaking her head. The old man did not say a word, but he just shrugged his shoulders.

Mum hustled us off as she instructed us, "You have been gone so long! You poor kids, you are both frozen solid and soaked to the skin. You will be lucky not to come down with head colds. Off to change into dry clothes, you two! I have it all laid out in your rooms."

It felt good to get out of those cold, frozen clothes, and to warm up in the nice, fresh, warm clothing. We explained the day away and the old man must have taken a magic memory pill because he suddenly remembered the dummy kid on the hill! He spun the story of how my sister expertly steered the sled to safety and saved the clueless kid's life.

He was simply amazing.

I often thought that he should have pursued a career in law because he could weave a tapestry of words that spun together like the finest cloths. Mum shook her head a few times, but it all passed, and she focused her attention on getting us warmed up and fed.

"Tomorrow is the big day, kids," the old man loudly proclaimed after dinner, as he settled into his chair in the living room. "The key is to pick out a fresh tree! We will get a good one. I will make sure of that."

He had put his favorite record by Harvey Crooner, which was, *A Happy, Happy Christmas,* on his trusty Victrola, (he insisted on calling his record player a Victrola) he plugged in all the lights on his Christmas village, and was settling down for a late afternoon nap.

"It is better to go for a tree on a Sunday, anyway," the old man explained, as he started to go off to nightie, night land. "Saturday is the busiest shopping day, and the con artists who run those tree stands put all the dried up, old, relics of trees out on Saturday to get rid of them."

I nodded at the old man's theory. It seemed very reasonable to me. Then again, I was a dopey ten-year-old kid, and I am not sure that I knew much at this point in life. I wondered why he had not mentioned that theory before, but I dismissed it; after all, he was a Christmas tree expert.

I sat on the floor with my sister, staring at the village and dreaming of Christmas magic. After being out in the cold, snow, wind, and going up and down that hill about fifty-two thousand times, sleep came easy for all of us.

Before I knew it, I was asleep and in my bed. This was one Saturday night that I did not argue with going to bed early.

Chapter Four

The Tree Adventures Continue

Sunday morning came, and I awoke in my bed to the sounds of banging of pots and pans in the kitchen. I pulled the shade up and stared out the window. The glass had frosted heavily, and it appeared to be cold and dreary outside. I put my eyeball up to one little corner of the window that had not yet frosted over, and I could see that the snow from yesterday had tapered off. It was only a few inches deep, but it was just enough to put a fresh, white coating on top of the frozen piles from the big snowfall earlier in the week.

I climbed out of my bed and wandered down into the kitchen where my parents had whipped up a breakfast of bacon, eggs, and toast. My sister was already at the table eating, and I suddenly realized that I was as hungry as a bear.

"Good morning!" The old man shouted. "Sit down and eat. We will be heading out for the tree shortly. You need to get some food in you. It is really cold out there."

All the energy expended from yesterday must have depleted my food tank, as I sat down and gobbled up my first helping of breakfast and asked for more. While we cleaned up the dishes, the old man had already dressed in his winter coat and hat and was heading out to clean the snow off and warm up the 1964 Putter Classic model 200.

I leaned an ear to the window, and heard the car groan, moan, and then on the third try, puffed off into some sort of compression.

So far, so good!

Maybe this day will be the long awaited, happy Christmas prelude that we had been waiting for.

My sister and I, under our mother's careful supervision, were dressed in our heaviest, available winter survival gear. I pulled out a spare set of gloves from my drawer. I was down to my last two pairs, so I was sure that Mum wanted to sew them onto the end of my nose so that I did not lose them this time around. We trudged outside to meet the old man in the driveway.

It was a cold, raw, and overcast day and it was the kind of day that you felt all the way down into your bones.

The Putter sat in the driveway, struggling to idle, and keep warm. The heat from the tailpipe had melted a little warm spot in the snow.

"Let's go, kids," the old man instructed us, as he had finished scraping the windows and we all piled in. The old man hit the push button transmission button for reverse. We waved to Mum in the window, and we watched as she mouthed, "Good luck," through the frosted window glass. We were off on our mission to pick out the tree.

"Last week, I saw a Christmas tree stand set up over by the Foodworld store in the corner of the shopping center. From the road, those trees looked pretty good. I think they were really fresh," the old man pointed out the window in the direction that he was heading.

Ah hah, it seems as if he was keeping a close tab on the local Christmas tree market after all. It was apparent that he had been performing advance reconnaissance in anticipation of our ultimate real Christmas tree victory!

The Putter moved slowly along over the crunchy snow. The vehicle did not move very fast on the warm, sunny days; on cold days, it just barely rolled along until it finally warmed up, which was generally in late July.

We made our way up the main road, towards the Foodworld parking lot. One right turn, a traffic light or two, and we were there.

"There are the trees, over there." I pointed to the corner of the lot.

"I know, I know where they are, don't go getting all excited now," the old man said as he spun the steering wheel across the parking lot and turned the car towards the tree stand.

In the far corner of the parking lot, you could see some wooden stands nailed together like tent poles. It seemed as if there were hundreds of trees leaning upon them. A string of dimly lit red and green Christmas lights waved and glowed through the frosty morning. They hung over the trees like a sad beacon for Christmas.

There was a large, black iron kettle on the far end of the tree stand, with an enormous fire glowing underneath it. There was a vapor of steam rising up from the kettle high into the cold air. We could also see a few men inside the stand, as well as what appeared to be some Christmas tree shoppers, walking around the outside of the trees. Two men were standing over by the huge kettle, stirring the contents inside of the pot with some long wooden sticks.

We were all staring at the trees and dreaming of Christmas tree wonder; the three of us were lost in the dazzle, hopes and dreams of Christmas tree joy. The old man cruised by when suddenly, we heard a man yelling and hollering. We all turned and looked around to see where the yelling was coming from while the old man stopped the Putter in a drive aisle right in front of the tree stand. The sudden calamity of the man yelling had startled all of us, including our father.

"What is all that yelling?" He asked as he gently braked the car to a stop, and his head spun in all directions as he tried to figure out what was going on.

Looking out the rear window of the Putter, we spotted a man charging across the lot from out of the wooden stand yelling and waving his arms.

"What, are you crazy?" The man was screaming as he stomped his boots hard on the lot and made his way towards our car. I looked at my father, he looked at me, and I shrugged my shoulders.

My sister piped up from the rear seat and asked, "Who is he yelling at, Dad?"

The old man turned and said to us, "I don't know, but he looks like he is some kind of whacko." He turned the window crank knob on the Putter, until the window was down, and he stuck his head out in the direction of the shouting man.

"Can I help you, chief?"

The old man had a habit of calling every unidentified man that he ever met "chief." Anyone and everyone were always addressed, "chief" and this angry guy was no exception.

The man approached the car and stood within a few feet of the driver's side door and he stopped. We could see he was a tall, middle-aged man with a crew cut, and a very angry look on his face.

"Oh, and you're a smart guy too, with the chief thing going on, huh? Who do you think you are? Coming through here speeding that fast! What were you dreaming about while you were coming through here a hundred miles per hour? You could kill somebody," he screamed at the old man and then folded his arms across his chest and leaned back on his heels, looking at our father.

"Can't you see there are shoppers and little kids all around here for Christmas?" He asked as he stomped his feet upon the ground. Obviously, this was a really upset and worked up man, who looked as if he was going to blow a gasket.

The old man looked around the car, and then he looked at both of us. My sister and I both shrugged our shoulders.

The old man then turned back to the angry man, and he said, "Look, chief, I don't know who you think was speeding, but it was not me. This car is a hunk of junk. It barely can go forty miles per hour on the highway. And that's with a tailwind. I was just driving along here looking for a place to park, and I was not speeding. You must have me mixed up with another car because it was not us!"

I thought to myself, how it was very unlikely that you could ever confuse the 1964 Putter Classic model 200, with its multi-shades of a blue color paint, with another car but I kept my mouth shut.

"Don't tell me what I saw," the angry man said as he now stomped closer to the side window.

Now, there were many things the Putter could rightly be accused of; being a hunk of junk, smoking like a forest fire, causing a traffic jam as it puttered along at a maximum speed of twenty-five miles per hour, being an inferno in the summer, being a freezer in the winter, but speeding, I do not think so. The Putter could be driven on the highway, and the car would eventually make it up to about forty miles per hour, if the road was perfectly flat, and you did not have to hit the brakes for about two or three miles.

There were little kids on tricycles, kids on Pogo sticks, and folks on the riding lawn mowers that could outrun our 1964 Putter Classic model 200. This had to be the first speeding accusation in history for a 1964 Putter Classic model 200!

That was the end of the ballgame! The old man and the angry parking lot man now were embroiled in a heated debate! The angry man had stuck his face in the driver's window and was blasting away at the old man. There was spit flying out of his mouth like a fire-breathing dragon.

Those little drums on the side of the old man's head were beating like tom-toms, and he was fighting back with, "CHIEF THIS AND CHIEF THAT! DON'T YOU TELL ME HOW DAMN FAST MY CAR WAS GOING!"

On and on and on it went. . ..

There was nothing such as a little, happy excursion for a

Christmas tree to perk up your day and fill you with holiday cheer!

I sat there and looked around, while the old man stated his position so eloquently, and in my little kid mind, I recognized many of the men standing around the tree stand. Some of them were now ducking under the wooden stands and making their way over to the car in order to see what this verbal disagreement was all about in the parking lot. My eyes then caught the sign standing next to the Christmas tree stand. I read it aloud in the car, "Annual Policemen's Benevolent Association Christmas tree, and chili-cook off sale."

Oh no, I thought, as I studied the faces of the men as well as the angry man with his head in our car! I played a lot of baseball with the Police Athletic League in town, and I recognized some of the men as my coaches. I then put the pieces of the puzzle together as I realized that all of these men were policemen in town. I then looked closely at the angry, bellicose man, who was now face-to-face with our father in a red-faced dispute and realized that he was the chief!

He *was* the Chief of Police!

The old man had now made Henson family history because he had locked tooth and nail in an argument with the actual police chief!

"Dad, I need to tell you something," I said while I tugged on his coat. "Dad, will you please listen to me?" I pleaded.

The old man turned to me quickly, and only briefly addressed me before he went back to his debate. "Not now, kid! Who do you think you are, chief? Coming along here as if you are in charge of everything. I suppose ya think ya are a big hotshot around here? And furthermore. . .."

"Dad. Dad." I tugged at his arm in a desperate attempt to save us. Someone had to prevent the old man from going to the clinker.

"Dad!" I screamed, and finally managed to obtain his attention. I leaned over into his ear and whispered, "Look at the sign, Dad, this is the police sale and that guy you are fighting with and calling chief, well, geez, Dad, he is the police chief!"

The old man shut his trap quickly. He screwed his lips up like a corkscrew, and he stopped yelling in mid-insult. I spotted his eyes dart over to the sign, then back to the angry man in front of him, then to the herd of clandestine policemen approaching the Putter.

The flustered and angry police chief leaned back on his heels, reached into his pocket, pulled out his wallet, and displayed a big, giant gold badge.

"Let me see your driver's license, pal!" the chief yelled. "I am the police chief around here! The bad news for you is that, I am in charge! I know what I saw!"

Oh, boy, are we in trouble now! It sure was going to be hard to explain to Mum how we went out to buy a Christmas tree, and the old man ended up in the clink. The old man sat back in the driver's seat and you could see the little wheels spinning in his head. He was shocked, and he was stunned. His mouth quivered, and his head went back and forth like a ping pong ball in a championship match. He looked at me, then turned and looked in the back seat at my poor, horrified sister.

I could see the wheels spinning in a different direction now as he whipped up a quick strategy for this situation.

No one could maneuver like the old man, and this little debate was testing him to his maximum squirm setting. Now, as quickly as you can turn on a dime, the old man shifted gears. Once more, that old charm and gift of gab came through.

"Oh, well, I am very sorry there, chief. You know something, sir? Ah, ah, in looking back at the situation very carefully. Perhaps, I did go a tad too fast. It was just that we are very excited. I want to buy some trees for the kids here, and I may have not been paying close enough attention. You see, I am also checking these trees out for all the guys in the shop, where I work. I plan to first buy some trees from you and then tell the guys in the shop to all come here to support your wonderful organization."

The chief put his gold badge away, and his body language changed. The tone of his voice was different now as he spoke. "Oh well, you want to buy some trees and some more for the men in your shop?"

The old man put the Putter back into the drive gear and said, "Yeah, yeah, yeah, please just . . . let me just park over here, and I will . . . come on over."

The chief looked at the old man and spoke, "Well, there is a slight chance that you are correct. Maybe, it was not exactly your car that I saw speeding along here. I may have gotten it mixed up with that other blue car I saw. Say, exactly what color is this car of yours, anyway?"

He stepped back from the car and he almost smiled as he scanned the Putter's exclusive, custom paint job. It was painfully aware that to the loyal and dedicated police chief, the prospect of selling a large quantity of Christmas trees far outweighed the possibility of enforcing the speeding laws in shopping center parking lots.

He waved to the old man to park the Putter in some spaces next to the end of the wooden fence and he began to walk over there.

"Park this pile of junk over there and I will meet you," the police chief bellowed as he turned to check on his backup forces.

The old man nodded, smiled, and as soon as the chief put his head down and was a safe distance away from our car, the old man punched the gas pedal and rolled down the parking lot aisle.

The police chief and the rest of the policemen now all realized that the old man was making his escape, and that he had no intention of parking and then buying any

Christmas trees. Realizing the charade, the policeman chased us, trying in vain to get a good look at his license plate number, but the old man eluded them, he whipped into some vacant parking spaces and darted back and forth, until he lost them in and amongst the cars.

The last I saw; they were all hollering and waving their arms in the air as he slipped the Putter out the back exit of the lot. My sister and I had ducked down so that the policemen would not recognize us, and I would at least have a slight chance of playing baseball next spring. I wondered how the old man planned to disguise the appearance of the 1964 Putter Classic model 200 around town from the police force, but that would be another adventure for sure. For fifty bucks, he could always paint the car black.

As we made our escape out the back of the lot, I could hear my sister begin to cry from the back seat, "We are never going to get a real Christmas tree!"

That was it.

All the stress of sled explosions, irate police chiefs, sick looking, formerly beloved, fake trees, cars that would not start, keys lost in the snow, all culminated in an outright old man explosion.

The old man's relief valve blew off. "Forget all of this! We will get a new beloved, fake tree! I should have just bought it the other day!"

His merry Christmas holiday cannons were unleashed as on and on and on he went.

"We are heading home, and we will go out and buy a new beloved, fake tree tomorrow! I do not care about the half-price sales after Christmas! Forget all about these stupid-ass dried up, old, relics of real trees! They burn houses down anyway!"

This incident had now fired up the old man, and he was blasting us. He then suddenly looked at me and he surprisingly asked, "Do you have your damn gloves? You have not lost them, yet have you?"

I held both of my gloved hands up to show him as I nodded my head.

"And Paulie, keep your mouth shut about the words that I just said. You are always too honest and spill your guts to tell your mother all the details of my vocabulary!" I nodded my head and swore my mouth to silence.

Thank goodness that I still had my gloves. The old man may have turned me into the police chief for punishment. I just sat in the front seat, wishing that I could melt away and hide. I was sorry that I ever heard that there was such a thing as a real Christmas tree.

The entire time that the old man was letting loose, my sister was crying her eyes out in the back seat.

Christmas tree procurement really cannot be so hard, I thought to myself. I am certain that purchasing a real Christmas tree is usually not this difficult. It was just that in the wacky world of Henson, common, ordinary, and everyday things turned into all-out adventures. Millions of people jump merrily in their cars at Christmas time, throw a rope and blanket in the trunk, go to a lot, pick out, and buy a tree. They then tie it up on the roof of the car and head home, singing Christmas songs together in the car, while sipping hot chocolate. They all then celebrate a wonderful holiday, as they all dance and sing happily around the Christmas tree, while the father of the family happily smokes a pipe.

It all seems so simple, easy, and fun.

Ordinary people do not have these kinds of adventures like us. In fact, this was turning into a mega-adventure.

How does this stuff happen to us?

Chapter Five

Fresh Trees?

Sisters are great, and my sister was no exception. If I had been crying, the old man would tell me to calm down, or to shut up, or he would have simply ignored me.

Not with my sister. She was his little girl.

She had whipped up a storm of tears that melted the old man into a puddle. She had played her cards to perfection. It was a fantastic, tragic display of crushed, real Christmas tree expectations at just the right moment. Eventually, our father calmed down, and he stopped his ranting and raving. He realized that my sister was very upset, so he finally broke down and told Dottie to stop crying.

He took out a box of tissues he had stashed under the front seat and handed them to Dorothy in the back seat.

"Here. Stop your blubber gushing. Blow your nose," the old man said to my sister. "I know of another spot over by Saint Peter's Catholic church on Chamberlain Avenue, over on the other side of town. It is far away from those crazy police guys."

The old man's voice was calmer now as he worked to diffuse the situation.

"I passed it the other day on the way home from the shop. Let's go over there and see if they have some fresh trees."

I perked up now and came out of hiding in the front seat. "Yeah, Dad, let's go over to the church. They would not sell us a dried out, old, relic of a Christmas tree," I reasoned.

My father just looked at me out of the corner of his eye, as if he really did not agree.

"I think the church is the place to go. It is much better than those police guys," I continued with my sales pitch for the church.

Somehow, I did not understand the logic in that statement, other than the fact that the church would never allow unscrupulous Christmas tree sellers to be in their parking lot! It seemed to have worked since the old man had pointed the car in the direction of the church. My sister had perked up now, as the rainstorm of tears had stopped, and we were back into the Christmas tree fray. The Henson's traditional Christmas train had made it back onto the track.

We pulled into the church lot. It was becoming colder and colder, and the air was heavy and wet. It seemed as if it could begin to snow at any moment. This tree display was a similar type of Christmas tree set up to the display we had seen over by the policemen's Christmas tree sale. The display had hundreds of trees, all leaning on wooden frames scattered in rows over in the far corner of the church parking lot. Similar to the policemen's display, the wooden tree frames also had strings of Christmas lights hanging above them, supported along the top of the wooden posts. They were a lot different from the policemen's area, though; these strings of lights had many colors and were a lot brighter. The lights broadcasted Christmas loud and clear in the cold air as they swayed back and forth in the wind.

The old man parked the Putter. We all climbed out of the car, and we made our way over to the tree stand. The excitement was now building, as we finally had arrived at a real Christmas tree lot, and we were closer to buying the tree!

This lot also had a big, giant kettle cooking over next to a little trailer parked on the lot. This kettle did not have chili cooking inside of it, instead the kettle was steaming, crackling, and it smelled fantastic, as if it were a huge, burning, open wood fireplace. The blue smoke was rising up from the kettle, high into the air, and the enticing aroma of burning pinewood was an enthralling experience for the senses.

"These trees look and smell fresh, kids! I think we can find something here," our father said as he led us closer to the rows of trees. The optimism was growing!

Just when we were close to the trees, around the corner from behind one of the wooden posts, there appeared a giant mountain of a human being. He came walking out from under the frames, and he ducked under a wooden frame that seemed as though it was ten feet in the air.

Ten feet in the air and this giant man had to duck under it!

He seemed, as though he was the tallest, largest man in the entire world. In addition to being ten feet tall, due to his huge girth, he must have weighed an enormous amount of weight, He wore a wool hat upon his head, and from what we could see under his hat, he had thick, black hair, and a wiry, black beard covered his entire face. Somewhere, buried amongst the beard and fur on his round face, we could see two big, shining eyeballs peering back at the three of us. On his feet, he wore big, brown, logger boots, and he wore a massive wool overcoat. Covering his hands were thick, black and grey work gloves that looked like giant hockey gloves on his huge hands.

He looked, as I imagined, that a modern day lumberjack person would look. I could see him in my mind, sawing down giant one-hundred-foot-high trees in the woods and single-handedly carrying them to stack them on the back of a truck.

"HELLOOO AND MERRY CHRISTMASSSSS!"

He bellowed in a loud, booming voice that shook the trees right out of the wooden frames, and echoed for miles into the cold Christmas air.

"Welcome to our Christmas tree stand! Where we sell only the freshest trees in town!" He met us at the side of the entrance to the trees, patted both of us gently on our backs, and said, "Hey there, kiddies. Do you want a real tree for Christmas?"

We nodded our heads in agreement, while we stared up at the giant behemoth of a human being. The truth was that we did not intend ever to disagree with the giant.

As the well-trained and fresh tree theory, subscriber kids, we were, we both spoke in unison, "We want a tree, but it has to be a fresh Christmas tree!"

The giant bellowed out a loud, booming laugh and the very ground shook under our feet. He then looked at our father and said, "Of course you do, kids! You do not want a dried up, old, relic of a tree! Dried Christmas trees can burn your house down!"

It was true! The giant had confirmed all the old man's theories!

I heard the old man mumble, "That's right. . .."

The giant cut him off. "Youse kiddies and your dad have come to the right place. We only sell fresh trees here. My brother and I have been selling trees here at this lot for forty-five Christmas seasons in a row. My brother cuts the trees down in the mountains of Pennsylvania and northern New Jersey and brings them down here every day. In fact, look at these fantastic trees! There is just something about Christmas trees, the smell, the sawdust, the beauty of them all. I live for this time of the year!" The giant continued as he turned and pointed at a row. "These trees just came in about one hour ago."

The old man was stunned at the size of the giant Christmas tree seller, and he slowly recovered at the sight of the huge man. The wind shear and air movement when the giant spoke could blow you over, and the old man held on tightly to the wooden frames with his hands in defense of the shock and concussion of the giant's voice hitting the air.

When he could finally speak, he shook his head in agreement and said, "I know that you have been selling trees here at Christmas time for years and years. I pass this way on my ride home from work at the shop and I pass your Christmas tree stand here."

"That's right!" The giant loudly agreed.

"We have been here all these years, and we happily give a little money to the church, and we make a little money ourselves. However, the main reason we do this, is that we want customers like you to have a great Christmas. We love Christmas! It is the one time of year when joy and peace shine down upon us all. It is not about the money we make . . . it is about this," the giant explained while he waved his arms and hands around as if to show us his kingdom of Christmas tree magic. "You see, any trees that may not sell because of one reason or another, and are no longer fresh, we throw them in the big kettle over there."

He pointed his huge arm and finger at the big cooker that we had seen when we first walked on the lot.

"We only sell the freshest trees."

We just stood there as if we were dopes in awe of this massive human being, with our mouths wide open, listening to his testimony of fresh trees, wondering how someone could actually grow to be this big.

We finally returned to reality when the old man came over and pushed us down the first aisle of trees.

"Well, let's take a look," our father said as he strode into the first row. The snow on the ground was now pushed into piles under the trunks of the trees, as they all stacked neatly in their wooden cribs. The entire time that we strolled within the display, the giant was still ranting and raving about trees.

"Yeah, yeah, yeah," the old man said. "Let me concentrate here," he complained as the giant man was getting on his nerves. The giant man seemed impervious to the cold as he just kept walking along with his coat open and a wide smile on his face. The wind whistled as it sent a deep, freezing chill through the racks and rows of trees, but he maintained an almost constant sales pitch to us. We walked up and down the rows as we looked at Fraser firs, Scotch pines, and Balsams.

Oh, the aroma! It was like Christmas for the senses.

The old man was mumbling to himself about how he was not buying the giant's sales pitch, about being in business to make sure we had a great Christmas, as he was growing skeptical of the giant's banter.

"No, I want a Scotch pine," the old man said emphatically. "They stay fresher longer than any other tree."

The giant shook his head in agreement, smiled, and he acknowledged the fact that the old man knew his trees.

Our father grabbed a Scotch pine tree from the rack.

"Now, watch carefully youse dopey kids," the old man said as he spun the tree in his hand and picked it off the ground.

The giant, my sister, and I stood and watched as the old man then picked the tree up in the air a foot or so, and gently tapped the trunk of the tree on the ground a few times.

"You see. This is how you test the tree to see how fresh it is. If a lot of needles fall off, then the tree is a dried out, old, relic, and it is not fresh."

The old man then bent down and very carefully examined the ground underneath the tree where he had tapped the trunk on the pavement. We all bent over and peered at the ground to study the needle accumulation.

The old man ran his hand along the ground, stood up and he seemed satisfied as he reported, "A few needles fell off, but this tree looks good."

The giant bellowed his sales pitch once more, "I told

you, sir! We only sell the freshest trees!" The old man shook his head in disagreement, as his cynical senses of Christmas commercialism had yet to dull from the giant's enthusiasm.

"Sure, you do," was all he said as he waved us on.

We went up and down the rows, checking this tree and that tree, and watching while the old man tapped various trees individually on the ground, while testing them for freshness. All the while, the giant man followed us around, talking and working hard to sell us a tree.

Finally, a tree in one of the last rows caught the old man's eyes. He pulled it from the wooden rack and checked it out carefully. He spun it around a few hundred times, checking the shape and size. He then tapped it on the ground and examined it closely for about ten minutes, going over every single branch.

"I think it is a good one," the old man reported. My sister and I cheered and clapped our frozen hands together. It looked like we had finally reached the end of our adventure!

"That is a very expensive tree," the giant said ominously. "Those are a little different from our regular pines. Those particular special Christmas trees are selling for fifteen dollars."

Well, when the old man heard the word, "expensive," his ears perked up and a puff of steam came out the top of his hat. There was nothing that our father enjoyed better than working a deal, and he instantly feigned shock and horror at the price as he answered, "Fifteen dollars! Are you kidding me, chief? I will give you eight bucks for it!"

The bargaining began, as the giant man shook his head and said, "I cannot take eight dollars for that, it is an expensive tree that I could sell for a full price in a few minutes."

"Sell it to whom? There are no other people here. All right, chief, I will up the amount to thirteen bucks for it right now," was the old man's quick reply.

"You got a deal!"

The giant clapped his gloves together, and it sounded like thunder. Sawdust remnants and bark from old Christmas trees filled the air from the force of the giant's gloves, hitting each other.

The giant shouted, "Let's tie it up on your car and get the deal done."

In one swoop of his massive hands and arms, he scooped the tree up like a feather, and effortlessly flung it over his shoulder. We all followed the happy giant as we could hear him still bellowing on and on about wonderful trees and Christmas. We all continued to follow him, and we made our way out of the Christmas tree maze. My sister and I jumped for joy, and we were hugging each other and dancing around, while the giant and our dad tied the tree up on the Putter.

Finally, absolutely finally, after begging and pleading, near death on a sled, lost keys in the snow, mistaken identity by irate police chiefs, and other endless maladies, we had now purchased a real tree! Even more important was that the old man checked it for freshness with his special freshness technique and it had passed muster as a fresh tree.

We saved Christmas!

In addition, as a bonus, our house would not burn down to the ground, because we had picked out a fresh tree from the honest, Christmas loving, giant!

The old man gave the giant the dough, shook his hand, and we jumped in the Putter, crossed our fingers that it would start, and we took off.

"Merry Christmas!" The giant shouted and waved to us as we pulled out of the lot and onto the road.

The giant was such a happy man, and despite the old man's skepticism, I could not help but think that he truly did love Christmas and Christmas trees.

We had the radio tuned again to station WPAT, and we were all singing Christmas songs as the car made the way back to home. It looked as if it was a fantastic end to a great day. We had all put what we would come to call the "famous police chief incident" behind us, and it was long gone and forgotten now.

I figured that I would deal with it come the springtime and baseball season. I had already come up with a plan that I would tell the police coaches on the ball team, that the driver was my long-lost uncle, or some other unknown person who had kidnapped my sister and me, if any of them by chance recognized me.

We pulled in the driveway, and the old man honked the car horn in joy while happily announcing our arrival. We ran out of the car shouting and yelling for our mother to come out and see the tree. The tree was still tied up on the car, and Mum put her coat and hat on, and came running out into the snow.

"Take a look here, honey," the old man said as he proudly pointed at the tree. "I picked a winner here!" It was as if he had bagged a prize deer at a hunt and was pointing it out to everyone, as the pride was just streaming down from Heaven to his soul.

"Oh my, it is fantastic! What a wonderful, Christmas tree. You must all be so hungry! You were gone a very long time. I was starting to get worried," our dear Mum proclaimed, both her excitement at the sight of the tree and an element of concern about how long we had been gone.

My sister piped in with the beginning of the tale of the police chief incident, "Oh, you should have seen what happened over at the Foodworld!"

Oh no! I did not intend to tell a soul or jump in on this explanation after the lecture that I had received, so I kept my trap shut.

The old man interrupted her, "Yeah, yeah, yeah, well, it takes time and different places to pick out a fresh tree, there are tons of con artists out there, you know how it is!"

Our mother had a funny look on her face as her husband had diverted all attention back to the tree and squashed the story.

"I am trying to keep supper warm and I did not know how long you were going to be," she said, as she helped the old man untie the ropes for the tree that attached around the front bumper.

Once loose, the old man whipped the tree down from the roof of the car and yelled, "Look at what a fantastic fresh tree we got!"

When he dropped the tree down upon the ground, the trunk of the tree struck the driveway hard, and a few little needles fell off the tree.

"Tinkle, tinkle, tinkle." we heard the sound of a few little needles as they dropped off the tree to the ground.

The old man's head instantly turned around, his eyes popped out of his head a little, and he asked, "What was that?" The old man had ears as sharp as an owl, and his eyes were better than a hawk's eyes at one thousand feet.

"Oh, it was nothing, just a few little needles fell off the tree," I said, reaching down to the ground, scooping up three or four of the needles to show him.

The old man immediately erupted into loud shrieks. "A few needles! A few needles! Wait, a minute. There were not any needles falling off when we tested the tree over at the Christmas tree lot."

"It is only a few, little needles, Dad. It is not a big deal," I attempted to head him off at the pass on this one with a slight amount of reasoning. Looking back, for my age, I was a wily kid.

"Wait, wait, wait a second here, Paulie, don't tell me, I am the Christmas tree expert around here," and with that, he dug down, buried his face in the tree and started to examine the branches. He picked up the tree, he tapped the end of the trunk on the surface of the driveway, and a few more tiny needles fell off the tree onto what remained of last night's snow remaining on the ground. The old man frowned and looked at the three of us standing there in the cold air.

It may have been my imagination, but it suddenly felt a whole lot colder.

His eyes darted back and forth in his head, and he licked his lips as though this was of some growing concern. The driveway now was mostly clear of ice and snow. It was down to the bare asphalt in spots, and the old man picked the tree up, and moved it to a bare location and once more, he tapped it on the surface.

He looked directly at our mother and said, "I don't know! These needles are coming off all over the place."

Mum looked at him and answered, "Well, honey, it is just a few needles. They are bound to fall off any tree. You can go right now, over to the pine trees on the side of the house that are growing in the ground, and you could tap those branches, and I bet that a few needles will fall off of those trees too."

The old man was already shaking his head as he dismissed Mum's theory. "Nah, nah, nah, believe me. I checked this tree before we bought it, and there were no needles falling off of this tree," he said while still shaking his head back and forth.

I started to get a strong sense of uneasiness. I glanced over at my sister, who had a horrified look on her face, and I knew in my heart that this adventure was not ending as quickly as we had thought it would. The search and quest for a traditional Christmas was not so easy to find!

The old man then picked up the tree and bashed it on the surface of the driveway, harder and harder, like a tomahawk.

"See, see, see! Come over here and take a look at these needles coming off!" He screamed as he subjected the tree to a grueling ritual of freshness testing. He stopped while we all peered at the ground where he had been striking the tree on the driveway. He then pointed at a small, little, scattering of about ten or twenty needles lying upon the ground, and dramatically proclaimed, "Look! The needles are falling all over the place. This tree is falling apart!"

I gave it my best shot at this point and decided to pipe up with a little observation. "I do not know if you are supposed to hit it that hard on the driveway, Dad."

He ignored me now, with his eyes fixated on the tree, and the drums on the side of his head in full beat and rhythm, he was now picking the tree up over his head in the air, and coming down with it like a sledgehammer on the driveway.

"See, all these needles are falling off," he exclaimed, while holding the tree up with one hand and looking at all of us for some type of response.

Oh no, it is not over yet, I thought.

My sister took off, and she ran into the house screaming and sobbing her eyes out. She had finally cracked, and had reached her maximum level of fun, within the punishing quest for a traditional Christmas.

I hung in there because someone had to take one for the team, and I seemed to be the most likely victim.

"Look," my mother decided to wade into the fray, "I really don't think that hitting it that hard on the driveway is really something that you should be doing."

The old man snapped back, "I know about fresh Christmas trees! You are from England. You do not know about Christmas trees! You have them stupid ass Boxing Day trees or hollies or whatever."

"We have Christmas trees in England, my dear." Mum corrected the old man.

Beaten for a mere second at his flawed logic, he jumped back in. "Well, you do not know about these American Christmas trees like I do, and the tree has to be fresh, or it can burn the house down!"

Oh no! Not that again!

Here we are full circle, and right back where we started from, with the original, burn the house down scenario. At least, he had yet to proclaim the tree as a, "dried up, old, relic," therefore, there still was an outside chance that we would be all right.

The old man stood there staring at the tree, spinning it around and around while studying it from every angle.

"This tree is a dried up, old, relic!"

Well, so much for that faint glimmer of hope because there goes the final stake in the heart of this Christmas tree.

Mum also retreated into the house, leaving me to fend for myself. I think the comment about her heritage had sent her off in a bit of a tizzy.

The old man stood there with his hands on his hips while he studied the tree for a long time. I stood there with a stupid look on my face, with my feet freezing in the cold, while saying prayers under my breath, which I had learned in church Sunday school, pleading for some type of divine intervention to glue needles back on Christmas trees.

The old man suddenly looked at me and said, "You know, maybe, it got a little dried out on the roof of the car, while we were driving home, and it just needs a little water. Run down to the basement and fill up the pail that we keep next to the boiler full of some water and bring it back up here."

I nodded my head. Off I went in a flash to the basement, to obtain the pail. Once more, my storied career as a tool fetcher continued. I knew the name of every tool in his workshop and toolboxes. Since I was old enough to walk, I had been assigned the job to go back and forth and bring various tools ordered up by the old man, while he was embroiled in hand-to-hand combat with some malfunctioning mechanical device, which was usually his primary foe of the 1964 Putter Classic model 200.

I went down into the basement and filled the pail with

water from the faucet by the washing machine tub. I grabbed the full pail of water and dragged it with all my strength out to the driveway. Luckily, I was big and strong for my age. We picked the tree up, plunked it in the water, and the old man leaned over the pail, watching it while picking at the needles.

"Look, the tree is drinking the water," he said. Being a stupid kid, I leaned over and studied the water. I was almost thinking that I would hear a sucking sound or actually see something, but I did not notice a thing.

My mother stuck her head out the window, saw what we were doing, and called out that supper was ready.

She put a happy twist on the situation. "Oh good! The tree just needs a bit of a drink, honey. It will be fine now. Let the tree have some water, come inside, eat, and warm up. You can have a few Big Boulder beers and relax. I am sure the tree will be fine."

Mum was once again going to resort to some covert strategy in order to win this war. The old man seemed satisfied, and he was content for now to let the tree sit in the pail of water.

The entire time during dinner, the old man's eyes were going back and forth in his head and he was shoveling in his food like a madman. Every few minutes, he kept getting up and looking out the window at the tree sitting in the pail in the driveway, as if he was expecting to see something different. He began a long speech and sermon, yapping on and on, about how the tree has to be fresh. Once more, he was repeatedly dwelling on the whole house burning down idea.

My sister and I looked at each other and shook our heads. I had to think how our beloved, fake tree that looked a little weird would have been a lot easier than all of this had been. My mother was working hard to calm the old man down, but it was to no avail.

As soon as he was done with supper, he grabbed his hat

and coat and motioned for me to do the same. We both ran outside to check on the tree. Sure enough, the old man pulled the poor tree out of the pail and he started with his freshness testing. The same procedure started as before, as he was now banging it repeatedly, harder and harder, on the driveway.

"Nah, nah, nah, this is not a good tree, it is not fresh. Look at the needles coming off," he cried.

I had to admit, there were a couple of little needles coming off, but they did not seem to be too excessive to me. I stared at the ground under the tree and noticed that there may have been ten or so needles sitting in the snow where the old man had bashed the tree trunk. The old man was now raising the tree five to six feet in the air, and he was ramming it down on the ground like those giant ram machines that you see putting in bridge piers along the highway construction zones.

Needles were now flying everywhere.

"This is the way that you have to test it for freshness," he kept repeating to me. He had hit it so hard and so many times that the base of the trunk was now starting to split and break apart. The old man stopped, and he sat down on a snow pile. He was breathing heavily now, and he shook his head while he looked at the tree as it leaned on the pile next to him. I think he was exhausted from the tree testing that he had been performing.

"We have to take this tree back to the lot. It is a bad tree. That giant must have gotten this one mixed up with one that he was going to burn in the big kettle." My father became angry now. He removed his wool hat, and he looked at me while wiping sweat off his forehead.

Freshness testing is hard work.

"This is a dried up, old, relic of a tree, which will not last until Christmas, and the holiday will be ruined!"

I shuddered in horror at the mere thought of a ruined Christmas and having to wait an entire year to have this much fun once more.

I looked at him and said, "Well, what is the giant man going to say? It still looks like a pretty, nice tree to me, Dad." I continued my weak effort to plead in the tree's defense.

My comment must have sparked an idea, as I saw him glance at the tree and then back to me. The old man popped up from the snow pile, clapped his hands, and said, "Go and get my pliers, go get the needle nose, and the regular pliers."

"Pliers, Dad?" I was clearly puzzled.

"Yeah, yeah, yeah, and hurry. It is getting late, just go and get the pliers!"

I ran down to the basement, grabbed the requested varieties of pliers, brought them back up as quickly as I could, and gave them to him.

He grabbed the now officially proclaimed dried up, old relic of a tree, and held it up with one hand on the trunk. I watched in amazement as he put the pliers down near the trunk of the tree and clamped the jaws around one single branch of the tree. He then worked the pliers back and forth and pulled them towards the end of the branch, stripping the needles off the branch in one long swoop. It was like people eating corn on the cob during a summer picnic.

"ZZZZZIPPPP!"

Needles went flying everywhere!

He moved to the next branch and, "ZZZZZIPPPP!"

More needles went flying. He stripped the branches cleanly, right down to the wood. I was wide-eyed at the needle stripping procedure.

"Come over here and hold the tree, while I work the pliers. Spin the tree as I move," the old man instructed me.

Around and around and around he went, with me moving the tree as he worked through stripping each branch of needles.

ZZZZZIPPPP! There soon was a huge pile of needles lying under the tree and the tree was now looking like a bare skeleton.

ZZZZZIPPPP! ZZZZZIPPPP! ZZZZZIPPPP! Soon, the tree was now a mere shell of its former self. The poor, defenseless Christmas tree stood there, with about twelve needles remaining on the entire tree on a few random branches.

I did not say a word; it was, in fact, beyond words, while I stared at this former, glorious tree, now stripped bare in a mad rush of overzealous, freshness testing.

Nothing proclaims Christmas more than a bare skeleton of a dried up, old relic of a Christmas tree.

The old man stood back and looked at it in a satisfied manner. He tugged at his pants, straightened his wool hat, and reported, "You see, I was right, it was not a fresh tree."

He grabbed the bare tree, tossed it back up on the top of the Putter, and tied it off. One could hardly even tell that it had once been a Christmas tree. It was a sad, skinny stick with a few measly branches, with some sparse needles, a few bare twigs, and a long, bare trunk. Mum had now appeared in the driveway, and she looked at the tree in horror. She also could not say a word. She remained speechless and she could only point at the poor, bare tree. The shock of the sight of the tree had stolen all of her words.

"We are taking the tree back," the old man yelled. "I told all of you that the needles were going to fall off. Youse guys, did not believe me!"

She stood there amazed, not saying a word, as we jumped in the car and backed out of the driveway.

Chapter Six

The Defining Christmas Moment

The entire time, during the ride on the way over to the Christmas tree lot, the old man went on and on, preaching to me about how the giant was going to give us a hard time, and how it will be impossible to get our money back.

"This is how the evil world ruins Christmas!" He screamed. "All people care about is money. I knew that he couldn't care less about fresh trees and making sure our Christmas was a great one! Did you see how he tore that money out of my hands? The money grubbing, greedy, giant . . . he ripped it right out of my hands!"

I nodded my head in agreement as the old man checked me for a confirmation of what had happened.

"It was all an act with that supposed love of Christmas trees. Not all the actors are in Hollywood, Paulie. Remember that!"

He then continued, with a long diatribe of other reasons as to what has happened to Christmas due to money grubbing, commercialism. His hands gripped the steering wheel like a vise, and he was blowing steam off like a teakettle. It was clear that he was suiting up in his best suit of armor to get ready to do battle with the giant at the lot who had fooled him into buying a non-fresh tree.

"You see, it is all about the money nowadays. No one cares anymore about the true meaning of Christmas. All that talk and mumbo-jumbo sales pitch he was giving us about Christmas was a fraud!" I listened carefully to the lessons the old man taught to me and nodded my head in approval. All the time, I was actually wondering just how this whole fiasco was really going to transpire, once the giant sees what is left of our tree.

In a huge coup, my father came up with a stirring patriotic idea that, "The government should step in, and come up with laws and rules for selling fresh Christmas trees to prevent the ordinary guy from being taken advantage of."

I was just learning about government in school, and this did seem like a good idea, so I shouted back, "You're right Dad, I agree." After all, I reasoned, the old man had served in the military. He was a solid patriotic citizen, and he knew about the government. If I had an American flag handy, I would have waved it in the air, as if we were going into battle, defending all honest citizens across the country against evil Christmas tree sellers!

We pulled into the lot and we both climbed out of the car. It was now early evening, and it was bitterly cold. I stomped my feet on the ground just to make sure they were still attached to the rest of my body, because the Putter's heater left a lot to be desired, as far as actual heat output was concerned. The multicolored Christmas lights above the tree stands glowed happily in the early evening air. We walked towards the trees when sure enough; the giant appeared from under the cover of evergreens. There were not any other customers in sight in the lot, and we were alone to do battle with the giant.

I imagined that this must have been how David felt when approaching Goliath on the open battleground.

"HELLOOO AND MERRY CHRISTMASSSSS! Hey, youse guys! How are you doing? Merry Christmas!"

The giant was waving when he saw us. He had a big, broad smile on his enormous face.

"What did you come back for, another Christmas tree? Do you need another tree? Merry Christmas!"

The giant was bellowing on and on as he walked

towards us, his breath steaming in the frosty air. In what I hoped was a comforting sign, he seemed as happy and jovial as he had been earlier in the day.

I had a bad feeling about the situation, as I could picture in my mind the giant thrashing and pulverizing my father right here in the church parking lot. The old man, of course, was a pit bull and the giant's huge size did not intimidate him in the least in his quest for a fresh tree. He had come too far to allow a little thing like the largest human being in the entire State of New Jersey, who could squash him like a grape, to stop him in his endless pursuit of a traditional Christmas.

We stopped in our tracks as the giant came closer and stood in front of us.

"No, we did not come for another tree," the old man answered. "I have a problem here, a very serious problem."

"What, what . . . kind of problem?" The giant stopped in his tracks and looked down at us mere miniature creatures, with his smile fading to a surprised look. He clearly was very upset when he heard that we had a problem.

"Let me show you there, giant, chief guy. It is easier . . . if I show you," the old man said, as he waved for the giant to follow us to the car.

The old man had tagged the giant with a new name.

I ran ahead and untied the ropes that held what used to be a Christmas tree on the car. The old man grabbed it, dropped it down to the ground, and stood it up next to the car for the giant to see. There the tree stood, in all of its very sad glory, a tall, lean, needleless stick. It was now a tortured victim of the old man's harsh and brutal, fresh tree testing capabilities.

The giant took one look at the tree and just stopped and stared with his mouth wide open. "What the heck happened to your Christmas tree?" He bellowed aloud the question in his huge, deep, earth shattering voice.

The old man prepared to dig in, and I faded back to the

car for safety in anticipation of the profound explanation that was coming.

"Well," the old man was stammering a little here, but swiftly regained his composure, searching deep within his very soul for that usual razzle dazzle, "I do not think it was a fresh tree. I guess when we were driving it home, the . . . wind . . . it must have dried it out, and all the needles fell off."

The giant gawked in horror and shook his head at what used to be our Christmas tree.

"I have been selling trees for over forty years and I have never seen anything like this! There is hardly even a needle left on the entire tree!"

The giant was clearly shocked at the sad condition of our tree.

"Do you mean to tell me that you drove home and when you went to get your tree off the car, this is what it looked like?" The giant was now intently studying the remnants of the tree and scouring over the branches.

The defining moments were now here, and my father answered as he very strategically expanded upon the exact details of our afternoon, "Yeah, yeah, yeah, I guess it was dried out and old. You sold us a bomb of a tree. You must have gotten it mixed up with the trees that your brother cut down in Pennsylvania today."

My father was digging in now, getting ready for battle, studying the giant's face, and body language for a twitch or hint of what was to come next. I just looked around, with my heart pounding, planning an escape route in case the giant exploded like a huge atomic bomb.

I also hoped and prayed that the old man did not call him "giant, chief guy" again.

The big giant looked around the tree, pulling and tugging at the branches, with his big, huge eyeballs popping out of his head in clear amazement at what had happened to the tree. He stood up and turned towards us. I felt my heart rise up in my throat, and I prepared to make a run for it.

"I never have seen this before, and I sincerely tell you that, I am really sorry about this. I feel terrible." The giant buttoned his overcoat up, as if a chill had suddenly penetrated his, until now, impenetrable, cold defense shields.

"Huh?" The old man could barely squeak out. He was shocked at the humble response of the giant.

"Yes, I told you that we pride ourselves on only selling the best and freshest trees around. My brother and I have not stayed here for all these years by not treating people fairly and honestly, you know. What is important here is that you are happy, and that you and your family have a great Christmas with a beautiful, fresh, Christmas tree."

The giant turned and pointed his long arm at the tree stands.

"You and your son . . . please go back in there and pick out the type of tree that you want. I am just going to take this tree and throw it into the kettle over there and it will be a done deal."

The giant finished speaking, he picked up the stick of a tree and walked towards the kettle. I looked at my father and he was standing there, amazed at the giant's words. His eyes met mine, and I could see that they were clearly different. The defensive posture was gone, his guard was down, and he was relaxed at the sudden realization that the giant man was not going to battle with him at all. A smile broke across his face and a mellow, happy look came over him.

"Wow, thank you," was all that the old man could manage to say. It was as if he was too stunned at how this had transpired to find any other words to say.

My father motioned for me to follow him into the rows of trees as he started to scan the trees and pick out a replacement. I did not say anything. I just followed him up and down the rows of the trees. He quickly identified a tree right away and pulled it out of the racks.

"This looks like a good tree," the old man said. "It looks just about the same size and shape as the other one."

I nodded my head in approval. At this point in the game, I was not about to disagree with anything. He gave it a few little half-hearted taps on the ground with his infamous freshness testing, but nothing like he had done before. He was strangely quiet and subdued, and he was not saying much of anything. When he reported that this was a good one, we each grabbed an end of the tree and carried it out of the rows towards the kettle area.

The giant was still holding the old tree next to the iron kettle, and he was studying the branches very carefully when he spotted us heading towards him. When he saw us, he quickly stood up, and he tossed it into the kettle fire with a quick little flick of his massive arms. The fire glowed and crackled with the new wood thrown upon it.

"You got one, huh? That sure was quick!" The giant was back to his usual jovial, happy, loud self. "It looks like a nice one, and it is fresh too," he reported as he grabbed the ends of the branches, feeling the needles with his gloves. We carried it over to the Putter and tied it up on the top of the car.

My father followed him back to the kettle, turned to him, and said, "You know something, giant, chief guy . . . I want to pay you for this Christmas tree."

The giant shook his head and said, "No, no, no, you do not owe me anything. That first tree was a mess. You were correct that I must have had it mixed up with an old one. Handling all these trees, I am bound to make a mistake or two." The giant smiled, and he chuckled at the thought.

Right then and there, in the middle of this Christmas tree lot, it finally happened.

After all the effort, old lights, new lights, lost keys in the snow, fake and real trees, miniature Christmas villages, fake tree scent, sad and angry people, near and actual disasters, fights and debates, what the old man had really been searching for in his heart this season came over him. Christmas spirit took over his soul.

The Christmas spirit of giving and caring about the actual holiday finally came through.

The struggles to find a real Christmas tree and to recapture a traditional Christmas had been worth it.

The giant had treated the old man, just as people had treated each other years ago, when the holiday meant so much more than just how much money you could extract from someone's bank account.

My dad broke out into a giant smile. The giant man with a heart of gold Christmas tinsel put his giant limb of an arm around my father and said, "Merry Christmas to you and your family."

My father pulled out fifteen dollars from his coat pocket and he stuck it in the giant's coat pocket. "No, no, no," my dad insisted. "You take this money and you have a merry Christmas. Wait right here, please, wait right here."

The giant waved to indicate that he would, but he seemed a little puzzled.

The old man ran over to the trunk of the Putter and yelled back once more to the giant to stay there. That he would be right back. He opened the trunk, and I watched as he reached down in a box that he had in there. The old man had told us earlier in the week about how each year the big boss in the shop where he worked handed out gifts of expensive bottles of whiskey to whomever they thought were the best workers in the shop that past year. The old man had received a bottle, as well as a huge, twenty-five-pound turkey, which we were going to have for our Christmas Day feast. The old man was proud of his accomplishment, and had made a big deal, while telling all of us of his good fortune over supper one night.

Out of the box in the trunk, the old man pulled out the

bottle of booze. He ran back over to where the giant and I were standing. I could see the bottle gleaming in the night, reflecting in the glass, the many colors of the Christmas lights on top of the wooden stakes. The bottle had a big, red Christmas bow tied around the neck of it.

My father handed the giant the bottle of booze and he said, "Merry Christmas to you!"

The giant held the bottle up, read the label, and whistled. "Wow, I cannot take this. It is a very expensive bottle of booze."

My father answered, "No, no, no, you take it, it is so cold out here. The afternoon is gone now, and this is a terrible night. It is so cold. Please take a drink of this and stay warm. I want you to have it as a Christmas gift." He smiled at the giant and convinced him that he should have it, as the old man stammered out, "Merry Christmas to you giant, chief guy and, well . . . thank you."

Before you knew it, they were the best of friends, and they cracked open the bottle over in front of the fire. The giant had grabbed two glasses from inside his trailer. They poured the whiskey, and made a Christmas toast to each other. They were both laughing and talking about the local football teams, baseball teams, and all sorts of subjects about the old neighborhood.

I just stood there amazed at the entire event, and at what had transpired right before my eyes. I took it all in as a fond memory, the fire roaring in the kettle, my father next to the giant man, both of them standing there, laughing and sipping some Christmas cheer, framed by a backdrop of soft Christmas lights and hundreds upon hundreds of now officially confirmed; fresh Christmas trees.

They shook hands and exchanged well wishes for the season one more time. We got back in the car and started the engine.

I turned and looked one last time and we waved at the giant man waving back to us, bellowing, "MERRY

CHRISTMAS," as only he could, into the frozen air.

As we turned onto the main road radio station, WPAT cooperated with a timely selection of "The Christmas Tree," and the old man whistled along with the merry tune.

"Boy, that giant, chief guy is one nice, Christmas lovin,' guy," the old man said as he beeped the horn with a goodbye signal, and we turned for home.

In the old man's custom, New Jersey language, no one could have captured the giant's spirit more eloquently.

Chapter Seven

The Christmas Spirit

My sister and mother met us in the driveway as they heard the old man beeping the horn violently to signal to them our triumphant return. He jumped out of the car and we untied the tree as the old man was beside himself with joy.

"That giant, chief guy over at the lot there is the greatest guy in the world! Just look at this tree, what a beauty!"

My sister and mother clapped their hands in joy and sensed that this had finally ended the nearly impossible real Christmas tree mission.

We carried the tree into the living room, and that night, we put the fantastic new Italian lights on it. Neither my sister, nor I, even stepped on a single light bulb, and we managed not to have any errant lights stuck in our ears or hair as we assisted with the light installation mission.

I never said a word to anyone about the old man giving away the bottle of booze that he received from the shop or paying the extra dough for the tree. I knew that somehow, and in some way, the money and the booze actually bought something more than just a tree for the old man.

He actually had bought his Christmas spirit back.

The old man was happy and full of holiday spirit. He was helping with the tree and house decorating while singing aloud to all kinds of holiday tunes.

The next morning, the old man took a rare day off from work, and since we had finished school last week, and we were now on Christmas break, we could all be together as a family. This was truly a monumental moment in Henson's family history! We had a huge tree trimming party, and we decked out the tree with all kinds of special ornaments and garlands. The old man spun one Harvey Crooner Christmas record after another on his Victrola all day long. My mother cooked up a dinner feast of her famous Shepherd's Pie recipe and a warm apple pie for dessert.

I have to admit that the old man chugged more than just a few Big Boulder beers here and there. I swore I saw him in the kitchen, testing out one of those dreaded, "too sweet" Dingleberry beers. Regardless, the old man remained full of spirit, in more ways than one!

It was a wonderful day.

That night, we turned out the lights in the house, and stared in awe and wonderment at how breathtakingly beautiful the real tree was. It was the most fantastic Christmas tree that I had ever seen, as it glowed there, twinkling as if it were a bright and clear beacon of the season.

I watched as the old man tossed that crazy, artificial tree scent away in the trash, as he realized that this tree had a built-in scent! My mother proudly reported that she was looking forward to not having a headache all Christmas season this year.

Our traditional Christmas, although it was a struggle to achieve, really turned out to be one of the best times of our lives. The old man sat there in his chair for a long time that night, enjoying a few Big Boulder beers, (after a brief taste-test, those Dingleberries were once again, deemed as too sweet) playing his records, and just admiring the tree glowing in the darkness. My sister and I fell asleep under the tree, and Mum woke us both up and pushed us off to bed.

Christmas Day came and went, and it was a great day. Mum had prepared a fantastic turkey dinner to remember, topped by cakes, pies, and other fabulous homemade desserts. The next day, for our mother's English holiday of Boxing Day, Mum prepared another fantastic roast beef dinner with Yorkshire pudding, and topped it off with a dessert of a Christmas plum pudding that was one of her crowning moments!

All the visitors and family who came by our house, both on Christmas Day and Boxing Day, admired what a glorious tree we had this year. The old man would never hesitate to tell the long story of the quest for the tree, and by now, the story had grown in details by leaps and bounds.

The old man's storytelling magic had turned it into a wonderful tale of adventure and folklore. I stood in the doorway as he spun tale after tale to my grandparents, uncles, aunts, and other family and friends, of how he backed the police chief into a corner, and forced him into submission, and how he rescued us from near death on the sled, (sleigh) with his lightning quick speed on the icy hill! He never hesitated to tell everyone about the "giant, chief guy," who was now at least eleven tall, and how when he laughed, the ground shook.

The tree remained fresh and proud, as it was the day when we picked it off the lot. The old man would pick at the needles once in a while and test it. He kept the water filled every day, but he was convinced that we had picked a good one. The tree easily fulfilled the requirement of the old man's New Year's Day rule, and it was still fresh and bright when the holiday season finally ended.

The old man became a little teary-eyed when it came time to take all the decorations down. After New Year's Day, he sadly packed up his Christmas village and packed it away for another year. Then we turned to the tree. We helped him take off all the Italian lights, the decorations and tinsel, and we packed them away in boxes. We returned all the furniture to the living room, and Mum was happy to see her house back to normal, or at least as normal as a Henson household could be.

It is always so sad when Christmas finally does end; this year was no exception. The old man then slowly and sadly lowered the tree to haul it outside to the trash.

The conversation during the process was all about what a special tree that was, how wonderful the giant was, and what a great, traditional season it had been. The old man had even reluctantly conceded that there were just a few people left on this good, old planet who celebrated Christmas for what it really was. He restored his faith in Christmas, and to a certain extent, even his faith in people.

Instead of tossing our special tree in the trash heap, as millions of other families did, lining up spent, dried up, Christmas trees up and down the roadways, he took the tree outside and he cut it up in the backyard alone by himself. He stacked the little pieces and logs up in the back of his garden shed. During the spring and summer, he would break them up and toss them in his compost pile for his garden.

I think he felt that by doing this, he kept a little piece of that special tree with him forever more.

My mind spun back to where I was as I realized that I was standing out in the middle of the shopping center parking lot, next to the Christmas tree stand.

Oh boy, time is ticking here. I did linger too long, after all.

Out in the front of the rows of trees, I spotted a family with a young father and three young boys, checking out the trees that were closest to me. They were picking out individual trees, and the father would grab one and hold it up, while everyone checked it out. He was holding them up one-by-one, as they checked how tall they were and how wide they were. I could not help but stop there and watch the scene unfold.

The father was chatting away about a tree he was holding, "I think this one will fit nicely in the corner of the room." The boys nodded in approval and just then, they happened to all look up and spotted me looking their way.

I spoke out, "Hey, how's it going? I wish you grace and peace as well as a merry Christmas to you and your family. You know, you want to make sure you get a fresh tree."

The father looked up, and he answered me, "Merry Christmas to you too, Father. Yes, we want to get a Christmas tree that is fresh, so it looks good and lasts all season."

I had not hidden my clerical garb! I was always being confused for being a Catholic priest. I was not going to correct them. In the grand scheme of things, it really did not matter.

I nodded my head in agreement and told him, "You know, a good way to test it is to pick up the tree and gently tap it on the ground, to see if any of the needles fall off."

"No kidding. I never thought of that before. That does sound like a great idea. Thank you," the father said as he gently picked up the tree and tapped the trunk on the ground, as the young boys watched intently.

"Now . . . not too hard," I cautioned, "you just have to tap it really, really, gently."

I think he got a fresh one.

THE END

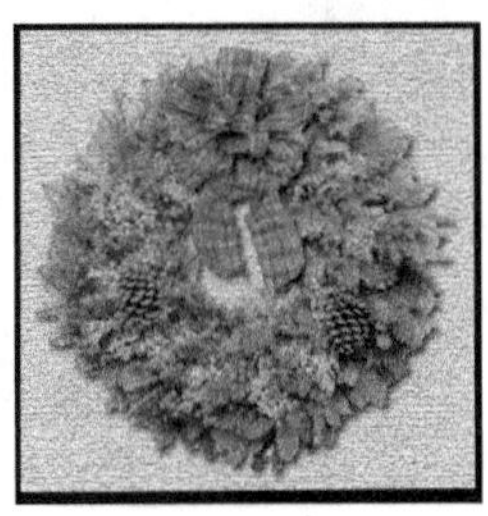

The Collector

Chapter One

The Elderly Man

The doctor placed his arm around the elderly man who was sitting upon his examination table and said, "You're really in good shape. I do not see any major problems. All of your tests came out excellent for a person of your age. I think that you just have to exercise a bit more. I think, if you go out walking and increase your walking regiment, then this pain in your legs will go away. You need to increase the circulation."

The doctor walked over to his table in the room, flipped through the medical records, and scanned them once more.

"That is what I am going to prescribe, my friend. I am going to prescribe some aspirin and exercise."

The elderly man protested back to the doctor, and he said, "You know, doc. I have been walking almost every day. Ever since my wife passed away, I take the dog out three or four times a day and I do errands. You know . . . I go and visit with the neighbors. I keep moving around."

The entire time the elderly man was speaking, the doctor was shaking his head back and forth.

"No, no, no," the doctor said. "Just going around the

block is not going to do it. You have to work hard to increase the amount of exercise that you get and broaden the walking program. If you do that then, I am sure the pain is going to go away."

The doctor waved the elderly man down from the examination table and said, "Let's see you again in a few months and see how you are doing."

He put his arm around the elderly man and walked him out to the patient waiting room. He handed the elderly man's medical chart to the nurse at the front desk, and said to him, "You have to put your old ways on the shelf and remember, what is old is old, and what is new is new! If you can increase your walking program, say, up to two or three miles, then that would be fantastic. Please take it slowly, build up gradually and I promise that you are going to feel like a new man."

The elderly man and the doctor shook hands and exchanged goodbyes. After settling the paperwork with the front desk out the front door, he went.

The elderly man walked outside and into his car. He shook his head, because he did not want to listen to what the doctor was saying.

"I had hoped to just take a pill or two," the elderly man muttered to himself and he chuckled while he started the car. He rode home, thinking about what the doctor had said to him during the entire ride back to his house. When he arrived home, he took his old dog out for a walk. It was not that bad a day weather wise, so he thought; well, I will just go a bit farther, maybe out to the main street. The two of them did set out on the journey. They puttered along slowly, made it out to the main street, and then headed back home.

He was exhausted and his dog was exhausted too.

When he got home, he sat in his favorite chair, took his shoes off, and rubbed his ankles, while he noticed how the swelling had recently increased in his ankles and feet.

There was no doubt as to how badly he felt right now, the longer walk had taken quite a bit out of him. He rubbed his ankles and feet and observed how sore they really were. The elderly man shook his head and thought to himself that the doctor must be mistaken; he really does need more than just some silly exercise program.

He lived in an urban area on the older side of a small city in Morris County, New Jersey. It was the only city in the semi-rural county, a small city, but a city nonetheless. He had lived here his entire life, having long since retired from work. His wife passed away a year or so ago, and it was just him and his faithful old dog now. His children had all long since grown up and moved away to seek different employment opportunities and to find new lives in other areas.

All of his children had moved out of New Jersey, and the elderly man had not been very happy about that, but he had to admit to the fact that with the types of work that his children were involved in; there was not much in the way of viable employment here. In recent years, the local economy had taken a terrible downturn and the cost of living had risen dramatically. His children checked on him via the telephone once a week, but the elderly man mostly just kept to himself.

He had a couple of buddies that he met at the Veterans' Hall for a chat once or twice a week, and he tipped a few beers with them, but he really did not socialize that much.

He attended church on Sundays; it was a Lutheran church out on the outskirts of the county. It had been slated for closing a few years back, because of a number of issues, but it recently had experienced a revival, and now the congregation was bursting at the seams. A new pastor was recently hired, and he had done an outstanding job of bringing the church back from the brink of extinction.

The elderly man was thrilled about the improvements. The church was important to him and his family's history there was a big part of his life. He had been involved at first when the church was in the process of revival, but now that it had for the most part smoothed out, he had faded away to the background.

His family were all charter members of the church, and their roots were there for many generations within the congregation. These days, however, he did not have the energy, or the desire, to be involved in anything except for simply attending the Sunday services.

The new pastor was young, smart, and dynamic, and he really liked the young man. The two of them had connected, and he supported his new ideas and energy, but other than attending services, he was not interested in some of the behind the scene's drama of operating a church, even if he was a charter family member.

He did, however, tell the young pastor that he was there for him, if he ever needed the support, and the young pastor seemed to appreciate the comment.

The church world, behind the scenes, could be tough, with maneuvering and politics and it could quickly grow wearisome. He was happy now to stay out of people's business and keep the same old routine, and a very small circle.

The elderly man's real love and passion was baseball, and he sat in his chair and watched ballgame after ballgame during the season. He was not much for the other sports, but baseball was his love. He did have to admit that maybe he did sit around an awful lot, watching and enjoying the baseball games on television. The more he thought about it, then the more he knew the doctor was correct that he spent too much time in front of the television.

Sighing loudly while he rubbed his feet, the elderly man vowed to give it a shot and see what he could do to increase his physical regiment. The elderly man remembered what the doctor had told him when he had instructed him not to push too hard, to let the strength come a little at a time, and he followed the doctor's guidance. Some days, he took the old dog with him, but other times, he would just go alone. If it was a pleasant day weather-wise, he would walk just as far as he could before he started to feel that it was too much. It was late spring and the summer heat was right around the corner. The elderly man knew that he would not want to be out there, if it was one hundred degrees and the heat was blazing down, or the humidity was stifling. Right for now, though, the weather was very pleasant for walking.

As he continued his regiment each day, the elderly man had to admit he felt that he was getting a little stronger, and as of late, some of the swelling pain in his ankles and feet had slightly reduced.

He kept at it, and he promised himself to go a little further each day. He became dedicated to the new program, and his dedication, as well as his regimentation, not only seemed to improve his physical outlook, but he also felt a little better emotionally.

The elderly man walked, and he walked.

As he made his way, his old mind wandered, and he noticed things that he would normally bypass in his car and never notice, or at least, would never give a second thought. He noticed the streets that he had known so well since he was a child was now rundown, and the old neighborhoods in the city were becoming tired and worn.

Many of the original families had long since moved away, and the houses that they had previously kept maintained and in tip-top condition were now in disrepair. The new occupants did not have the same pride in ownership that the other generations had in their properties and homes. The lawns were full of weeds or were overgrown; fences were broken, missing pickets, and were in need of paint. Roof gutters were falling down and litter strewn all about the lawns and front sidewalks.

Many of the houses were an outright mess; it was obvious that severe regression had taken place over the last few years. It was quite sad for the elderly man to observe, and he was surprised that it had taken his new walking regimen for him to notice this.

He must have had blinders on as he rode by in his car, but now, while he moved along on the walkways, it became quite apparent to him.

Each day, the elderly man would go a little farther, and he found himself plotting a new course or direction for variety in his venture, as well as the opportunity to check out new areas along the way.

The elderly man also noticed how people no longer cared any more, or they were generally apathetic and not concerned about the environment. He noticed how folks tossed their trash around, and carelessly tossed old cans, bottles, and general trash around. He thought to himself, how people just did not think about the quality of life and appearance of the old city any more in this modern day and age.

"There is no longer any pride in this place," he would mumble. One day, as he was preparing to go out on his daily excursion, he had an idea that maybe he could make a little difference. The old gent cared. He remembered how pristine the old city streets had once been, and what the areas looked like when folks took pride in where they lived.

"A twofold mission," the man said before he set out on his daily mission.

He tucked a large plastic trash bag in his back pocket and mumbled, "No one else is going to pick up some litter, so maybe, I will pick some trash up as I go along, and make just a little difference here and there."

He theorized that the bending, stooping, and additional movements would only add to the exercise program. It seemed as though; the elderly man had convinced himself that all of this was truly worthwhile as he left for his daily walk.

As he made his way along, when he spotted a can, trash, or bottle, he would bend down, pick it up, and place it in his bag.

Oh boy—he had better rethink this plan!

He realized very quickly that the bottles made the bag too heavy and this truly would add to his exercise regimen! When he arrived home after his initial collection mission, the elderly man shook his head at the amount of trash he had collected. He threw it out in his garage with the rest of his household trash.

Despite the physical exertion, the man could not contain the fact that he was happy and, to some extent, fulfilled inside. He had made just a little difference, and he felt as if for the first time in a long time, he had a duty, as well as a little objective. Staring at the mound of trash in the bag, it made him feel better, knowing that even at his age, he contributed in some small way. He suddenly had a small purpose in his life and he felt as if he had a mission.

He went into the house, fed the dog, and eventually made his way to his chair. The elderly man took off his walking shoes, and he noticed how the swelling in his feet, as of late, had reduced greatly.

In fact, he could visibly see that the condition was greatly improved, and the swelling was reducing on a daily basis. When he rubbed his ankles, he observed how they were no longer sore, and the muscles seemed to be becoming tight and strong.

"Maybe, the doctor was right after all," he said aloud. He was surprised that the exercise program had indeed helped so much. The elderly man was very pleased; he felt a lot better and was becoming stronger every day.

The elderly man knew that the hot weather was right around the corner and his precious baseball season had already begun. Very soon, the weather would not be quite as attractive for walking, and the lure to just stay in his chair and watch the baseball games would be strong.

His mind wandered to baseball, and for some reason, he thought about the old ballpark on the other side of the city. He had not been there for many years. In fact, he could not even tell you how long it had been since he had seen the park.

He realized that he never even passed by it in his car. Perhaps, even in his mind, he purposely avoided it, since it was a link to his past, his faded youth, and a faded memory.

The park was in an area of the city that he avoided, and it was not on any routes that he ordinarily traveled. He always went to the same places, the same stores, church, the cleaners, the same old stops.

"I wonder how the park looks now," he said; as he reached down to comfort the old dog at his feet. The old dog lifted his head and looked at his master, as though he, too, was curious. Thinking about the baseball field and the park, he wondered if he could make it on foot. It would be a very long walk for him, and he was not sure that he had trained enough to conquer a walk of that distance.

Still, he was curious about it and he wondered what the park was like after all of these years.

His curiosity had been aroused, and the fact that the park was a long hike for him was even more intriguing. It was as if he set a goal in his mind and it stuck in there as he sat in his chair. Slowly, the elderly man drifted off to a nap and for a quick visit to his past while in dreamland.

The old park was a place where the man had spent a large part of his childhood; playing baseball, playing football, hanging out; it was a place full of memories for him. Tucked in a gentle corner of the old city, it was perhaps a little more than a mile or so from his house, and he could not help but think about how important a place it had been for him when he was young.

Memories and the past came back to him. He had spent his entire life in this city. He grew up in this very neighborhood, worked for a company here, raised a family here, and retired here. He thought how it was very strange that he never even thought of the park until now, and he actually wondered what had suddenly inspired him to have such strong thoughts of visiting this, until now—long, forgotten place.

When he woke up, the elderly man vowed to make it a goal to make it to the park on foot.

The next day he set out, but the effort and distance were just a little too much for him to endure. He made it about halfway, but had to give up and turn around. He realized that as well as he was feeling that he was not quite ready for that type of distance.

Each day, he would try, and each day, he went a little farther. He was glad that he had set such a lofty aspiration of completing the journey to the park, because it gave him something special to look forward to as the ultimate sign of his conditioning. It had certainly broken up the same old boring routine, consisting of the same old walks and streets that he had now grown so accustomed to during his ventures.

Each day over the next few weeks, he grew a little closer to his final goal, as his body and legs grew stronger and stronger. His strides became longer, very steady, and he was feeling wonderful. Some days, poor weather interrupted his walking, but for the most part, each day he crept closer to his purpose of reaching the park on foot.

One day almost to his own surprise, he was there! The park was right there in front of him! The elderly man broke into a big smile, because it had been many, many years since he stood on the edge of this park. He strode confidently as he walked closer to the edge of the street opposite the park. He was amazed because he felt as if he could still walk these sidewalks blindfolded!

The park was large, and it had two baseball fields, with one each at opposite ends. One field was a regulation-size baseball field, with a little league sized baseball field on the other end of the park. The park was a little unusual because standing out in the outfield on the far end of the park was a house. The man chuckled while he stood looking over the field, remembering how his goal as a left-handed hitter was to sock a home run over the fence, and have the baseball land in the side yard of the home. He remembered how one or two great hitters in his youth actually knocked a ball so far that they bounced the baseball off the roof of the house. He had managed only to hit one or two homers in the yard, but nonetheless . . . he had done it!

The elderly man was a child once again, and he was reliving fond memories as he gazed out at the field.

When he saw that the little children's playground next to the house was still there, he shouted aloud, "I wonder if the field house is still standing, the one with the plaque that had the great Zambino's inscription on it!"

His childhood professional baseball hero, Louis Zambino, had actually visited the field, dedicated it, and stood right at home plate for pictures and interviews. The plaque mounted here commemorated the great event.

The elderly man moved closer and closer to the field and he crossed the street until he was actually standing within the confines of the park. As he drew closer, he stopped and focused past his euphoria, and realized what it was that he was actually looking at.

Curbing his excitement, the old man stood there and looked around at the condition of the park. There was trash all over, the grass was high and not maintained, and there were bottles and cans strewn all over.

It was not a pretty sight.

The end of the park had a war memorial monument and a flagpole that had been there for as long as the old man could remember. It honored the war dead from the city, with names of the fallen soldiers added to the plaque, as the various wars throughout history occurred. It was to the man, who was a war veteran himself, a holy place, a place of honor, and of deep appreciation. It was a focal point for the park and a very famous landmark in the old city. Years ago, whenever there were pictures taken of the park, this monument was always the prominent feature of the photographs.

The elderly man spotted an old hobo sitting on the steps of the monument drinking from a bottle covered with a paper bag. He was horrified to see that all around the base of the war monument were strewn old bottles, papers, and mounds of assorted trash.

In addition to the condition of the war monument, the baseball field was a mess; the grass was spotty and almost nonexistent. The trees were not trimmed and the benches that lined the fields were falling apart. No one was playing baseball here. In fact, it looked as if a game had not been played on these fields in many a season. There were no baselines, the player benches were missing, and only some posts remained in the ground as a painful reminder of the seats where baseball players waited for their own individual moments of glory. The backstops behind home plate at both of the fields were falling down, and large sections of the wood behind home plate had rotted away and were now missing. He noticed how the old, cut up fire hose that once lined the backstop to deflect the baseballs and to soften the blows had rotted, and now was peeling away from the backstop.

The elderly man sighed, became quite forlorn and upset, as he mumbled, "What has happened here in front of my very eyes. Has this old city given up on itself? Doesn't anyone care about it anymore?"

This was not what he had expected, but being honest with himself, he did not know what he had expected to see after so many years. As he stood there on the sidewalk lining the park, he knew that this was certainly not what he wanted to see.

He walked over to the field house to see if the famous brass dedication plaque of the great Zambino's famous visit remained on the side of the building. He knew what event the plaque had recorded; he had virtually memorized the words as a youth. The old man was horrified when he saw the plaque covered in graffiti, and you could hardly even read the writing. In fact, you could barely tell that it was a special plaque at all.

The park was a complete and total mess, a sad sign of urban decay, a testimony to budget cuts, lost priorities, and apathy.

As he stood out there next to the large field, his mind wandered back to when he played ball here as a teenager. He had been a great player in his youth, a shortstop by position, and in his day, he was one of the best players this area had ever seen. He really thought he could have made it in the big leagues. He had been a slick fielder at shortstop, and he could move to his left especially fast, and scoop up the hardest ground ball or line drive. Once he fielded the ball, he could throw the ball like a rocket, as he had possessed a strong arm. No runners could outrun his throws to first base; he would throw the batters out right and left! The elderly man also remembered how good a hitter he had been. He had been a clutch hitter who would always come through whenever his team required him to deliver a key hit.

The elderly man could feel the smooth wooden handle of the baseball bat in his hands, and the sound of the crowd cheering from the now vacant bleachers that suddenly filled with old ghosts of the past swirling around and haunting the old man.

Very clearly, he saw the faces of teammates, key adversaries, and opponents from other teams that he recalled. He could see the team's managers and coaches, who were, of course, now all long gone. The memories of big games, the big hits he got in key moments, and the joy of winning championships, all came rushing back to him as he stood there. In his mind, he heard the crack of the ball hitting the bats, and all the joy of laughter that comes from winning games, as well as winning championships!

With great fondness, he recalled marching in parades in his baseball uniform with the championship trophies carried proudly in the bed of a pickup truck in front of the team.

Oh my, what glorious times those were!

If only he could have taken the time to enjoy them and hold those times deeply in his heart way back then. Now, they are only fond memories, shadows of his past, dreams of when he was so young.

All the good times that he had on this field, it was to him a very sacred and holy place. The elderly man always thought that if only he had managed to get a break, he could have made it to the big time. However, the big war came and then the draft. He had to fight a war, survive, then return home to a young family, and he had to make a living.

He postponed baseball, and this time it was forever. It now existed only in his memory, in his mind, and in his book of time.

The sadness that the elderly man felt was heartbreaking. His eyes welled up in tears, while he stood there on the edge of this field full of memories, with the wind blowing a little breeze that gently moved the few remaining, tiny wisps of hair that he had left on the top of his head.

He now wished that he had never come back to the park. He would rather that the field and the park would have always remained the same as he had it in his mind's eye. It was now his wish that it could have stayed there, unchanged and untouched forever. The park's condition was crushing to the old man's spirit, and he realized that it had wounded a part of his soul deep inside, when he saw the sad state of the condition of the field. The old man no longer felt that spring in his step, as he had been feeling the last few weeks.

He felt weighed down now with old age and his own mortality.

He could not believe the state of disrepair that his beloved field had fallen into, and as he stood there, he suddenly remembered the trash bags that he now always stuck in his back pocket for his long jaunts. In a burst of energy, he grabbed the plastic trash bags from his back pocket.

It was strange that in his dismay; he had forgotten that the bags were even there in his back pocket until now, but he started instinctively to pick up some litter, cans, and bottles. It seemed as if there was an endless supply of trash as the man picked up one paper, bottle, soda and beer can after another. Keeping recycling in mind, the old man put cans in one bag, and the litter and bottles in another. The elderly man was lost in his new mission, and he quickly went to work, picking them all up one by one.

A sad reality had come over the old man as he now realized how seriously things had changed in his home city; he just had never opened his eyes enough to see it. He realized that the park had become a hangout for teenagers, up to no good thugs, and homeless folks. It was very plain and simple that it was a disaster. The budget cuts in the city have ruined the park, as well as the city, the old man thought. They have let all the maintenance go and now have allowed it to fall into a sad state of disrepair.

The elderly man stood up from his trash collection mission and he stretched his back muscles out. He thought how sad it was that the city did not even care to cut the grass or weeds that now overran the entire field. It was the icing on a very miserable cake.

The man spoke to only his memories and almost

shouted aloud, "The grass has not been cut here for months. I am so disgusted that I am going to write a letter to the council and mayor!"

With some element of satisfaction, he thought that would do the trick, as he went back to his work, placing more and more cans and trash into his bags, but he knew it was much more than that. He knew in his heart that would be fruitless. No one would even respond to his letter. There was probably no money left in budgets for park maintenance and upkeep. Jobs had become scarce these days and budget cuts were deep; recreation and parks were low on the list of priorities when the fiscal crisis hit, and he knew that there was likely no money for the park during these difficult and desperate times.

This city, like so many old cities in the country, was going through tough times and the tax base had shrunk over the years. Folks had moved out of the city proper and out to the suburbs on the edges of the county where his church was. People did not want to live in the old cities any longer, nowadays; they wanted the fancier, larger homes that they now built out in the nearby suburban areas.

The old man continued to work. He did the best he could, and he filled his trash bag with cans. He realized that in his zeal to clean up the park that he had a flawed plan. He was no longer a few blocks away from his house, where he could carry the trash bags home easily. The bags with the bottles were heavy, and the park had not one single trash barrel around to dispose of the trash. He was sure that was part of the problem of why the park was so full of litter.

"How stupid is this that there are no trash cans around!" The old man shouted out in disgust.

The bottles were much too heavy for him to lug back, so he would need a different plan for them, but one or two bags full of cans he felt that he could easily handle. He threw the sack of cans on his back, and he dragged the full bag of bottles behind him.

Across the street, and down the road a little from the park, was a large warehouse and the elderly man, with some great effort, dragged his bag full of bottles into the loading dock area. He spotted a man working on the dock and asked him if he could dispose of the bag of bottles in his trash dumpster. He did not want to impose upon the warehouse man by throwing too much in the way of trash in the dumpster, so he decided to ask to throw only the bag of bottles in the receptacle. He explained to the warehouse man that he had cleaned up the park a bit and gathered some trash.

After all, the cans were light. He could set them out for recycling, and it would help with his exercise program to carry something back home.

"Go ahead there, old timer. Throw as much as you want in there," the worker said as the elderly man explained that he had collected them from the park. "Good luck with that mission," the worker said rather sarcastically. "The place will just be full of them again tomorrow!" The worker shouted at the old man as he saw just how hard he had worked on collecting the trash. "I applaud your efforts, so go ahead, and use the dumpster anytime. I do hate to say it, pal, but that is just a dump now, not really a park. I do not know why you would even call it a ballpark."

The elderly man thanked him again, and with his bag of cans in tow, he turned in the direction of his home. The old man just about forgot about his various ailments, as he now had a mission. The old gent now had an even greater purpose in his life, a goal to make the old ballpark better through his own efforts.

Each day, he made his trek to the park and each day; he felt better and better. Each day the collector did what he did the best these days; he collected! He did write a letter to the mayor and the grass at the park got cut; not a fancy cut, but at least, it was cut.

He would repair some things with a little tool pack that he tucked in his pocket. He would tighten a loose sign, install some screws into loose slats on the benches, he would prune some tree limbs with a little folding saw he carried, and of course, he would pick up the cans, bottles, and trash. He did the best he could at making things look a little better. He would chase away thugs and teenagers and reprimand them when he would see them throwing trash about. Each day, he felt that he was making an effort to improve the park's condition.

After a day's collection, he would drag a bag of bottles and trash over to the warehouse rubbish dumpster, and each day, he would bring home another bag of cans.

On a weekend afternoon, a few weeks after he began his clean up mission, the collector was sitting at the bar in the Veterans' Hall having a beer with his best friend. The collector told his friend about the horrible condition of the park as well as his one-man mission to clean it all up.

His friend shook his head and agreed that the trouble lies with the city itself.

"There are no jobs, there is no money, and things just keep going downhill. Perhaps, our time has also come, my friend. Maybe, it is time for us to sell our homes and leave this old city," the collector's friend said, as he listened to the collector's testimony.

His friend had little optimism and little in the way of positive energy, as he continued with his blunt opinion. "Yes . . . maybe, it is just time for us old guys to pack it all in," he said.

The summer was now upon them, and the weather was beginning to become hot and humid. Soon, the days would be long and sticky, and it would not be the type of weather that an elderly man should be out in, performing strenuous exercise. The collector told his friend that he knew he could not continue to make that long trek in the heat, and he lamented that if he did not get out there all the time, then the park will become a mess once more within a few days.

"It seems as if the park is dependent upon me. I am the only one who cares," the collector complained.

While sipping on his beer, the collector's friend said, "Well, it seems to me that you get a tremendous amount of exercise just by picking up all that trash, fixing things, and then dragging it all around. Why are you still obsessed with walking? Why not just drive your car over to the park and then load the bags in your car? It would be easier, and I am sure the warehouse people would appreciate you not filling their dumpster all the time. You started out on an exercise mission, and now it has changed into something completely different for you."

The collector's friend put down his beer and looked at the collector, as if he just had a sudden thought come upon him. He seemed surprised by his own idea, as he pondered it for a moment before he spoke.

Before taking another sip of beer, the collector's friend said, "You know, you should take the cans over to Hardy's recycling center, over on Ryerson Street and he will give you a few bucks for the scrap metal. What in the world are you doing with all those cans, anyway?"

The collector laughed as he said, "I had been taking them out to the trash, but actually I have been lazy, and there is quite a pile in my garage that has accumulated. I need to get rid of them now that the hot weather is here. I will have a big, stinky, mess on my hands soon. When you take a look at the situation, I suppose that I should be a good steward of the Earth and recycle them in bulk too."

The collector's drinking companion nodded his head and agreed.

"Hey, take them over to Hardy's and get a few bucks for them. It is not too much, but for all the work that you are doing, you might as well buy a six-pack of beer with the money. I will tell you another thing about Hardy's recycling center," the friend continued to say between sips.

"He is working hard to bring in new business, so he has this little niche where he gives all his customers one of those lottery scratch-off cards with each drop off. He is working hard to keep his customers from going out to the fancy new automated place out on the highway. Who knows, maybe you will win a million dollars from your cans!"

They both laughed at the thought and finished their beers while embroiled in other conversations. It had been a productive meeting over a few beers as the collector came up with some very good ideas for a plan going forward. His friend's advice had been good advice for sure!

The collector had agreed with it all and he implemented the advice right away. The next day, he loaded all the cans in his car and took them over to the recycling center. The attendant took the cans, measured and weighed them, and gave him a receipt to bring to the cashier. The cashier handed the collector a few dollars, and he even received the lottery ticket, just as his friend told him he would.

The collector had a smile on his face when he arrived home and threw the dollar bills and the lottery ticket in an old cigar box that he kept in a desk drawer. He laughed at his little part-time job that he had now created, when the fact of the matter was that he really just had hoped that it would be his little contribution to the good of the city, as well as his own health and well-being.

Each day when he felt well enough, and the weather cooperated, he made the trip to the field, and collected what he could. Once a week, he would bring the cans to the recycling center, and then place the money and the lottery tickets in the cigar box. This went on and on. While the summer waned, and the fall of the year was upon him. Almost every day, the collector was out there on his personal mission, doing what he could do to improve the ball field. He had taken this very seriously, and in some way deep down, he felt as if it restored his soul and revitalized him.

One day, he was quite amazed when he opened the cigar box that he had now taken for granted, and he finally came around to actually counting the money in there. He then remembered the lottery tickets, and he sat on the edge of his bed scratching off the little boxes one by one.

"What a kick this is, these things are a joke, no one actually wins at these silly games," the collector said negatively as he looked at ticket after ticket that had resulted in one loss after another.

The old tickets slowly accumulated in a spent pile, as ticket after ticket, yielded no wins, until he was down to only two or three left in the box, and one left in his wallet from the most recent trip.

When all the tickets in the box were confirmed losers, the collector opened his wallet and tried the last one.

He scratched at the little boxes with the edge of a coin and, to his utter amazement—there was a match!

"Wow!" He exclaimed. "The ticket is a three in a row match! A one-thousand-dollar winner! How about that one?"

The collector stared at the winning ticket in amazement at how his luck had changed! The collector was laughing so hard now that even his old dog lifted his head and came over with his tail wagging, realizing that something good had just happened. Perhaps the old dog could not understand it, but he still wanted to share in the happy moment with his master.

The collector could hardly contain his excitement at his sudden good fortune.

Now, the collector was retired on a solid pension, and his money needs were stable these days. He thought, 'what would he do with his little cache of unexpected wealth?' He sat on the edge of his bed tapping the top of the little cigar box, thinking, and thinking. The collector felt a feeling of warmth and reassurances come over him. He smiled, as he knew that the answer would not come quickly, but something inside of him was telling him to wait, and that the purpose for all of this would come along eventually.

He was not sure why, but he said to himself, "A good cause will come along and maybe this money that I have collected, will help somebody. I just know it will, I just have to wait for a sign and for a cause."

He tapped the top of the box once again as if to reassure himself that he would find a clear purpose for the money, and then tucked the cigar box back away in the drawer. The lottery ticket he put back into his wallet and he figured cashing that in could wait until the next day.

The collector's legs were strong now, and the muscles were firm and lean. His pain had almost disappeared, and his overall health had improved dramatically. His doctor visits were quite amazing, and the doctor was very proud of him.

"See, I told you," said the doctor, as he beamed at the collector while glancing over his latest test results. "These are the kind of follow-up visits that doctors dream of! You just needed to get out there, get some motivation, and get yourself moving around. Now, with the winter coming, make sure you keep up some kind of exercise."

The collector nodded his head and smiled. He was not sure if it was his attitude that had changed his physical health, or a combination thereof, but he was a believer.

The doctor continued with his instructions, "If there is ice or snow, then be careful, do what you can, maybe a stair climbing routine, or other indoor exercises, so that you do not regress backwards again."

The collector smiled back because he did feel so much better.

He told the doctor, "Honestly, I have to admit that I did not think it was just a lack of activity. I thought that your idea of some exercise would not do a thing to improve my leg pain. I am a believer now, and my exercise led to so much more. I have a bounce in my step, a purpose in my life, and it opened my eyes to an awful lot of things that were going on."

The doctor smiled at not only the collector's health but also at his positive frame of mind.

The collector was satisfied, but with winter coming, he knew that he would have to curtail his regiment. He wondered, and he worried about how the park would fare until he could once again resume his work in the spring.

Chapter Two

The Young Father

A few miles from the collector's home, in the mill section of the old city, was a factory. It was an assembly line and production type factory, and it was one of the few places left in the city these days, which employed numerous people. Until a few months ago, the business was doing fairly well, but recently, all the workers had noticed that the orders for production had slowed considerably. The terrible economy of the entire area and the rest of the country had finally caught up with the little factory.

Rumors had started to grow of layoffs, the possibility of the release of workers, and the rumor mill had increased to a fever pitch over the last few weeks.

It was now December, and only a few short weeks before Christmas. Rumors such as this, especially at this time of the year with Christmas right around the corner, caused quite a stir and considerable uneasiness throughout the workforce.

A foreman for the factory walked across the production line floor at the height of the afternoon's production run. He walked very slowly, with a sad and distressed look on his face. He went up to a specific machine where there was a young man operating it and he tapped the young man on the shoulder. The foreman motioned over the noise for him to shut down the equipment.

The foreman said to the young man, "Come on into my office, I have to speak with you for a moment."

The young man knew by the look on the foreman's face

that something was wrong. This was not going to be a pleasant conversation. He reached down, shut off his machine, and followed the foreman back to his office.

The foreman pointed to the chair in front of his desk, and motioned for him to sit, while he closed the door to the office. The foreman went around the back of the desk and sat down in his chair, as the young man took up the chair in front of the desk. The foreman looked down at some papers that he had on his desk and he shuffled at them nervously.

He then finally looked up at the young man in front of him and said, "Look, I am very sorry. Please do not take this wrong because it certainly is no reflection on you at all. You have been a very good worker here, and I feel bad about this, but. . .." The foreman was struggling greatly with this conversation.

"I have to lay you off from your position here today. I just received some mandatory layoff orders that came down from the main office, and I have no choice but to go through the shop according to seniority. Unfortunately, you are one of the least senior persons that I have on the production floor, so I have no other choice or decision that I can make."

The young man felt his throat close up, and he started to hold back some tears.

He replied, "But, it is a couple of weeks before Christmas, and I have two little kids and a wife. Where am I going to find a job? It took me six months to find this job, it is not good out there, and with it now being Christmas, I am sure that no one is hiring."

It was a heart-wrenching scene. You could sense the desperation of the young man and his immediate shock and despair.

The foreman said, "Please believe me, I feel bad for you. I am not a mean-spirited man, but I have my job to do too. The way things are looking around here, I may not even have a position come New Year's Day."

The foreman looked away from the young man for a few moments. He had fired many folks over the years and furloughed quite a few too, but this one really hurt him. He liked the young man, and he was a very good worker, but as he had told the young father, there was very little that he could do.

He continued and said, "It may be only a little something, but there is a two-week severance package based upon your time of service here. . .."

The foreman's voice trailed off, as it was clear that he did care, and that this was a painful discussion for him to be having. The foreman fiddled with some papers on his desk again, so the young father could not see his face.

When he had gathered his thoughts and frame of mind, the foreman looked up and said, "You are a hard worker and a smart young man. I will provide you with a great reference. You will find something and land on your feet. If I can do anything for you, then, please just call me."

The foreman handed the young father a paycheck and another envelope across his desk as he told the young father, "The main office will process and complete your final paperwork."

With that, the foreman stood up, extended his hand, and wished the young father good luck.

Down the hallway, the young father walked slowly towards the main office and he did not know what to say or do. All he could think about was how he would explain this to his wife and children and tell them the horrible news. He went to the main office and collected his paperwork. He was almost numb while the woman in the main office explained the particulars to him about his severance and medical benefits. He sadly gathered up his paperwork and personal gear and made his way out of the main office.

On the way out, the young father saw the foreman in the

hallway. The foreman half-heartedly waved and once more, he said, "Please, call me if you need something."

The young father nodded, but he doubted that it would ever happen.

The young father went to his car, climbed in, and started it. He was numb as well as torn apart and devastated. This was the last thing that he ever thought would have happened to him right before Christmas. He had always worked hard, the boss had said it himself, and he was a reliable worker. He was never late, worked every minute of the day; he kept his mouth shut and kept his nose to the grindstone. There was no justice to this situation at all. It had been a painful lesson in life for the young father.

No one really cared about you; numbers were really all that mattered in this world anymore. He drove the car out of the factory parking lot and he headed towards his home.

The entire way home, his mind was reeling with ideas, and he thought about what his next move would be. He had no plan, and that was the frightening part. He walked in the back door of their small apartment and sat at the table in the kitchen.

He was home early and his wife was, of course, very surprised to see him. She knew from the look on his face that something was very wrong.

The young father took off his hat and coat, and he sat there with his hands folded and a dazed look on his face. Their children were in the other room, doing their school homework, and he motioned to his wife to close the kitchen door, so that they would not overhear the conversation. The young father told her about the layoff, and that the factory was in big trouble. He knew there were no jobs around and that this was about to become a very difficult time for the young father and his family.

He felt sick to his stomach, and he felt a pain inside of him that he could not describe.

His wife sat next to her husband, took her apron off, and

she put her arm around his shoulders.

She loved her husband very much, and she always supported him.

She smiled at her husband and she said, "It will be okay. You will find a job. There is something out there that will come along. I just know it will."

The young father shook his head and said, "I have no plan. I do not know why you still believe in me. I don't even know what to do."

The young father put his head down to hide his eyes from his wife.

"What are we going to do for the kids for Christmas? I know we bought the doll for our daughter, but we have not bought anything else."

He thought about their young son, whose love was baseball, and how his son desperately wanted a new baseball glove for the upcoming season. His old glove had worn out, and it was too small to fit him any longer.

The young father looked at his wife and said, "I have to do something . . . at least to get the baseball glove. They each have to have at least one present under the tree this year this Christmas."

His wife did not reply. She only hugged her husband and tried to absorb some pain that he was feeling. His mind was spinning, and all he could think about was how he would provide a Christmas for the family, food for the table, how to pay the rent, and where he was even going to look for a job. He thought about affording winter clothes, and about all the other things that young fathers had to provide and earn money for their family's needs.

He sat at the table for a long time.

He tried to hold back his tears and emotions in front of the children. The children could sense that there was trouble in the air, but their mother had prompted them to be wary and support their father.

The young father looked across at the little Christmas

tree that they had put up in the living room, and how the family had, just a day or two ago, been preparing for a big celebration.

Now, it seemed so bleak, so worn out, and Christmas would be mired in misery, while everything seemed so wrong.

Chapter Three

Pastor Paul John Henson

In the rural section of the county, on a large property that was just off the new highway, on the very remote outskirts of the same city; stood Reunion Lutheran Church. The church was nestled in a hidden enclave of woods and natural beauty. The charter for Reunion Lutheran Church was one of the oldest in the area, but this church building and the surrounding campus were not that old. It was in fact, a newer structure in the reincarnation of the church.

Reunion Lutheran Church's origins were deep in the past. In fact, the church was old and it spanned many, many generations of families. When the congregation originally started the church on a location in the downtown section of the old city, the name of the church was First Lutheran Church. When the church grew larger, the congregation decided to move out of the downtown environment of the old city, and build a larger church and campus in this section of Morris County, New Jersey. There at the new location, the leadership decided to change the name of the church to Reunion Lutheran Church. This was to signify the reuniting of the congregation within the new facility and property.

Reunion Lutheran Church had enjoyed twenty years or so of great prosperity in the new location, with a fantastic campus and sanctuary, a dynamic pastor, and a young, vibrant, and exciting congregation. Then, the State of New Jersey had come through the area with a new state highway. The resulting highway construction had cut off the church from the main access roads. State officials, who had promised to repair the access to the church, which the highway had cut off, had broken promise after promise, and the situation deteriorated. The years rolled by, the access to the church never improved, and the demographics of the church and the area changed. The new highway had made the church and the grounds almost impossible to reach. To arrive at the church, you had to wander off the main roads, then up and down a maze of side roads, and side streets to enter through a backwoods entrance and exit.

It was a difficult situation, and slowly, the lack of road accessibility, as well as apathy and change, caught up with Reunion Lutheran Church. The pastors moved on, the young families grew older and moved on, the congregation shrunk down to horrifying numbers, and the money dried up.

The buildings and campus had fallen into a terrible state of disrepair, and the management and supervision of the church reverted to the guidance of the district bishop's office, led by Bishop Werner Beck Clodhopper Von Houten in Newark, New Jersey. They had no permanent pastor, and very few members remained who actively attended services. Bishop Von Houten had slated the church for closing, and then he would authorize the eventual sale of the buildings and property.

That plan, however, had changed dramatically and rather suddenly. . ..

It changed on a Monday morning in the bishop's office when Bishop Von Houten made the fateful decision to send his newly ordained, young, and currently unassigned pastor out of the district office and assign him to Reunion Lutheran Church. The plan was for this young pastor to guide the small remaining flock until the bishop could arrange for the lengthy process of closing the church down.

The young pastor, Reverend Paul John Henson, had a

strange, convoluted sort of background, and he had come to ordination through a long and storied process. He had no current full time assignment, and he worked for the bishop directly, while filling in here and there until his full-time status could be determined.

Bishop Von Houten had noticed that there was indeed something very special about this young minister. He had not seen anything like him in his forty years or so of working in the ministry. He had a difficult time at first in understanding him, but he knew there was a special touch from God that guided this young pastor. It truly seemed like everything he did was somehow strangely inspired and God given. Bishop Von Houten noticed how difficult situations or impossible assignments did not discourage the young pastor. He always kept his spirits up, came up with a plan, and then charged ahead every time. The bishop was a believer in the hand of God guiding Pastor Paul John Henson.

He had seen enough to convince him that something unusual followed this young man around.

The plan to send Pastor Paul (the young man truly disliked the title and address of Reverend Henson; he much preferred the informal address of Pastor Paul) had been almost magical for Reunion Lutheran Church. Pastor Paul was different, in fact, at first glance; you would guess him to be anything but a Lutheran pastor. He looked more as if he was a leftover hippie from the 1970s, with shoulder-length reddish-blonde hair, a full beard and mustache, and a tall, muscular, lean build. He was very strong with a powerful handshake, and an athlete's body. He was a very handsome man. The young ladies all would swoon at the sight of the handsome Pastor Paul, and then groan in disappointment, when they found out that he was married to an attractive, blonde-haired woman, who was as beautiful as he was handsome!

The young pastor was smart, dynamic, and a powerful

speaker. To say that he had an interesting background before his present career would be a slight understatement. Before entering the ministry, Pastor Paul John Henson had a long career as a professional ice hockey goaltender, until a terrible knee injury forced him into an unexpected and early retirement. The rumor was that he was within a step or two of the big leagues at the time that he was injured. Despite his career being cut short, all the opinions of the experts who had seen him play were that he had been quite the player. Even though he fell short of the big leagues, he was a legendary goaltender; in fact, most experts who had seen him play labeled him a superstar in his abilities.

Retooling his life, he returned to where he grew up in Paterson, New Jersey, and he had made a decision to enter the ministry. To be certain; it was a most interesting change of direction! He had married a few years earlier before coming to Reunion Lutheran Church, and he now had two young children, a boy, and a younger girl, who, along with his wife, resided in the parsonage house on the church property.

One of the most unusual things about Pastor Paul was the dynamic circle of friends, associates, and others that seemed to be part of his entourage or "team." Pastor Paul was a born leader and his energy, personality, quiet insight, and zeal carried over to everyone who met him.

Pastor Paul John Henson was able to transform Reunion Lutheran Church and spare it from closing. Somehow, within a short period, he had repaired the buildings, and through his many connections, he remarkably had the missing road built, and many other achievements. He returned to the church once again, into a wonderful, vibrant, and dynamic congregation.

Old members returned to the fold, new members recruited, and soon Reunion Lutheran Church was once again bursting at the seams. It had only convinced Bishop Von Houten and others that the hand of God led and guided the young man in all that he did.

It had been a very remarkable transformation.

The bishop left Pastor Paul there to continue to lead Reunion Lutheran Church, and to see what he could do to continue to lead them into growth and prosperity.

Now, two years or so after bringing the church back from the road of ruin and certain extinction, many things had changed. You see, life has many challenges, and human beings have short memories. A handful of the same members of the congregation began to forget the past success of Pastor Paul. Some members, who had praised him for his dedication and his saving of their beloved church, had now grown cold and, in some cases, arrogant, obstinate, and demanding of the young pastor.

Until his entry into the ministry, Pastor Paul's past training was under a completely different background, and his years of playing ice hockey at a professional level had prepared him for many challenges that he could use in his new career.

The parallels that would occur between his two very different lives, sometimes, amazed Pastor Henson. His background was all about teamwork, growing together, and relying upon each other for strength, success, and backup. He had little explanation as well as patience for the silly quibbling and nit picking that had crept into the congregation as of late.

It seemed as though a small group of old members who he referred to as "the old guard," had risen from the ranks. Their main purpose seemed to be to argue and debate all the new ideas of Pastor Paul, as well as some newer members. Pastor Paul felt there was nothing wrong with the influx of new ideas that came with the newer members because he felt it was a natural progression as the church grew.

However, the old guard was stuck in their old ways, and when any mention of changes, new programs, or innovative methods occurred, the old guard did a wonderful job at discounting and discouraging the new ideas. They were a small group, which in fact, yielded quite a bit of power.

It seemed as though they had magically forgotten what the young pastor had done for them, with the pastor's success at revitalizing what had been a dying church and fading membership. Pastor Paul was a thick-skinned man, who was used to critics. He brushed aside a lot of the criticisms and attitudes, but the infighting and silly debates had become wearisome. Still, Pastor Paul resigned himself to not backing down from anything, and he charged ahead.

It reminded the young pastor of what an old hockey coach had told him many years ago, after he had allowed a weak goal, scored during a critical game. The coach told him, "Paul, they never remember the spectacular save that you made last week, or even just a game or two ago, when you preserved a win. They only remember the goal that you just gave up. Shake it off; the next save will be the game winner."

The coach had spoken very true words; Pastor Paul always remembered them and kept them close to his heart for inspiration in difficult times.

Inside Reunion Lutheran Church on this overcast, cold, December afternoon, in the senior pastor's office, Pastor Paul John Henson sat behind a large oak desk. The young pastor was working on preparing his sermon for this upcoming Sunday worship. Advent sermons can be tricky and difficult sometimes.

How do you put a new or interesting twist on such an old story that folks have heard so many times before?

The young pastor was pondering this one, and he set his pen down, shook his head, and rubbed his eyes. It was becoming late in the day now, and this sermon was just not coming to him very easily. No matter how hard he tried and worked along the edges of the story of a young virgin and her husband . . . it just was not working.

He pushed the paper aside. This reminded him of another time in his life when a sermon just would not come to him, and when that sermon finally arrived, it was a good one. In fact, that sermon was the reason he even had a job today. He knew that a sermon would eventually materialize. It was actually something else that was bothering him this afternoon, and it really had very little to do with sermons.

He looked around in his office and he knew the real reason that he was struggling. He thought about how right at this moment, he truly was unprepared to be the pastor of this particular church. He was puzzled now at how he should best handle the situation. He had done a wonderful job at revitalizing the church when it was down for the count, but it seemed as if he was struggling with providing leadership now that the church had settled back into a normal state of affairs. Now, despite all of his background, experience with team building, and experience with difficult life situations, the young pastor could not figure out the small group that seemed to be gaining momentum in opposition to him. He felt himself wandering, dreaming, and he wondered if he had made the correct career choice after all. There was little doubt in his mind that after his initial success at Reunion, he now had stalled in his leadership. He sat at his desk, trying hard to fight off doubts that he was not supposed to have entered the ministry after all, and other serious thoughts that had entered his mind quite often these days.

Paul John Henson was smart. In fact, he had graduated number one in his class in seminary, and he was proud of his education. The pastor could even teach Luther's small and large catechism largely from memory and had been a superb student. He received this very tough assignment to resurrect this parish shortly after graduation, and he prided himself on the success of the challenge. It was what made him tick, and this particular challenge was stirring up his competitive juices. He was not the kind of person to back down from anything. In fact, he was quite fearless, but he needed to be careful. After all, he was now a minister and no longer an ice hockey goaltender!

It was very strange though. Pastor Paul, after his first year here, had noticed a significant change in the overall attitudes of many of the church members. Once the bedlam of pulling the church all back together had simmered down, and Reunion Lutheran Church returned from the brink of extinction, it seemed as if the magic had died. Once he had revived Reunion Lutheran Church, and when the wayward members came back to the fold, Pastor Paul realized that it was actually an old and very established congregation.

While his professors had prepared him well for all the theological angles, they had not prepared him for the internal politics, the turmoil, and behind-the-scenes management of such an old and established congregation. The infighting and the division of factions within the various families and groups that now attended the church surprised Pastor Paul. He watched in amazement sometimes at how a congregation that had families that went back a few generations within the church family was really a group divided, and how contrary to the gospel, some of them acted. Sometimes, he felt that preaching the gospel here was almost a lost cause. He knew that he should not feel that way and he prayed about it, spoke with his wife often about it, and tried hard to work through it.

At times, it seemed to be so silly to him the subjects that would cause the groups to erupt into huge debates and confusion.

His congregation, and other listeners to his sermons and speeches, told him many times how dynamic he was in the pulpit, and he played his speaking talent as his strength. He composed impassioned sermons that preached unity and teamwork from the pulpit, but it seemed to be to no avail.

A week or so ago, he called upon one of his old professors at seminary and discussed the situation with him, and the professor encouraged him, but offered little in the way of direction or advice. He briefly mentioned the issues to his boss, Bishop Von Houten, but the bishop was not the type of man who provided that nature of guidance. He was gruff, and at times, the bishop seemed uncaring. In the bishop's opinion, his job as bishop was to provide advice to the business angle, and leave religious guidance to God and the pastor's own decisions. The young pastor received the message from the bishop loud and clear, so he did not dwell on the issue with him.

The young pastor worked as hard as he could to feel as if he belonged, but being a young man, he brought with him modern and new ideas that sometimes met with strong opposition. Every single new idea that he presented met with strong resistance from the old guard within the church. They pushed back; hard, often, and whenever they could.

"That's not what we used to do, and that is not what we do here," were the common cries that Pastor Henson would hear over and over, whenever he introduced a new thought or idea. The pastor became disgruntled, and he felt his spirit becoming downcast. But he would never give up.

To give in was not an option that Pastor Paul Henson would ever consider. He had faced a lot more difficult and tougher situations than this one, that was for sure!

He picked his pen back up and felt as if a sermon had started to come to him, but the words quickly faded. He crossed out the lines he had just written and laid his pen back down. He thought to himself, how would he change the attitudes here, how do I bring new ideas here, how will I stop the infighting and gain acceptance? What words or passages from the bible would strike a chord amongst this difficult congregation?

He picked up his Bible, and went through it, page-by-page, not really looking for anything in particular, just searching for some type of inspiration.

The young pastor prayed aloud, "Oh Lord, just guide me. Point me in the right direction, and provide me some form of inspiration, direction, and guidance. Perhaps, it will come in the sermon this week, or in some other new ideas. I need to bring this church to the next step. Guide me, oh Lord, and I will follow the lead."

Pastor Paul knew that in some situations, events, and times in his life, he had encountered certain situations that he could never explain. He just knew that he was about to go with his instinct and that God was in control. He knew that the events of the past week had contributed to him struggling today and to him feeling such a disturbing negative attitude in the air of the church. He was a positive person, and negative thoughts and mind-sets were a disruption to him.

He thought about the meeting that he had attended earlier this week with the annual Christmas committee. It was this meeting event which had triggered his current frame of mind.

This committee was a large group, staffed with old guard church members who would serve in large numbers. All of them felt that the annual Christmas committee was one of their favorites to serve upon during the church year. The church had Christmas traditions that went back for years upon years and the old guard loved them! They covered (and debated) everything from the way the church was decorated, to what meals were served at the annual Christmas dinner for the congregation. This committee was a hornet's nest, full of opinions and debates.

It all seemed so silly and contrite.

The pastor was bored stiff with the arguments during the meeting as he tried to play referee to each side in the little disputes. In addition, some old battle axes that were serving on this committee felt the sudden need to use this forum to express their strong opinion of their pastor's hippie appearance, and were quite outspoken as to how he looked and acted. They were conservative, and they had no trouble stating their opinion that Pastor Paul Henson needed a good haircut and trim!

Whispered comments from one or two of the old guard group of conservatives, such as, "He is older now, and he should now begin to look and behave as a conservative Lutheran pastor," and other comments were strategically loud enough for the pastor and others to overhear in a sidebar conversation. He just laughed at all of that nonsense about his appearance. He had faced that all of his life, and he was not about to change now! It would not be the first time that people had judged Paul Henson on how he looked on the outside rather than what he was all about on the inside.

That was generally a very poor mistake to make.

It was at this meeting, the young pastor had first presented to the old guard, as well as the rest of the committee members, an idea that he had for this Christmas season of a new program of outreach to the community. He spoke in front of the group as to how the area and nearby city were suffering from the current poor economic conditions. Pastor Paul spoke of their neighbors being in need. He emphasized how jobs were very difficult to come by during these turbulent times. Pastor Paul presented the idea to them with an impassioned speech filled with biblical quotations, and examples of helping the poor and downtrodden. He was amazed as he spoke that some committee members were already shaking their heads and the body language that broadcasted disagreement, even though the young pastor had barely even started to convey his idea.

Some members of this committee, and the old faction of

the church, were fairly well off financially, and had some old money tucked away here and there. While the church was not overflowing with cash, since they had recovered from the years of dwindling membership and near extinction, they certainly were not doing too badly.

The pastor felt they were in very good shape and his boss, Bishop Von Houten, agreed. It was a rare time indeed, when Von Houten agreed with anything or anyone, especially Pastor Paul! However, the bishop was thrilled at the miraculous financial turnaround that Pastor Paul had managed to achieve here at Reunion Lutheran Church. Pastor Paul also felt lucky to have such a position that paid a decent salary in this very difficult economic environment.

With those ideas in mind, he worked their good fortune, in comparison to others in the nearby communities, into his presentation. He painfully reminded the members of the committee how just a few short years ago, this wonderful church was ready to fall into extinction forever more, but it had rebounded, and then restored to glory in service to the Lord.

Perhaps some poor folks out there needed the same kind of small hope to trigger their own comebacks in their own lives. He hoped that the analogy would strike a close chord to the members, but it seemed to fall upon deaf or uncaring ears. Pastor Paul was amazed at that fact, as he found it to be almost unbelievable that some of these folks could choose to forget how badly and close to ruin they were just a short time ago.

What is wrong with them, he thought?

The idea for the Christmas committee that he was presenting was very simple; it did not seem as if he was asking for very much. The young pastor wanted to have a Christmas giving tree program, where they could invite people from the town who were down on their luck and struggling. In addition to assisting those in need, he also felt that the church could attract some new parishioners. He explained that during difficult times, families and persons often look for support from church and from God.

"Reunion Lutheran Church may be able to help these persons with a new church home as well as spread the gospel messages," Pastor Paul said.

Pastor Paul told them how the giving tree would be an outreach program, a mission of sorts. Any people who registered would receive a ticket with a number that matched presents and gifts gathered under a large Christmas tree in the main church assembly hall. He gave them a brief description of a sermon that he was working on to convey just the right message of hope for the Christmas season. He felt it was an important mission opportunity for the church to be able to provide a little something for their spiritual needs, and to present a small gift at Christmas to those who had nowhere else to turn.

After the presentation had finished, Pastor Paul sat back and listened to the debate begin. The old guard members, as usual, erupted into debates, fights, and heated discussion. Some outright did not agree with the entire idea of this giving tree and they were very vocal in letting everyone know that. The factions squared off around the table, in order to debate every angle, and dissect this new idea. Some did not like the idea of strange and desperate folks coming in off the street and into their church.

"That work is better off left to the homeless mission's downtown," they cried.

"Way too much money to spend on this type of mission," was another complaint that received support from many of the attendees.

Others did not like a program that seemed to advertise and promote the more secular aspects of the Christmas season, and they felt it was wrong to be giving presents out within the church confines.

Pastor Paul at first just sat back in amazement and took

it all in. He then decided that he wanted to bang some of their heads together to knock some sense into them. He breathed deeply and calmed his emotions, and then slowly he joined in the discussion. He brought scripture as well as their mission outreach obligations into the mix.

Slowly, after the long, involved, and heated discussions, some members started to soften as the pastor fought back.

How he wished that this committee included his best friend, Harry M. Redmond Jr., his wife, Rose, as well as the pastor's wife, Binky. He knew that if Rose, Binky, and Harry were sitting here, then the old guard would have had a good fight on their hands!

The pastor's wife, Binky Henson, was a striking woman, who was smart, dynamic, and precision in her thoughts and in her focus on details. She would compete and usually win with anyone in a one-on-one debate. However, Christmas committees staffed with old, cranky crab-apples were not exactly the Redmond's cup of tea, and Binky was busy with their young children. Therefore, Pastor Paul needed to defend his ideas on his own.

Pastor Paul was no slouch on his own, and he circled the wagons and defended his idea. Besides, he was not without his own group of supporters. There also was a group of Pastor Paul advocates serving on the committee who loved the young pastor and they joined with him to rally support for the idea. Slowly, the idea started to gain approvals, with one or two old guard members reluctantly agreeing that it was a good idea for community outreach at Christmas time.

When the time came for a vote, the committee approved the idea for a giving tree, but with some conditions regarding the funding of the event.

One of the male leaders of the old guard, a middle-aged, loudmouthed, gentleman named, Christopher Johnson, stood up and proudly announced, "You cannot use any church or mission funds to purchase secular gifts, such as toys or other such items. Only use the church and mission funds to purchase food, clothing, Bibles, religious materials, or essential items. In the committee's opinion, the church money can never be involved in promoting a secular aspect of the sacred Christmas holiday."

Pastor Paul and a few committee members protested. The pastor felt that it was a special time for families, and there was no harm or biblical reason against providing toys to some needy children who may have no other gifts at all. The majority of the members agreed that the toys were a nice touch, but they would not agree to allow any church funds to purchase them.

After many intense discussions and a long, tedious, boring meeting, Pastor Paul realized that you had to select your battles and start new ideas slowly. At least he had received approval to conduct the event. Pastor Paul knew that he had won a major battle with the old guard.

In the next day or so, the event organizers received the church mission funds to purchase wholesome food and warm clothing, as well as supplies, such as wrapping paper and tags to support the program. They all agreed that they would advertise the giving tree in the church bulletin, as well as the local newspapers. They also agreed to hold the event on a Saturday evening a week or so before Christmas.

Back at his desk, Pastor Paul realized that he had made some progress and his mood changed a little. Since the night of the meeting, he had heard the whispers in the congregation this past week about the giving tree event. Some persons were for it, and some were still firmly against it, but he would give it his best shot. If the Christmas giving tree event was a success, then perhaps, it will become an annual event.

Suddenly, an idea for his sermon came to him. Even though it was early in the Advent season for speaking of the visit of the Magi, he wrapped into the text, an angle using the visit of the three wise men as a prelude into announcing the giving tree event to the entire congregation.

Just as he began to write his composition, the young pastor's secretary, Martha, tapped on his door. Martha had a few questions about the giving tree. She had been typing up the church bulletin and needed some additional information, which Pastor Paul gave to her. He also gave her the title for his sermon for inclusion in the bulletin, which the young pastor titled "Giving Back."

Sunday came, and Pastor Paul John Henson was in fine form as he preached his sermon. Worship services right before Christmas tend to have outstanding attendance, and this particular Sunday, the church was almost full to capacity. He looked over the congregation as he preached from the pulpit and he tried to gauge the mood of the folks in attendance. When the offering collection time came, he noticed the coffers were full and the plates were overflowing. He looked down from his pastor's bench as the plates passed through the sanctuary aisles. Pastor Paul stared at his young children, and his beautiful wife, beaming at him from her usual seat in the congregation, while seated next to his best friend, Harry, and his wife. He was a lucky man, he thought, to have such family and friends. He almost missed the doxology blessing of the offering signal from his acolyte because he was daydreaming so much about his good fortune!

As he sat on his pastor's bench, right before the final hymn, he thought to himself that perhaps he had received the answer to his prayers. He felt positive about the current direction and he just needed to keep up the momentum. It was as if he returned to his hockey playing days. He knew that all it took sometimes was one win after a losing streak. You gain momentum, and the season can turn around very quickly.

After the processional, Pastor Paul took up his usual

weekly position at the church exit in the narthex. He was greeting and meeting with the parishioners as they left the sanctuary. Of course, some came by, shook their head, conveyed their misgivings about the giving tree event, or complained that it was too hot or too cold in the building. Some passed by and told Pastor Henson that he needed a haircut and a shave. The choir was too loud, or too soft, or a laundry list of other issues that were wrong in their eyes.

One old guard church member came through, voiced to him that it was a nice sermon and a powerful message, and complimented the pastor on his speaking abilities, "But I do not think this giving tree is a very good idea. This church has been here a long time, and we have gotten along fine for years, without all these new ideas and frivolous spending of our mission money."

The young pastor only smiled, but deep inside he wished he had his goalie stick handy, so he could give the old sourpuss a good whack on the backside.

"God, forgive me," Pastor Henson whispered under his breath as he crossed himself. He smiled and put on a solid face of support, while deep down inside, he once more felt the pressure and his spirit fading.

Deep in his mind, as he smiled and mumbled back to the persons that he was greeting, but he could not let go of the thought that these folks just do not understand how lucky they really were. They needed to hear some stories of life's pains and challenges to wake them all up, he thought.

He knew from his life experience that he needed some type of positive flow to change all of this negative energy, and he did not know right at the moment where he was going to find the inspiration for change.

In the receiving line, as the attendees came through one after another, Pastor Paul's mind continued to wander, as he searched and prayed for a magic solution to appear.

Suddenly, the young pastor looked up, and there standing in front of him was the collector.

This was the collector's home church, and he stood there right in front of the pastor with a big smile on his face. He shook the pastor's hand firmly, and Pastor Paul looked at him and patted him on the shoulder. Pastor Paul had known that he had not been feeling well a little while back with poor circulation in his legs, and now he was a bit curious, since the collector looked so well.

Pastor Paul was very fond of the collector because he was one of the few active longtime members who remained when he first arrived at Reunion Lutheran Church. He had been a very vocal and staunch supporter of all of his early efforts. He also knew that the collector was a charter member here; in fact, he was the only one remaining active in the congregation.

He was descended from one of the original families that had actually started Reunion Lutheran Church many generations ago. The collector carried an awful lot of influence here at the church.

The pastor knew that the past years had been difficult for the collector. His wife had passed away, right around the same time the collector's health took a difficult turn. Therefore, Pastor Paul was glad to see him looking so well today.

Pastor Paul exclaimed, "Wow! My goodness, you are looking great. How are you feeling?"

The collector answered, "I feel wonderful, Pastor Paul, just wonderful. I took up an exercise program, and I feel better every day!"

The collector continued with very strong enthusiasm building in his voice, "I have got to tell you, I love this new idea of the Christmas giving tree event. I think it is a fantastic thing!"

Caught off guard, the pastor broke into an almost suspicious smile and replied with some surprise, "You do?"

"Yes, yes," the collector continued. "I do think it is great.

You know what is old is old, and what is new is new, and sometimes, you have to move along and accept new ideas. Do not let these old curmudgeons push you around, and discourage you, pastor. They must have taken amnesia pills and forgotten all that you have done for us. You just bring those new ideas in here and you have my support."

Pastor Paul was now smiling broadly, and he thanked the collector. He laughed at the collector's comments because he had experienced folks who had taken amnesia pills a few times before in his own life.

The collector then asked, "I want to know if you will be in the office tomorrow? I would like to come by and chat with you a bit."

"Sure, of course. Yes, I will be in the office. I would be glad to meet with you, in fact—that would be wonderful. Please call Martha, with an available time and you can get onto my calendar."

Pastor Paul was clearly pleased at not only the restoration of the collector's health but also of his support of the pastor's idea.

Upon hearing that he had made a successful appointment with Pastor Paul, the collector tapped the young pastor on the back and said, "Merry Christmas. That was a great sermon and please keep up the good work. Do not ever cut your hair or shave. Come to think of it, I am thinking of growing mine the same way as yours. That way, I may be able to attract some of those young, single, ladies that stare at you!"

The collector winked at Pastor Paul and out the door of the church. The collector strode confidently, while quickly outpacing most of the parishioners, and even some of the younger folks.

Pastor Paul watched him for a bit with the smile still on his face, shook his head, and then went on to greeting the next person in line.

The following Monday, Pastor Paul was in his office

working on some paperwork. He had forgotten about his appointment with the collector, until Martha knocked on the door, and he looked up to see both Martha and the collector standing in the doorway to his office. The collector was smiling broadly and waving. Tucked under his right arm, near his shoulder, was a bag. The pastor stood up, smiled, and waved him into the office. The collector sat at the guest chair in front of the pastor's large oak desk.

After exchanging some pleasantries, greetings, and a quick discussion about the weather, Pastor Paul asked the collector, "So what can I do for you? What did you want to speak with me about?"

The collector smiled broadly. He reached down into his bag and pulled out the little cigar box that he had kept in his drawer at home. He then placed it on the pastor's desk. Pastor Paul did a double take glance at the appearance of the box, of which invoked a laugh from the collector.

"No, no, no, Pastor Paul. I did not come here to share a Christmas cigar or a cup of holiday cheer with you!"

"Well, I admit, that I do partake in a cup of cheer or two now and then, and I surely smoked a few cigars after a big win on the ice in my old life, but this was not what I expected," Pastor Paul chuckled.

The pastor continued to laugh, and then he listened intently as the collector continued to speak, with his hand still on top of the cigar box. "I heard about the giving tree and heard all the gossip and whispers among the congregation. I felt strongly that this was the situation that I had been waiting and praying for to come to me. First, I need to give you some of the past history, Pastor Paul."

The pastor sat back in his chair because he now was intrigued by this visit and the strange little cigar box that had been set upon his desk.

The collector continued, "I have been attending this church since I was a little boy. I think that you do remember that my relatives going back generations were amongst the charter members here. You can check the charter on file in the narthex and see their signatures. My family served a major role during the planning of the original church in the downtown section, and my relatives donated some of the original monies to build most of the original structure. I was baptized here, and I grew up here, was confirmed here, took my first communion, and took catechism here."

Pastor Paul nodded, to show to him that he did indeed know of the collector's background and heritage.

The collector leaned in over the desk now, and his voice grew serious and deep. "I was married here, my children were baptized here, and I imagine someday . . . that I will have my funeral here. You will remember that at the time you came here and worked so hard to bring the church back from the brink of despair that I was very sick, my wife had just passed, and I wished, hoped, and prayed that I could have done so much more to help you in your efforts."

Pastor Paul shook his head, and he spoke, "That is not true. You provided a tremendous amount of assistance, despite such a difficult time in your life. You were invaluable in your support at the time. Without you, our facility manager Mr. Dave Sharp, Mrs. Whipley, and a lot of others, this church would not be here right now."

The collector smiled. "You are very kind, Pastor Paul. Yet, I know that without you and your friends, and the hand of God that is upon you, we would not have a Reunion Lutheran Church. That is why . . . I had to come here. I owe you a great deal for coming here and for the work that you did to save our beloved, Reunion Lutheran Church. I cannot emphasize enough, what I mentioned yesterday, not to let these old folks bring you down, you just stick with where your heart is taking you and where God is leading you. You are a special man, Pastor Paul, and

I, for one, cannot even imagine what has gotten into these people around here to forget what you have done for us all. However, I do know that I have lived a long and full life, and I have seen how God sometimes tests people and certain situations come upon us all as part of these tests."

Pastor Paul shifted a little uneasily in his chair and he smiled a weak smile at the collector. The young pastor agreed, and he knew well of what the collector was speaking.

The collector leaned in and rested his folded hands on the front of the desk. "I think this giving tree is a great idea for Christmas and you have my full support."

The collector leaned back in his chair now and continued to speak. "I have friends on that Christmas committee and I heard what went on there. Some of these old birds should be ashamed of themselves, and the high and lofty opinions they bring in here. Why would they not let you buy some toys for the kids for the event? What was the reasoning? Do they not understand and realize that after all, it is, Christmas?"

Pastor Paul shook his head and answered, "They would only approve church funds for food and clothes, Bibles, and items of a religious nature. They felt utilizing mission funds from the church for toys would amount to promoting secular events with church money."

Upon hearing that, the collector laughed loudly, and he slid the cigar box across the desk to the pastor.

"Well, open that box, Pastor Paul," the collector proudly proclaimed. "There is a little bit of money in there. You take what is inside there and go buy what you want. You buy what you are inspired to buy. If it is toys, then it will be toys. If it is Bibles, then it will be Bibles. If it is food, then so be it. You will find inside that cigar box—what I feel you need right now to be quite useful for this event."

Pastor Paul opened up the cigar box and whistled as he picked up the money and thumbed through the bills that were in there.

"Wow!" The pastor shouted at the amount of money in the box. He then replied, "Thank you! My goodness, this is a lot of money! But I cannot spend it on toys for the event; the committee would have a fit."

The collector leaned back a bit in the guest chair when he heard Pastor Paul's comment and he smiled a little.

He turned and pointed at an oil portrait hanging on the wall of the senior pastor's office. The portrait was a depiction of when Paul Henson was playing ice hockey and the collector said, "Now, pastor, I have heard of your background. You were quite the player, if I recall correctly, it was number twenty-seven."

The pastor nodded to affirm the number that he wore.

"You were a step or two from the big time. I have heard the stories. I tipped a few beers with your best friend there, that wonderful and colorful character, Mr. Redmond, a few years back, when you first came here. He told me all about you. You are a folk hero to many, especially to Mr. Redmond. He told me where you two came from, what you did in the past together, and now I look and see where you are. You did not stand in front of hockey pucks without any fear for years on a professional level, because you were afraid of something now, Pastor Paul. Did you ever think that the pressure you are feeling as of late is part of God's plan? Sometimes people who just do not understand the true message of the gospel, probe for weakness, they push their own agendas for a reason, and when they find a weak spot, they bore in with a misguided effort, to have their own way. I may be wrong, but from what I can tell, I do not think that Pastor Paul John Henson ever backed down from any challenge, either as a pastor, or as an athlete, or as a man. Now, you are not going to allow a few old crows to change that, are you? What I heard about you from Mr. Redmond, is that you two, never really played by many of the rules. Now suddenly . . . you are going to play by them?"

The collector wiggled forward in his chair and smiled, then he added, "I do not think that will be the case."

Pastor Paul turned around, and looked at the painting on the wall of him, low in a goaltender's crouch in front of the net, waiting for a shooter to move in on him. He smiled, but he did not say a word. He looked back at the collector, who knew exactly what Pastor Paul was thinking.

The collector pounded the desk a little with his fist. "That is the spirit, Pastor Paul! This is no different from an ice hockey game, you need to stand up in the net and make the saves. I gave you that money to do as you want with it. After all, your instructions were *not to spend church money on toys.* Well, there isn't any church money in that box, Pastor Paul! If anyone challenges you on it, then march them to that charter on the wall in the narthex, and stick their stuck-up noses right in it, until you come down to my family name!"

On that note, the collector told the young pastor his story, right from the beginning. He told him about the doctor, his reluctance to begin walking, then how he grew stronger, until he finally made it to the park. He told him about his fondness for the park, his love of baseball, and his sadness at the condition of the park, then about picking up the cans and bringing them to the recycling center. He even told him about the lottery tickets and his good luck at possessing a winner. He also told the pastor about how he was saving the money and searching for some cause to contribute to and support. A cause that would be special. A special cause, he said, something, or someone that would fulfill the prayers that he had been saying for guidance.

The collector said, "When I heard your sermon at the worship service yesterday about giving back, it really struck a nerve in me. I read in the bulletin about the Christmas giving tree, and then I heard the story of what went on behind the scenes. I then knew that I had been led to where this money should go."

The collector stood up from his chair, leaned again over the pastor's desk, and placed both of his hands on the edge of the desk.

He was now trembling, and it reflected in his voice as he shakily spoke. "Please understand, this became so much more than exercise. It became a mission of hope. It was what I needed, to renew my mind, body, and my soul. It gave me purpose, direction in my life, and revitalized me, Pastor Paul."

The collector had tears in his eyes now, and his voice trembled, while he fought to find some more words, "I knew after hearing you speak about giving back, that as a long-time member here and a descendant of charter families, I should be supporting you and your new ideas and efforts. I needed to give the money to you so that you can do what you need to do. I have seen what you have done first hand. I know of your background, and I believe that the hand of God guides you and all that you do. I believe in you, Pastor Paul, and what you are led to do."

The powerful words, experiences, and testimonies of the collector profoundly impacted the young pastor. So often in his life, since he had met his friend Harry's first wife, Sky Blu Redmond, there were so many things that had happened to him that he did not try to explain. He knew just to go along with his feelings and instincts; it had served him well for many years.

He now felt bad for having doubted his choice of careers and allowing the negative energy of the old guard to affect him. The collector was correct in his analysis. Backing down should not be an option. Staying positive was the only way to be, and he vowed that he would stay that way.

The collector sat back down in his chair and he could tell by the excited look on the pastor's face that he had said the correct things. He knew now that this young man had been going through some inner turmoil of his own, and there was a connection between them, a sense of relief that God had answered both of their individual prayers.

The young pastor became even more excited as he reached down, obtained a newspaper next to his desk, and said, "Well, now. I think this is really becoming more amazing, you are going to find this article very interesting."

He opened the newspaper to a page, laid it open on the desk, and slid it across the desk so that the collector could read it.

"Read about that," Pastor Paul said.

The collector fumbled for his glasses, took them out of his shirt pocket, put them on, and started to read the newspaper. There in the newspaper was an article about the recent passing of a very wealthy gentleman in town. The gentleman was similar to the collector, because he also had grown up in the city, and could trace his roots here back to many generations. The collector knew him; in fact, they had played baseball in the city at the same park on the same fields. He was a little older than the collector was, but he remembered that he had also been an outstanding baseball player.

The gentleman had owned a quarry in the county and had acquired a huge fortune. When he passed, he left a large estate with specific instructions for his family in his will. He donated money to many causes, and one of them was his home city. Of the public monies that he had left, he allocated and set aside some of this money to fund the total repair, reconstruction, and revitalization of the park and baseball fields to its former glory!

In the article, was a statement from his widow, saying how her husband had loved the park, and played baseball there as a youth, and how he wanted to make sure that if the city could not afford to restore it, then he would like to be able to help them in the process.

The collector sat back in his chair. He sighed, and then

he laughed. The news was so surprising to the collector that he did not know what to say. A smile broke out on the collector's face and he finally said, "You know, Pastor Paul, if I had brought along some Christmas cheer, I would pour us both a glass to celebrate together. If there were cigars in that box, I would light one up now!"

They both laughed, and the collector had a hard time not showing that he was ecstatic to learn of this news.

The pastor looked at the collector and he said, "Prayers do get answered, my friend."

The collector nodded his head in acknowledgement. Both men stood up and shook hands.

The collector turned, walked to the door, then he spun around, and he spoke strongly and loudly, "Now, you do what you want with that money, and if anyone questions you, then you tell them to come see me. I donated the money, it did not come out of any church funding, and it is my wish that you do what you want with it."

The young pastor agreed, and told the collector, "Thank you so much. You have given much more than just this money. You have offered me your faith and support, and that means an awful lot. Please be sure we see you at the giving tree. After all you have done, I feel that you really should be there."

The collector started to say, "Yes," but then he stopped, and never finished the sentence. He seemed to be pondering the invitation for a time until he finally said, "Well, maybe. I will see what my schedule is like, but if I am not there, I know you can handle it! Always remember in life, pastor, that you need to always charge ahead. What is old is old, and what is new is new."

He smiled, waved, and out the door, the collector went.

Pastor Paul turned, and he sat at his desk. He folded his hands in prayer and prayed aloud, "Thank you, Lord, for steering me. Thank you for bringing me to where I am right now. I know that you have a plan. I will let you guide and steer me in the correct direction."

He grabbed the keys to his trusty old jeep, the cigar box, and his vest. He then walked out of his office and up to the church secretary's desk.

His secretary looked up, and he said, "Please have a nice evening, dear Martha. I will be back in the office early tomorrow, but right now, I have a special errand to run." She nodded and bid him a goodnight.

Pastor Paul jumped in his old jeep and headed in the direction of the toy store because he had an obvious mission and he knew what he wanted to do. Walking into the local downtown toy store, he felt alive, and as though he now had a vision of various toys to purchase, but he also felt a strong feeling that there was a special item that he needed to find, in and amongst all the others.

He just was not exactly sure of what that special item was, or what was driving him to purchase it.

He walked up and down the aisles of the toy store and he grabbed whatever he felt caught his eye.

He asked the Lord to give him direction. "Steer me as I shop," he prayed under his breath. He grabbed dolls, he grabbed board games, he grabbed general toys, and items that he felt were generic in nature, and would have an appeal to both boys and girls.

He was having a grand old time here! He then grabbed alternate toys, a boy and then a girl, a girl and then a boy. The young pastor was thrilled; he thought about what joy this will bring to children who needed some hope in their lives. The entire time, he was keeping a close watch on the funds, being very careful not to exceed the collector's donation. He had quite a bit left, and he counted what remained. "Wow," Pastor Paul was thinking aloud, "I have a whole carriage of toys here and still have a good amount of money left; I still need to buy labels, wrapping paper and tags." He turned down an aisle with his carriage and he noticed that it turned out to be the sporting goods aisle.

Pastor Paul looked up and saw that the aisle was aisle number twenty-seven. He felt a cold shudder go up and down his spine. There was that number once more. It happened to be a magic number in his life. It was also the number he wore as a goaltender during his playing days.

His wife and all of his close friends still called him by his nickname, which was "twenty-seven."

He knew that he had to go down this aisle.

He then remembered that the collector used to be a baseball player, and his fondness for baseball. Pastor Paul's eyes went up and down the merchandise, and he looked at the money he had left in his hand. He looked at the price tags for the goods and saw that most of these prices were higher and very expensive. He thought that he could easily spend too much and that he could be overspending the amount of money he had left.

Pastor Paul went to turn and leave the aisle.

He spun his carriage, and then he stopped.

Something inside his mind told him not to leave, but to turn back around. He turned, and his eye caught a baseball glove on the lower shelf. He felt it was strange that this particular glove was not next to any of the other baseball gloves. That fact seemed to be very odd indeed, and he swore that it had not been there before when he first rolled past this shelf, or maybe he just had not noticed it.

The glove was on sale, and the price was very reasonable for such a quality glove. He reached down, picked it up, and put it on his hand. The pastor had played a little baseball in his day, and he surely knew what a good glove was. He spent a good part of his life wearing a goaltender's leather catching glove on his left hand, and this did not feel much different from that glove did. He stretched his fingers inside of it. He tapped his fist into the pocket of the glove and shook his head in agreement that it just felt right. He could afford to purchase this glove, and still have enough money for the wrapping paper, labels, and other supplies that he still required.

He thought to himself that the collector would want this to be one of the gifts, and with that, he took off the glove and placed it into the carriage.

Pastor Paul made his way to the checkout, and he began chatting with the cashier who had seen all of the toys and goods, and then the pastor's collar on Paul Henson. The cashier put the pieces together that all of these toys and supplies were for a Christmas church event. Pastor Paul took the opportunity to put a big plug in for the giving tree. Even the cashier could sense the excitement in his voice while he explained about the big event. They checked out all of the merchandise, and he paid for the goods. He then placed all the toys and supplies into his jeep.

Once inside the vehicle, he counted the money left and was quite pleased with how it had all turned out. With the funds left in his wallet, he would place a portion of the money left over in the collection plate on Christmas Eve. The balance of the money would go toward the purchase of a number of Bibles to give out at the giving tree event. He felt he had done well, and he had everything that he needed.

When Pastor Paul arrived home, he burst through the back door, calling for his family, as he could hardly wait to tell them what had transpired that afternoon. His wife, Binky Henson, came running along with his son and his daughter, in response to his excited cries. Binky shook her head in amazement and his two young children, who had come out of their bedrooms to see what was going on, were thrilled at the story that their father told them. As Pastor Paul told his wife and children, the story of the collector and what had happened, they too were amazed at the words of the collector, and his mission of hope and trust in Pastor Paul. They all put on their coats and helped to carry all the toys and supplies from the jeep into the house.

Binky hugged her husband and gave him a kiss.

She was thrilled, and she told him, "You see, twenty-seven. Your hard work has paid off, and God answered your prayers, my dear Paul! This is where you are supposed to be, and what God wants for you. I knew that something would happen to bring some positive support back after all that you have done for the church. I told you that it was just a few malcontents there and that they really love you, just like we all do!"

Pastor Paul loved his wife more than he could ever describe. He was always thankful for all of her support and faith in him.

They all felt revitalized, and after dinner, on the floor of the living room of the parsonage, the young family gathered around and carefully wrapped all the toys and labeled them with tags and numbers. The Henson family worked hard and very carefully, to identify the gifts so that folks who requested a toy or specific type would receive a chance to select the correct one. They labeled each item "boy," "girl" and "generic," carefully numbered them, kept them all organized, and color coordinated. Tomorrow, he would bring them into the church and place them under the Christmas giving tree.

He knew that the night of the giving tree was going to be interesting, but he was ready for them all. He was strapping on his old pads, pulling his old goalie mask back over his head, and just as the collector had said, he was not backing down from his mission.

Once the old guard found out that there were toys included in the mix, then the fireworks would start. He was sure there would be a confrontation, but he had his answers prepared and he knew he had the collector's support.

The other people, who had volunteered to help with the event, were also hard at work at their own homes, just as the Henson family had been tonight, wrapping the food and clothes previously purchased with the approved funds. They also had taken the time out of their own lives to help with the mission, and they were numbering and labeling them as required in accordance with the system. Pastor Paul was thankful to those people who also had supported his hope to bring just a little joy to the community this Christmas.

That night, the young pastor got down on his knees next to his bed and prayed. He thanked the Lord for guidance; he added praise and hope for the collector.

Most of all, he thanked and praised God for his wife and family.

As he stood up from the side of the bed, he knew that somewhere, there were many people who needed help in this community during this holiday season.

He felt that the giving tree could be just what they were searching for in their lives this Christmas.

Chapter Four

The Giving Tree

The big night finally arrived. The turnout for the Christmas giving tree event was tremendous. It was a sad testimony as to how difficult the economic times currently were in the area.

Decorations of the wonderful Christmas season gaily filled the lobby of the church, and Pastor Paul and his wife had set up a table near the entrance, which had brochures and literature about Reunion Lutheran Church placed upon it. The decorating committee had set up a tall and wonderfully decorated Christmas tree in the fellowship hall of the church. All the volunteers who had agreed to help in the organization and operating of the event were hard at work, checking folks in and assigning tickets. The fact that the handing out of the gift tickets was very strategically organized; turned out to be a good thing since the turnout was so large.

All the lovingly wrapped and carefully placed gifts, food, Bibles, clothes, and toys looked wonderful and presented a heartwarming holiday display of hope, joy, and peace while they sat under the Christmas tree in a huge pile.

As the general public came in, you could hear the drone of their wishes in the background, "Thank you, merry Christmas. I need some food, please. I hope I can get some food. I hope to receive a warm hat because this winter has been so cold so far," and on and on it went, as each person was assigned a ticket.

The needy people of the surrounding communities had turned out in droves to see what, if anything, they could pick up for free. Some parishioners stood by on the side, and of course, the naysayers and gossip groups slowly gathered in clusters. They were whispering to each other and could not wait to see what would happen. Pastor Paul kept focused, stayed positive, and ignored the negative influences.

This was going to be fun, he thought.

The group running the event had organized this perfectly, and it was coming together nicely. Pastor and Mrs. Henson and their children stood on the sideline watching as the event unfolded.

The choir and bell choir performed. They each performed a few musical solos, and then performed a variety of songs together, with the bells as a cheerful musical backdrop for Christmas.

The time came for Pastor Paul to speak, and he kept his words meaningful and non-denominational. He shared some pointed words, his vision for the community, and Pastor Paul spoke of the mission of the church. In addition, his explanation of how the church had returned from nearly closing seemed to inspire the tattered group of visitors. Pastor Paul utilized the church as an analogy, and explained to the crowd how despite the odds, you can always rebound and come back even stronger!

The pastor told them how long they had been there, and why the congregation had decided to reach out to the community this Christmas. He told the crowd how he hoped that, if they were searching for meaning in their life, or a church, they would consider making this their home church.

Pastor Paul commented how the giving tree would supply something that they all needed for Christmas. Something for both the church, and for persons who were in need, explaining from the makeshift pulpit that he and the congregation of Reunion Lutheran Church hoped this event would make a small difference in all of their lives. The young pastor thanked them for coming, thanked the volunteers and the choir. When he had finished, he returned to the sideline of the fellowship hall and stood with his family.

Standing on the side, holding Binky's hand as she held their two children by their shoulders in front of them, Pastor Paul searched the crowd, looking at their eyes, and all he saw were sad, worn out, and weary persons. He saw older persons, and younger persons, he could pick out persons who were in trouble, as well as identify people with drug and alcohol problems.

He could see persons who had little or nothing at all and the pastor could see many people, who carried despair and sadness with them, and had brought it with them to the church tonight.

The pastor knew many of them would never make the church their home, but he thought at least for one night, some of these people would realize that God and other people really did care about them.

He also searched the crowd for the collector, and he thought just maybe he would attend, and he could thank him once more for his generous gift. Surely, he thought that the collector would be here tonight to see what it was all about, and to see what the pastor had spent the money on for this special Christmas event.

It was to no avail, as the collector was not anywhere that he could see, or he was lost in and amongst the crowd.

After the sermon and music, the giving of the gifts began. It was a simple procedure, and the event flowed smoothly. Each person, who entered the church this evening, received a numbered ticket, and upon hearing their number called, the ticket holder would hold up the ticket, then the lucky person would then come up to the giving tree, turn in the number, and request a specific type of gift, and receive the gift.

On and on it went, and the smile on the faces of the recipients was well worth all the hard work and effort that went into the event. One person received a warm jacket, and then someone received a basket of food, then a hat, and on and on it went.

As the Christmas joy spread, many other gifts were awarded and unwrapped. Another warm winter hat, a pair of gloves, and many other gifts went to happy recipients. The Christmas joy of gift giving, the spirit of the holiday, and the joy of the evening spread.

Happily, awarded to a young family and a thrilled little girl, was the first toy of the evening. Pastor Paul and the entire Henson family cheered aloud and clapped when they observed the first toy unwrapped, and the smiles in which it brought to the family. The lucky family who had received it was thrilled that they had received something so special for Christmas.

When the old guard members, who had gathered in a little group, saw the first toy unwrapped before their eyes, they turned around in horror and gasped. Chris Johnson and two or three of the leaders turned in the direction of Pastor Paul and they stomped up angrily to where they were standing.

"Oh boy, here they come! They are charging the net!" Pastor Paul laughed at the silly response of the group. "They are coming over now, Binky. That did not take too long." Pastor Paul whispered to his wife.

"Do you want me to handle this? I can take care of them rather quickly," Binky suggested.

Pastor Paul chuckled at his wife's defensive protection of her husband.

"No, please take the children over by the snack table. I have it covered."

Pastor Paul knew very well how tough his beautiful and sweet wife could be! Binky smiled, and hustled the two children away to have a snack or two, while her husband handled the onslaught.

Pastor Paul had his speech prepared; he knew that he could neutralize them very quickly. The first argument that he knew they would present is that he mishandled church funds. Once they accuse him of that sad fact, and step over the inappropriate line, then he happily would push the destruction button on them very quickly.

Sure enough, here they all came. He knew they had arrived right on schedule to place their own feet in their rather self-righteous mouths! They arrived, proceeded to call him out, and demanded an explanation as to what he thought he was doing by disregarding their instructions and utilizing church funds in a non-approved manner.

However, Pastor Paul was ready for them, and he was steadfast and ready in his defense. He calmly explained to them that no church funds were misused, and that the toys were a special request from a private donor who had supplied the funds with which to purchase them. He also explained that this gentleman was a long-time parishioner here. In fact, he was part of a large family of charter members. The charter member had met with the pastor in private, and he made the donation, as well as the request that the pastor used the money as he thought best for the event.

Pastor Paul confidently explained that, "I had made the decision to purchase the toys with the private money."

He then pointed out that the committee had instructed him not to use church money to buy toys, but they had left a loophole open, by not banning toys entirely from the event. He had played their own words against them, and they were not happy at how the pastor had played them like fine violins.

He did not release the name of the collector, nor did anyone ask him to identify him, but once the entire group realized the situation, they read between the lines. There was only one charter member who was still active in the congregation, so they all knew who had given the pastor the money. The collector yielded quite a bit of respect here, and they knew that the collector was a large supporter of Pastor Paul John Henson. They backed down rather quickly when they saw how confident the young pastor was.

Even the most hardened of hearts of the old guard were not about to question a donation made by a person whose families were charter members of the church. That was a battle they were not willing to take on since it would be questioning the very heritage of their church over such a silly situation.

They were not happy, but upon learning that Pastor Paul had not utilized any church funds to purchase the toys, and that this was a one-on-one agreement with a very long-time member, they realized that there was not too much that they could do. They could continue to protest, but the pastor had done nothing wrong.

While Pastor Paul tried not to be smug or gloat, he thought of how sometimes you have to fight back. After all, Peter did cut the ear off the Roman soldier, and Jesus healed it.

The old guard left, and they mingled in with the crowd, no doubt to find supporters with which to share their misguided complaints. Pastor Paul turned his attention back to what was most important, and that was how this Christmas event was going.

Binky rejoined him along with the two Henson children. One look in her husband's eyes told Binky all she needed to know of how the discussion went. She knew that her husband's eyes told his entire story, and she knew how to read them like a book. Binky smiled and hugged her husband because she knew it had gone well.

Pastor Paul searched the crowd, and he studied them as he stood on the side with his wife and family. He studied the crowd's eyes and remarked to his wife on how much despair and troubles existed, even at Christmas time in this tired, old world.

One after another, they came, and it seemed as if there were hundreds. The volunteers would call out a number, such as, "eighty-two!" Someone in the crowd would lift up a ticket with the number eighty-two, go running up to the tree, and request a type of gift.

The church member would say, "Merry Christmas" and give them the gift. It was quite a heart-warming event, and it made you happy just to see the smiles on faces for such a simple little gift or two. Pastor Paul had a well-thought-out vision for this event and you could see that the community needed this as much as the church did.

While the pastor stood on the sideline surveying the crowd, he noticed a young man. For some reason, the pastor identified with him immediately. Using a quick study, he categorized him as a young father. . ..

Pastor Paul watched him, and as he did, he felt a strange feeling come over him to study him and to begin to pray. The man was alternating between standing and walking nervously in the back. The young father paced back and forth with a number in his hand. He then would stand and lean on the back wall of the hall, shifting his legs nervously every few seconds.

Pastor Paul focused on him. He searched his face, and he noticed the weary eyes and the sunken lines. It was obvious that this man was very uncomfortable being here in the church this evening. He thought my goodness; this man is much too young to have such a burden. He noticed that he was wearing a wedding ring on his finger, and he would clutch the ticket with the number on it nervously, while moving it around and around in his hands.

Pastor Paul prayed to himself, "Lord, what does this young man need? What is his story? What is his situation?"

After praying, the pastor leaned over to his wife and

whispered, "I will be right back." Binky nodded at her husband and she watched as he made his way through the crowd. She wondered whom he was going out in the crowd to meet, and what had motivated him.

"Excuse me, excuse me," the pastor said as he waded through the lines and moved closer to the young father.

"Hello, I am Pastor Paul Henson," he said to the young father as he reached out his hand.

The man looked up; he seemed startled to see that the pastor of the church himself had come over by him. He wondered why, of all the hundreds of people here that the pastor felt as if he needed to walk over to him. That was very strange, he thought.

It made him very uncomfortable.

His plan had been to hide here in the back of the hall and to remain unnoticed and not meet anyone, not a single person, until the announcer called his number.

He shook his hand and answered, "Hello, Pastor Henson, I enjoyed your sermon. This is a nice church. This is a nice event for the church to sponsor to try to help people. It is quite the event."

Pastor Paul thanked the young father, and he then asked him, "What brings you here?"

The insight of the pastor, as well as his youth and size, startled the young father. He could not be much older than I am, he thought. Why do I feel as if he sees into my very soul, as if he knows why I am here already?

The young father put his head down, as if he was embarrassed and ashamed. He struggled to speak, and the words did not come easily. "Well, I, well. . .." His voice trailed off. The young father spoke again, and he stammered, "I never thought that I would ever be in a position like this, but a couple of weeks back, I lost my job and it has been rough trying to find something. I read about this event in the newspaper and I thought I would come over to see what it was all about and to pray. I will admit that it has been a long time between church visits for me, Pastor Henson. I am not proud of that, but it is a fact."

Pastor Paul nodded his head and said, "Please, call me, Pastor Paul."

The young father smiled. He liked this guy. The pastor was calm, but you could tell he was strong, tough, and confident. In addition, he did not look much like a stereotypical pastor, with his long hair and facial hair.

He told the pastor, "I figure it cannot hurt to pray these days, Pastor Paul. I need a job. I wonder why when we become desperate—we turn back to God? Why do we not pray in the good times as well as the bad?"

Pastor Paul nodded his head, and he understood now why the young father was in so much pain. He smiled and said, "We are all guilty of that fact, sir. We need to understand that Heaven is about joy as well as comfort. Please sir, let me have your name and I will place you on our prayer list. We will pray for you to find some type of employment."

The young father gave Pastor Paul his name. The pastor took some notes down and while he was writing, Pastor Paul continued, "I see by the wedding ring that you are married." He then asked, "Do you have a family?"

"Yes, a boy, and a girl," the young father replied. "Just on an outside chance I came here, not only to pray, but also to be lucky enough to obtain something for our son for Christmas. You see, right before I lost my job, we picked up this doll for our daughter that she wanted, and we were planning to buy our son his present, but we did not get around to it."

The young father bowed his head to hide his eyes from Pastor Paul and he continued, "Then, I lost my job and all the money dried up. Christmas is next week, and I was just hoping by chance that I could get something for our son here. I just made it in here in time for even receiving a gift, as the nice woman at the front who gave me my ticket, said that I received the next to the last ticket overall." The young father looked up and met the eyes of Pastor Paul and he found the courage to tell him, "Do you know what it is like, Pastor Paul, how difficult this is at Christmas time, to be so down in your spirit and down on your luck?"

Pastor Paul quickly searched his past, and a Christmas of a long time ago immediately came into his mind. It was a horrible time when his best friend's young wife had passed away, right before Christmas Day.

Pastor Paul felt the young man's sorrow, however, he also felt his hope, as well as what Pastor Paul perceived to be determination.

He then placed his hand on the young father's shoulder and said, "I do. I have been there a few times myself. Believe me, I understand, and I wish you hope, joy, and peace. I am sure you will receive something nice. There are many warm winter clothes there, food, and even some toys are still left. I am sure that your Christmas and job situation will work out. Please come and visit with us for a Sunday service."

Pastor Paul John Henson smiled at the young father and reassured him, "Please, do not be ashamed. There are many people in the same situation. It is really tough out there right now." He patted him on the back and wished him a merry Christmas.

The two men shook hands, and the pastor walked away, joined his wife, and told her a little of the story. Binky held her husband's hand, and she squeezed it as she felt his warmth and hope in his powerful hand. She thought about how her husband had such strength in his hands. Binky knew that he had somehow extended with his strength some hope, joy, and peace to the young father.

She just knew it had to have happened.

They continued to stand together on the sideline. They watched as, on and on, it went well into the hundreds, until the supply of gifts under the tree was dwindling. Pastor

Paul and Binky saw the young father receive a gift, but they could not see what it was, because he tucked it quickly under his arm.

He turned, paused, looked back at the Henson family. He waved to them, and he quickly disappeared out the front door and into the night.

Christmas Day arrived, and the church was full for all worship services. The chatter around the church this Christmas season was that the giving tree had been a huge success. The event had remarkably picked up some new members, and for many of the congregational members of the church, it turned out to be the highlight of the season.

Not only had Reunion Lutheran Church reached out to the community in a time of need, but all of those who were involved in the event felt a sense of warmth and joy and true Christmas spirit. It felt wonderful to have a chance to give back to persons in need during this special season.

Some of the old guard still hung in there and brought up the toy issue a few more times. They protested about the entire situation, but they were careful and less aggressive in their complaints. After not receiving much support, they gave up and let it all die.

Pastor Paul gradually realized that he was slowly winning them all over, and even some of the old guard members agreed that he was doing a wonderful job. Some of them even remarked how they actually liked having a long-haired hippie for a pastor! They all started to cooperate more and even started to agree with his ideas.

The Christmas season at the church turned out to be a huge success, and the Christmas committee even voted to keep the giving tree as an annual Christmas event. Pastor Paul knew in his heart that this was where he was making a difference, and that right for now, this was where he was supposed to be.

Just like the collector, this Christmas season had renewed them all in their minds, bodies, and souls. Things were looking good around Reunion Lutheran Church these days, and Pastor Paul thought back to what the collector had said to him, "What is old is old, and what is new is new."

Pastor Paul smiled at the meaning of the words, and he thought how true they really were.

Chapter Five

The Shortstop

The spring of the year finally arrived after a long, hard winter. The collector did the best he could to keep his legs in shape. He listened to the doctor and performed the stair program as much as he could. He went up and down the stairs when the weather was bad and when walking outside was out of the question. He kept himself loose and walked the dog when he could. He was careful not to venture very far on the snow and ice, not wanting to risk tumbling down and create a serious situation.

He knew that he was still in good shape, and he was confident that he could make it to the park. He really wanted to see what was going on over there, but he was careful to avoid the temptation to cruise by in his car.

His goal was to be surprised, and for some strange reason, he knew that he had to walk there on foot. He felt it was the only way to keep up with the spirit of the entire mission. He really looked forward to the day when he would be able to walk over to the park and see what had occurred there.

The word in the newspaper was that as soon as the weather had broken of snow and ice, work had begun on the revitalization and construction. The goal was, the newspaper reported, to have the fields ready for the baseball season. He read where the work progression was right on schedule, and that all the local baseball teams had signed up to use the new fields. The revitalized park was where the local teams now scheduled to play all of their baseball games this year, rather than the field they previously used last year, because this park was going to be such a beautiful showplace.

The collector was really beside himself with excitement as he read the articles and his excitement was building every day.

Finally, the spring weather had improved, and one afternoon brought a perfect day for walking.

"I can relearn the chattering language of the birds as I walk," the collector proclaimed and out the door, he went. His goal, of course, was to make it to the ballpark.

It was a warm spring day, quite lovely indeed, and the collector strode easily along. He smiled proudly; he walked along confidently, until once more, there he stood on the edge of the park. His legs had not failed him. In fact, he felt wonderful.

The collector stood there amazed, as it was perfect, even more wonderful than he could have ever imagined.

He crossed the road and entered the park, just as he had about one year ago, only this time it was very different.

The tears rolled down the collector's cheeks and his throat closed, as even from a distance, he could see the former glory of the park had returned once more. He was beside himself with joy, and the emotion was overwhelming.

The collector's eyes scanned the scene before him and he took note of the condition of the restoration. There were new trees planted along the park's interior edges, and the now pruned and shaped older trees remained along the perimeter while proudly standing in newfound beauty. The sacred war monument had been washed and cleaned, and had a fresh coat of paint applied. A brand-new American flag was on top of the pole, and it waved proudly in the warm, sunny afternoon breeze. The refreshed and polished names of the war dead on the brass plaque shone in the sun. All the heroes had their honor and glory restored.

There were new park benches equipped with new slats, and the fields were a crisp, beautiful green with brand-new sod and turf as far as the collector could see. There were flower displays in pots throughout the park, and they added a delightful color to the scene, echoing the beginning of spring, and a new beginning and a rebirth of sorts.

The collector just had to see the field house! He walked quickly in that direction. If he could have risked a fast jog, then he would have broken into one!

Sure enough, the original plaque hung on the side of the field house in cleaned and polished glory, and it was bright and pristine, just as the collector had remembered it! The words were still there, and the collector read them off partly from memory as though he was verifying they had not lost any of the original wordings.

They had kept the old plaque for historical reasons, but they had added a new plaque next to it proclaiming a rededication of the old park. The new plaque honored the gentleman who had donated the money to revitalize the park. The collector was happy; this was a proud and perfect accolade to such a fine man.

The field house was clean and freshly painted, and it had a new roof installed. The overhead door on the side of the building was open, and the collector looked inside. He saw a young man standing next to a workbench filled with tools, some lawn maintenance equipment, and a large riding lawn mower. The young man was busily working on a mower blade on the workbench.

The collector smiled, as he realized that this young man must be the new maintenance person, hired to be the caretaker to maintain the fields and the park.

The collector moved on because he did not want to disturb the man at his work.

He continued to walk and tour the fields, and he walked

towards the larger baseball field to check it out. There was new, fresh clay laid in the infield, a new backstop, and new bleacher seats. Even home plate and the individual bases were now shiny, untouched, and fresh! The player's benches were new and there was a brand-new chain-link fence installed in the outfield. The collector walked out to the pitcher's mound and reached down to feel the perfect grooming on the mound, and the new clay on top was ready for action. He touched the precious clay, scooped up a bit in his hands and let it sift back to the ground. He stared down from the mound into the batter's box and thought how the batter's box was, just as he remembered it.

The collector stood there in the middle of the infield and his mind was spinning with memories. He took a deep breath, and he smelled that spring season smell of fresh clean air and freshly mowed grass.

The collector surmised that there was no game scheduled at the big-league field, because he could see that the field had undergone some preparation, but there were no baselines or batter boxes lined yet. In fact, judging by the look of the field, it seemed as if there were no games scheduled for the next day or two. He turned around, and he could see some action and some teams gathering down at the little league field on the other end of the park. He thought to himself; my goodness, I can even catch a ballgame! This is going to be a grand afternoon.

The collector strode across the infield; he stopped at the shortstop position, and he imagined himself fielding a ground ball and throwing out a speedy runner at first base. He thought, how many times so many years ago, he had stood on this very spot and fielded a ground ball after a ground ball. He felt wonderful; this was such a great day!

The collector walked all the way down to the other field and he went over to the sidelines. He watched the teams arriving and young players walking with their families to the field, with bats, gloves, and baseballs in tow. The players were starting to warm up, and he admired the crisp new uniforms that they each wore. The uniforms had the names of the team sponsors stenciled upon the back, and the collector read them off aloud, very softly, to no one but himself. He read the quarry's name, a local auto repair shop, the pizzeria in the city, an electric company, and many more names of local businesses and companies. He thought how this was so good for this old, worn city.

Everything was fresh and new and revitalized.

He looked around and he saw that now both team's players were throwing baseballs around on the sideline. A pitcher was warming up with a catcher on the sideline, and he noted how the catcher wore a pair of brand-new, shiny, shin guards and he had a color-coordinated chest protector on. The collector noticed that the one team had "Bugs" emblazoned across the front of their uniforms, and since they were a big-league team that he rooted for, he decided to sit on their sideline.

He took a seat in the grandstands, and the collector decided that he would watch the entire game.

The game started, and the collector could see that the two evenly matched teams both had good pitchers on each side. As the game progressed into the middle innings, it turned into a pitcher's duel, until one team managed to squeeze out a run or two, with a couple of base hits here and there. For the most part, it went back and forth, as the score first went to one to nothing, then a two-to-one type game, with no team taking a clear advantage in the score over the other.

The collector sat there in the warm sun, enjoying this more than anyone could ever imagine. After his lifetime of playing and watching baseball, the collector could tell that this game would probably come down to the last pitch as well as the last batter.

He could just feel it!

He was sitting higher in the stands for a good view of

the rest of the grandstands as well as the ball field. From his lofty perch, the collector noticed a young man, an attractive young lady, and a little girl sitting next to the young man. The collector assumed that it must be the young man's wife and daughter, and they were watching the game together.

He then recognized the young man as the maintenance man that he had seen in the field house when he was touring around near the larger field. He must be now off duty for work, and he is watching the game, the collector thought.

They were sitting in the stands, right along the fence, next to first base and the three of them were cheering for the Bugs team very enthusiastically. The collector surmised that they were obviously family members for one of the Bugs players, since they were cheering for most of the players by their first names, and they seemed to know the Bugs manager and coaches.

The game was down to the last inning, and the Bugs were now protecting a two-to-one lead. There were two outs, and it was the bottom of the ninth inning, when the Bugs pitcher walked a batter, and placed the potential game-tying runner at first base.

The next hitter strode confidently to home plate. He could be the game winner now, and you could see that this young man was a good hitter. He glared boldly at the pitcher, dug at the dirt with his spikes, and climbed into the batter's box. Protecting a one-run lead with this batter at bat was not going to be an easy task. The young family was cheering loudly now, and the opposition bench and fans were all standing, cheering, and rooting for their favorite teams.

The collector leaned over with his arms on his knees, watching the pitcher intently, and he himself let out a cheer or two of encouragement for the Bugs. Now, the excitement of the moment caught the collector too, and he found himself absorbed in the game and tension.

The pitcher grooved a pitch in there and he may have gotten the pitch in a little higher location than he wanted to, and it was in the hitter's wheelhouse. The batter swung hard and smacked it hard towards the hole between the Bugs shortstop and second base. Just, when it looked like the ball was going to escape the fielder and be a clean hit, the shortstop dove to his left, scooped the ball up, stood back up on his feet, and threw a bullet to first base, just beating the runner.

"YOU'RE OUT!" screamed the umpire at first base and the Bugs team, fans, and player's bench erupted into joy.

The Bugs had sealed the victory!

The collector stood up, and he was cheering wildly along with everyone else, while the joy and excitement of the victory consumed the collector. He saw the young family jumping up and down and the young father was backslapping and congratulating everyone around him.

During the joyous celebration, the young father's eyes met the collector, and the collector yelled out to him, "Wow! What a play!"

The young father answered, and he said, "Yes, that is our son. He made the play at shortstop! Can you believe that play?" The young father was beaming proudly with a smile that was a mile wide.

The collector said, "Fantastic! That was a great play! That son of yours has some talent! Wonderful! It was simply an amazing play for him to have come up with the ball and then throw the runner out like that to win the game."

The young father said, "Yes, it really is a great day. It is amazing. You know . . . he has a brand-new glove there, he got a brand-new glove for Christmas, and we got rid of his old glove. It was too small, and it was falling apart. I really did not think that we could get him a new one this year, but miraculously, he got one for Christmas."

It was obvious that the young father was very proud of not only his son but also the fact that he had been able to give him a glove for Christmas.

The collector could tell that the young father was full of strength, hope, joy, and peace. He wondered where such a young man could have developed such strength and joy at his young age.

The collector nodded his head and said, "No kidding. That is wonderful. It must have been a Christmas to remember. It must be a good glove because he is certainly quite a fielder there." The young father smiled back at the collector while he recalled his fond memories of this past Christmas.

"You know, it is really good when the old is old, and the new is new," the collector said, as he started carefully climbing down the grandstand.

The young father nodded his head in approval and said, "You are right! I even landed a new job this spring too! I was lucky to get it, let me tell you. My old boss wrote me a nice letter of recommendation, and I received another letter from the pastor of our new church. Otherwise, without that support, I think that I would have just been in the mix with many other applicants. You are sure right on there, mister. I like that saying. The old is old, and the new is new . . . and it sure does feel good."

The collector nodded his head at the young man's good fortune and he told him, "Good for you there, young fellow!" The collector smiled, waved, and climbed down the rest of the way from the grandstands.

He said goodbye to the young father and congratulated him once more on the success of his son and on his new job.

The young shortstop's teammates picked him up and held him over their heads, and as the collector stood and watched the celebration, he saw the young shortstop's family rush to join him in the celebratory moment.

The collector thought, what a grand day it had been. He knew that in many ways, he was looking at a rerun of when he was young, and he could make the same kind of plays at shortstop.

"I would have thrown him out too. It must have been that new glove," said the collector with a laugh.

The collector stood on the sideline, staring out at the field for a long time, just thinking and taking it all in. The fields were all empty now, and the only noise was an occasional car that went by, and the sound of the flag on the monument flapping proudly in the breeze.

The collector then took one last look, and he turned and started to head for home. Then something else caught the eye of the collector while he started to walk away and he smiled broadly.

He noticed that lining the entire field, every twenty feet or so, were brand-new trash cans.

THE END

The Watchman

Chapter One

Always on Duty

Walter P. Thrump was like clockwork. You could set your watch to his exact, timely arrival in front of the corporate headquarters building of Substantial Industries Worldwide LLC. If Walter P. Thrump needed to report for the four thirty in the afternoon shift, then his twenty-five-year-old, simulated wood grain panel, station wagon, with bald tires, missing hubcaps, and grey duct tape plastered along the side to hold the fenders on, would pull up into the parking space marked, "Security Officer" precisely at four fifteen in the afternoon.

You could count on Walter arriving fifteen minutes early every time, no matter what the shift assignment for Walter turned out to be. Walter would not allow it to be any different. He was steady, consistent, and reliable. His old car just puttered along the interstate, all the way from his home in Jersey City, New Jersey to the location of his employment, which was in a small town located upon the border of New Jersey and lower New York State.

Distance meant nothing to Walter P. Thrump; he timed it just right all the time.

Walter P. Thrump never missed a day of work, never took a vacation day off, and he was never late. He proudly announced when he arrived, every single day, that he was never late, and he did not even own a timepiece or wear a wristwatch. He just had an internal clock that kept time forever in his head, and it was accurate to the minute.

This day was no different to Walter, even though it was Christmas Eve in 1991. This was a special day as far as his shift schedule, because Walter's supervisor had instructed him to arrive at two thirty in the afternoon for his shift, since the company was going to close early for the holiday. Walter was about to relieve the company's receptionist in the front lobby.

Mr. Thrump was a security officer for Substantial Industries, entrusted with the duties of providing security services for the corporate building and campus. His current assignment was to the main headquarters building within a large corporate office park that included two other buildings on the property. Substantial Industries Worldwide, LLC, owned, and operated all the facilities as well as the property. Substantial Industries was a very large, worldwide company that made this location their worldwide headquarters.

Walter P. Thrump was proud that his assignment was to the main corporate building, since it was the flagship of this property. He was also proud of the fact that he was now a sergeant on the security force, having received a pay raise, along with the rank and title, about one year earlier. He was in charge of the other two security officers that would be working during this shift. One officer had an assignment, directly across the street, in a large building opposite the corporate headquarters, and one security officer assigned to secure the large warehouse building down the road from him.

Walter took his job seriously, and when folks would ask him what he did for a living, he would proudly answer that he was, "A security officer."

If the person mistakenly changed the phrasing to something such as, "Oh, a night watchman," then Walter would shake his head and very adamantly correct them.

"No, I am not a watchman. I am a security officer!"

Walter P. Thrump was a serious man.

The old station wagon pulled up in front of the worldwide headquarters building of Substantial Industries, exactly at two fifteen in the afternoon on this cold, dark Christmas Eve. A long trail of blue smoke followed behind his car like a smokestack, as the old car puttered along. Walter parked it in the security parking spot, turned the engine off, and he listened as the engine coughed and sputtered, and spit out a big, blue cloud of smoke as it shut down. He grabbed his lunch pail and bags of supplies, his hat and coat, rolled down his driver's door window, and stuck his arm out of the window. He pulled the door handle, opened the door to his car, rolled the window back up, he climbed out and closed the door. The inside driver's door latch had been broken for a very long time, but it did not bother Walter P. Thrump in the least.

Walter proudly strode up the majestic stone steps to the front door and walked into the grand lobby of the corporate headquarters building. As was his custom, he stopped in his tracks, and then turned towards the receptionist sitting at the large front desk in the lobby, pulled up his coat sleeve, and looked at an imaginary watch that would have been on his wrist.

Judy Hicks had been the main receptionist for Substantial Industries for a very long time, so she was quite used to Walter's routine.

"Okay, please, check me, Judy. It is two seventeen in the afternoon, or my name is not, Walter P. Thrump!"

Judy turned from her seat at the front desk, reached over to the clock that was sitting on the counter, looked at the time, and she chuckled.

"Two seventeen it is, Walter! I have to say, I am glad to see you too. This means that I am out of here, and I am ready to begin my holiday." Judy smiled at Walter, and he smiled back.

"You are amazing, Walter, and let me guess, you do not have a watch on."

Walter proudly walked into the lobby and clapped his hands together while proclaiming, "Right on time as usual and no watch on my wrist, Judy! Walter P. Thrump is here and on duty."

Walter took his coat and hat off, opened the door to the security closet in the lobby, and hung them on the hook behind the door. He then grabbed his bags and lunch pail and set them down on the shelf in the closet. Walter closed the door to the closet and stared out at the lobby. He smiled, because there was nothing that he enjoyed better than to be at his post and on duty.

Walter was about sixty-five years of age, and he was small, no in fact, he was tiny. If Walter was five-foot-five that was a very tall estimate because five foot four was more accurate. He weighed in at about one hundred and twenty pounds if he was wet, had on a heavy winter coat, and had a collection of spare change in his pockets. The security uniform provider had a difficult time in finding a uniform that actually fit him since his waist was so tiny. The uniform that he had on today was close to fitting, or at least as close as they could come!

It hung on his frame like a large tent, and he pulled his belt up about four or five notches to clamp his pants to his tiny waist.

He wore the blue uniform proudly, as if he was a rear admiral in the United States Navy. He had a polished brass badge, which had his name and rank on it that he proudly displayed on his front uniform pocket, in the exact location as specified by his security manual. He also had a bright brass whistle that hung from his other breast pocket and it had a little chain to hold it in place that looped through the buttonhole. He had a craggy face, with a long-pointed nose, deep-set eyes, and a thick chock of brown hair, which he swirled over to the side. Framing his face on each side were 1970s style long sideburns. His hair was amazing because he had not one single grey hair in his thick mane. Just as he was proud of the fact that he never wore a watch, or was ever late, he was just as proud of the fact that he had not one single grey hair. Furthermore, he swore that he did not dye it. He would defy anyone to inspect it and find a single grey hair; he knew they just did not exist.

Walter had about two teeth left in his entire head; he just gummed his food to chew it. He did not intend ever to replace them. He did not care. Although he was small in stature, Walter P. Thrump was one tough, little, New Jersey guy. A criminal sneaking around the worldwide headquarters had better be careful with Walter P. Thrump on duty. The criminal could be gummed into submission, as old Walter would never give up without a major battle! He may not intimidate anyone, but Walter P. Thrump would never back down from anyone either.

Poor Walter only had one lung. About ten years earlier, Walter had to have a lung removed. He had developed lung cancer because of some by-products that he had inhaled after working for thirty years in a glass factory in Jersey City. He had retired right after his operation, and the glass company gave him a small settlement of money along with his pension.

It really was a small consolation amount, considering that he gave the company his dedication, a large part of his life, a lung, and thirty years of hard work.

He decided that security work was a better fit for him at this stage in his life. He breathed a little heavily now and then, but he was alive, and for that, Walter was very thankful.

All he ever ate were Big Bob's Famous Cheese Puffed

snacks and a sandwich that consisted of a single slice of Big Bob's extra thick bologna on two pieces of white bread with a single blob of mustard. The sandwich was always prepared and packed the same way, wrapped in brown waxed paper, tied up with a plain cotton string. All Walter ever drank was soda right out of the bottle, and coffee in his trusty, white, and red thermos, No one ever saw him eat or drink anything more or less; they all swore by the same testimony.

Walter was on duty this Christmas Eve, and the corporate headquarters building and campus of Substantial Industries Worldwide, LLC, could be in no better hands than they were, while in the hands of Walter P. Thrump, on this special night.

Chapter Two

Christmas Eve Falls Slowly

"Couldn't you have asked someone else to work for you, Walter? After all, it is Christmas Eve, my friend," Judy asked from her front desk position, while she unplugged her headphones and handset from the main switchboard.

"Christmas does not mean very much to me these days, Judy. I am just happy to be here to get away from my wife and besides, I earn holiday pay!"

Walter beamed proudly at the thought of the extra wage. He then turned to his security desk in the front lobby, turned on his two-way handheld radio, and bent over to plug in his telephone. After a few checks of his systems, he then checked his alarm panel, security logbook, and the closed-circuit television cameras. Walter sat at his post, and he was ready to go to work.

Walter thought to himself how he really did not feel anything about Christmas anymore. The holiday meant nothing to him these days, and it just was an opportunity to earn a higher wage for a day of work. At this point in his life, he was happy to have his job, and to Walter P. Thrump, his job was of the highest importance to him. Not that it was a silly old Christmas.

"I am serious. My wife and I have been married for over thirty years, and it is exactly like that country song of a few years ago, that was such a big hit. I loved that song. It was dead on." Walter P. Thrump was a music lover.

"What song was that, Walter?" Judy asked as she grabbed her coat and hat.

"You know, I think the song title was, All Those Things I Used to Love about You, Now Just Drive Me Crazy. I loved that song. I think it was by Big Tex and Linny. I wonder whatever happened to them?" Walter said as he sat there at his desk, and he looked as if he was pondering the fate of the singing group for a few moments.

"Walter, you are quite the character. I am sure you exaggerate, and your wife loves you very much." Judy smiled at Walter. "What did you buy her for a Christmas gift this year?"

"Nothing. I give to her what she gives to me. Nothing. I have not received a present from her or anyone else in years. No one cares enough about me or the holiday to even send me a Christmas greeting card."

Walter was dead serious, and he stated the answer in such an abrupt manner that Judy could not really doubt his sincerity. Judy looked at him from the lobby desk, and she felt a tinge of sadness for this little man. He seemed so dedicated, and he never, ever, was in a sour or poor mood. Surely, he had someone who cared. What a terrible feeling that on Christmas Eve, you are so alone that you actually looked forward to coming to work, rather than being with your family.

Judy did not know how to answer him; she just fiddled with her coat and continued to gather her belongings to prepare to leave for the day.

"Well, Walter, please help yourself during the night to some of this candy on my desk. Please consider my gift for you and enjoy it. I do not need to eat it and gain any more weight. After all, the holidays are here!"

Judy laughed and looked at the skinny little man seated behind the desk.

"Lord knows that you sure could use the weight now, Walter! Now, please tell me that you did not sign up for a double shift and at least you will be home on Christmas Day!"

"Negative on that fact, Judy. Sergeant Walter P. Thrump is on duty throughout. I tripled 'em up and will finally get to go home late on Christmas Day. It is just a day, Judy, just a day that is like any other day."

"I hope your boss realizes how lucky he is to have you as an employee, Walter. I know we all appreciate how dedicated you are. You have a merry Christmas and try to enjoy it." Judy smiled and waved as she left. Walter smiled at her, and waved just as his two-way radio crackled with some security chatter on the channel, breaking the silence of the squelch settings.

"Officer Russell T. Hall on duty here, at the one hundred building and checking in for my shift." The radio announced the arrival of another security officer at his post in the building across from the main headquarters.

"Roger, Officer Hall." Walter keyed the radio and acknowledged the check in.

"Officer Mendez on duty here and checking in, at the one hundred thirty-three building for my shift." The radio crackled once more with the last remaining officer checking in.

"Roger, Officer Mendez."

Walter was satisfied now, because his entire team had checked in right on time. He checked in Officer Mendez as well as Officer Hall, and he filled in the logbook. Walter wrote in his logbook in big, blocky letters and his boss always laughed at how perfectly he completed the book. Walter missed nothing. Not even a bug walking across the floor of the lobby escaped his keen and highly trained eyes. He proudly and carefully logged every detail of his shift. His beady, little, deep-set eyes were sharp, and Walter P. Thrump was always right on the stick.

The afternoon had been cold, cloudy, and it smelled as if it could snow outside. Sure enough, now that the afternoon was waning, it had turned even a little colder, and a passing snow shower dusted the ground with a little white powder. It was very appropriate for Christmas Eve in northern New Jersey.

Walter was on duty and he sat at his front lobby desk, watching the screens, alarm panels, and the employees passing by his desk. With the company closing early, it was an almost constant flow of employees who passed by Walter and his security post.

"Goodnight, Walter."

"Merry Christmas, Walter. Please have a good night. I am off until after New Year's Day. See you next year."

"Merry Christmas, Walter!"

On and on, the employees bid a Christmas greeting to Walter P. Thrump as he nodded, smiled, and exchanged greetings with everyone he could as they passed by, while still not taking his eyes off his duty assignments.

Walter P. Thrump never shirks his duties, even for Christmas greetings.

It seemed as though every single one of the employees knew Walter. Thousands of them who worked in this huge facility and they all could tell you who Walter P. Thrump was.

Walter was a legend. It was as if he was a celebrity in his own right!

Soon the afternoon was gone, and Walter's internal clock ticked off, telling him it was close to five o'clock. Very shortly, the nighttime housekeeping crew would be arriving to begin cleaning the facility. Walter would soon begin the activity that he enjoyed the most about his job; which were his building rounds. Walter loved poking around, punching his watchman's clock, checking every nook and corner of the building. Walter treasured the building tours and walking around, hoping to find something to act upon or react to.

The nighttime had now descended upon them, and the electrical timers clicked "on" in the front lobby. The timers powered the fantastic holiday lights that the facility maintenance crew had installed right after Thanksgiving, illuminating the entire lobby in a colorful and fabulous display of Christmas brilliance.

There were blue, red, yellow, purple, and green lights; all set upon the live evergreen trees in the lobby, and it was a breathtaking display. To add to the wonderful setting, there was also a huge, twenty-foot-high Christmas tree that was tastefully decorated and lit up in the front corner of the lobby. Fantastic lights framed huge wreaths that hung on the railings of the center staircase, and in the windows along the front lobby glass. Walter sat there at his post, surrounded by the holiday display as the holiday lights twinkled and illuminated every corner of the lobby.

It set the perfect tone for a Christmas Eve at the headquarters of Substantial Industries Worldwide, LLC.

Everyone admired them, everyone, except for Walter P. Thrump. He only focused upon his security duties and making sure that nothing unusual occurred on this shift to the facility and properties that he had been employed to protect. He knew that the cold, snow, and the wind that had picked up as the night fell meant that the potential for power failures, rattling doors, and false alarms were on the horizon.

This was all serious business to Walter P. Thrump, and he was on duty on this Christmas Eve to handle whatever serious crisis would arise!

Chapter Three

Making the Rounds

The cleaning crew arrived for the night shift, and Walter reviewed with the executive housekeeper, the extra log sheet left by the facility director, for any special housekeeping requests for this evening. Once Walter completed reviewing the details of the shift and explaining the special requests, the housekeepers began working in the facility on their individual assignments. Walter radioed across to the other building to Officer Russell T. Hall and informed him that he was going to begin his first building round.

Walter flung the watchman's tour clock over his shoulder and headed for his first punch station. He hit the north staircase, checked the doors, and opened the little punch station door. Walter took the little key from the station, inserted it in the clock, and turned it until he heard the telltale "click" advising him of a successful punch. Walter loved that sound, and he always proudly went over his punch tapes with his road supervisor, showing him his timely punches and expertly performed building rounds.

On and on, Walter went on his journey. The little man went up the staircases, across the floors, up to the north roof hatch, down to the south tower. He stopped by the accounting wing and hit the station near the restrooms that all the other security officers always forgot.

However, not Walter P. Thrump, he never missed a single punch key station.

Along the way, he checked everything, observed the

cleaning crew, checked doors, turned off lights; he was an efficient machine, tuned for facility security effectiveness.

Walter wandered into the sales executive wing and noticed at the end of the hall that one of the corner offices was still lit up. He walked down the hallway to investigate, and saw that it was Mr. Lathrop's office. Mr. Lathrop was a senior executive in one of the many sales departments, and Walter knew that he was a very important man in the pecking order of the Substantial Industries hierarchy.

Upon reaching the office, Walter peered in and noticed that Mr. Lathrop was still working at his desk. Walter gently tapped on the office door, and the executive looked up.

"Working late on Christmas Eve, Mr. Lathrop? You should head on home, sir. I am sure your family will be looking for you. Is everything all right, Mr. Lathrop?"

Mr. Lathrop smiled when he saw that it was Walter checking on him. He explained, "It is fine Walter. I just have these last paperwork assignments to finish and complete. As soon as I am done, I will be out of here. I am okay and thank you for checking on me, Walter. Please have a merry Christmas."

"Thank you, Mr. Lathrop. You too, and please call me on the telephone at the security desk if you need me. I will not perform another round until well into the morning, but I can hustle up here quickly if you need me."

Walter smiled, and Mr. Lathrop almost chuckled at the eagerness of the little security officer to jump into some type of action.

"Thank you, Walter. I will be sure to call you if I need anything. Thank you. I appreciate your attentiveness."

The executive went back to his papers as Walter waved and continued on his building rounds. He only passed the housekeepers now, as it now seemed as if all the other employees, except for Mr. Lathrop, had left for the holiday.

Walter returned to his front lobby post and he radioed

over to Officer Hall to report that all was clear. He filled in his logbook, and carefully noted everything he had noticed on his round, even the fact that Mr. Lathrop was still in his office.

Walter pulled out his small transistor radio and placed it on his desk. He tuned across the A.M. radio dial, but all he seemed to pick up was Christmas music. Walter sighed and finally decided to concede defeat. As much as he was not into Christmas, he had to admit that it was Christmas Eve. Therefore, he left the radio tuned to one A.M. radio station playing Christmas music very loudly and clearly, even inside of the steel encased building. Walter thought it was very strange that he could receive the radio station signals so strongly this evening, as he usually tuned in a large amount of static inside the building.

However, tonight the reception was clear and strong.

"It must be good radio wave propagation tonight," the little man mumbled.

Most of the housekeepers were now completing their assignments, checking out with Walter, and leaving for the night as the cleaning duties slowly dwindled down. Soon, the executive housekeeper checked off on the log and work orders. She then bid Walter a holiday greeting, and out the door, she went too.

Walter was alone in the lobby once more, just him and his radio, his alarm panels, his camera screens, and the fantastic Christmas lights twinkling all around him.

As Walter sat at his post, the radio station played a particularly stirring rendition of, "It Came upon the Midnight Clear." The song played on and on, and it was so captivating that it melted even the Christmas hardened heart of Walter P. Thrump.

The little security officer's eyes remained on his screens and alarm panel, but his mind wandered away for a few moments. It may have been the snow, the lights in the lobby, or the music over the radio, but for just a few moments, Walter allowed his security focused mind to wander back to happier Christmas Eve gatherings with his wife and young family.

In his mind, there he was, in the living room in their first house together. He was sitting in front of the fireplace. The fire roared and projected warmth that he imagined he could feel even now in his legs and feet.

He could build such roaring fire.

His wife was there next to him, watching his son who was about seven years old, and his daughter who must have been about five years old at the time. The children were playing on the floor right in front of Walter and his wife. A fresh-cut Christmas tree proudly stood in the corner of the room, decorated with strings of multicolored lights and homemade ornaments. The Christmas tree stood there glowing and twinkling, broadcasting the season as if it were a beacon of hope, joy, and peace.

Walter's mind would not stop taking him back in time, so he rubbed his eyes, sat back in his chair, and tried to focus on the security screens. He could not focus. It was hopeless. His mind took him back once more, and he found himself staring at the large Christmas tree in front of him in the lobby of the building.

The Christmas ghosts swirled around the little man's mind. Back he was again, in the same living room. Look at how his wife was so beautiful and take a look at me too! Young, handsome, and still with that full head of hair. The children laughed, rolling on the floor in front of them, eating cookies, and drinking warm milk.

"Daddy, it is time for you to put the star on top of the tree!" Little Walter shouted to his father as his sister jumped up and down.

"Do it now, Daddy, do it before Santa Claus comes, and he sees our tree without a star!"

Mrs. Thrump carried the ladder in and set it next to the tree. Walter picked up the star, climbed up the ladder and he carefully placed it on the tree, then he snaked the electrical cord down the back of the tree, and let it hang near the electrical outlet. Walter climbed down, moved the ladder, and then plugged in the cord as the star flickered to life.

He turned out the lights in the little house, and the Thrump family stood and cheered at how fabulous the Christmas tree looked, with the star brightly glowing on top of it.

A beacon of hope, joy, and peace for all.

Mrs. Walter P. Thrump clapped her hands together. "Time for bed now, children! Take up your glasses and plates and bring them to the kitchen, then kiss your father goodnight. Off to bed now!"

The two youngsters moaned and groaned, but they followed their mother's instructions and off they were. Both of them stopped by Walter and gave him a kiss and a hug.

"Tomorrow is the big day now, you two. Off to bed so that Santa Claus does not pass you by!"

Upon hearing their father's words, the two young Thrump children ran across the room, up the stairs they went, and you could hear their tiny feet run across the bedroom floor above the living room.

Soon it was silent.

Now tucked safely into their beds for the night, dreaming of a special visit, and the wonders of the next day, it was obvious that the two little Thrump children had heeded Walter's warning.

Walter's wife came down the stairs after tucking their two children in, and she stood in front of Walter and smiled. In his mind, he could clearly see her face, and she was just as beautiful as the day they first met.

Then . . . the Christmas ghosts were gone.

Walter's mind returned to his duty, and the song ended on the radio. He felt just a slight pang of sorrow in his heart, at the times that had passed him by, and where he was now in his life. It was so long ago, but he still remembered somewhere deep inside of him what it meant to be loved, and to give love at Christmas time.

"Security Officer Hall, calling into the one hundred one building. Come in, Sergeant Thrump."

The two-way radio on Walter's desk crackled with the radio call, and Walter forgot Christmas ghosts and memories and jumped into action.

"Christmas nonsense," he mumbled. He grabbed the radio, keyed the microphone, and responded.

"This is Sergeant Walter P. Thrump. Go ahead, Officer Hall."

"Permission to go on dinner break. Officer Mendez is on duty here at one hundred building for duty fill in."

"Roger, Officer Hall. I will log it. Permission granted to go on dinner break. Are you coming over here to the one hundred and one building?"

"Roger. On my way, Sergeant Thrump. I will meet you in the lobby."

"Roger. Out." Walter made the notes in his logbook and then walked over to the security closet and pulled out his hat and coat and he put them on. He took a large broom from the closet and walked through the lobby towards the front door.

"I need to broom off some of that dusting of snow on the front steps, so Officer Hall or someone else, does not tumble down," Walter spoke the commands aloud to no one except himself.

He quickly dusted the snow off the front steps and walkway, made his way back into the lobby, put away the broom, jacket, and his hat, and grabbed his lunch pail and bags. He went back to the security desk, pulled up an extra chair next to his, and waited for Officer Hall to arrive.

This was to be his Christmas Eve feast. One slice of extra thick bologna on white bread, with a blob of mustard, some

Big Bob's Famous Cheese puffed snacks, soda, and a swig or two of coffee. Just what he had every night. Christmas Eve or not, that's exactly what Walter P. Thrump wanted.

Chapter Four

Up on the Roof

The front door opened. Walter heard the jingle and jangle of keys as he looked up from his screens and alarms to see Officer Russell T. Hall stride into the front lobby. Russell carried his lunch pail with him and he looked over to Walter and waved.

"Hey, Walt. How is it going tonight? Quiet, huh?"

Walter looked over to Russell, nodded his head, and smiled. He tapped the seat of the chair next to him as an indication that he had prepared a chair for Russell at the security desk for this Christmas Eve feast.

Russell T. Hall was Walter P. Thrump's only friend. They had known each other for the entire time, each of them had worked at this site, which was about six or seven years, or thereabouts. It is not as if they were bowling buddies, drank beer together, or anything of that sort. It was just that the two of them ate dinner and lunch together when they shared shifts and chatted about general things.

Except for his wife, Walter never really chatted with anyone else, or associated with any other person, except for Russell. It often felt as if Walter spoke to Russell, even more than he did to his wife! Walter had another good friend, who had worked here at Substantial Industries for years, but he sadly had passed away suddenly this past October. Walter missed him a great deal. By some sort of sad default, this made Russell the nearest person to being a friend that Walter P. Thrump had.

Russell was tall, well over six feet, and this was in sharp

contrast to his friend. He was of a medium build; had thinning white hair, blue eyes, and he wore black-framed eyeglasses. He was in and around the seventy-year-old mark in age, and he was retired from a military and police background. Walter was clearly impressed when Russell showed Walter some pictures of when he joined the military as a young man. The pictures showed an impressive young man, who was handsome, tall, and strong. However, even at seventy years of age, Russell was still a handsome man.

Walter considered Russell an excellent security officer, always on time and always doing his job. He was a good one, and Walter was proud to have him on the crew. Russell only worked here and there, as not to interrupt his pensions or government monies, but he did enjoy the work, and escaped out of the house for a mission on occasion.

He would tell Walter whenever Walter would ask him how much longer he planned on working, "Forever, Walter. People are like dogs, they need a job, if a dog does not have a job, then they grow lazy, old, and mean."

We all need purpose in our lives, and Russell T. Hall was no exception.

"Officer Mendez is in place over there, Walter. I briefed him, but it is very quiet tonight. I will trade places with him when I go back to the one hundred building, so that he can grab some chow. Officer Mendez said that the warehouse building is also very quiet, nothing going on, and all the warehouse workers have left for home now."

The two other security officers in the remaining buildings switched places and covered the two smaller buildings whenever the scheduled dinner, lunch, or coffee breaks occurred. Walter stayed at the larger building by himself and covered the flagship.

Walter was pleased with the report. "Good, yes, that is very good. We do not need any adventures tonight. Mr. Lathrop is still in his office upstairs. He will most likely go out the side door to the executive lot, but I will check his office on my next building tour around one in the morning."

Russell shook his head and said, "Lathrop is still working, huh? Oh boy, he will be in some serious trouble for working so late on a Christmas Eve."

Walter nodded his head in acknowledgment of Russell's statement and he reached down into his pail and pulled out his soda and the sandwich wrapped in wax paper, tied with the plain cotton string.

"Yeah, yeah, yeah, for sure, Russell. I think Mr. Lathrop is going to be in some major trouble. His wife is going to have a fit, working this late on Christmas Eve. I bet that he is in big trouble already because it is getting so late now."

Russell chuckled at the sight of Walter's sandwich and his concern for the executive's welfare. He shook his head gently back and forth while he settled into the chair and he sat next to Walter.

Russell pointed at the sandwich and said, "I would have thought that you would change up for a Christmas Eve meal tonight there, Walter. I see that you decided to stick with the same old, same old."

Walter shook his head as he responded, "No reason to change. Christmas is just another day, nothing special to me anymore."

"Oh, I see, Walter, and I imagine you have another identical sandwich packed for your Christmas Day celebration for the next shift as well." Russell took a bite of his sandwich and a spoonful of fruit out of a cup while waiting for Walter's answer.

Walter nodded his head in agreement, as if there was no other alternative at this point.

Russell frowned at Walter's response and told him, "Christmas is what you make of it, Walt. If you have had bad experiences as of late, stay positive, and something will come along to change your mind. You know Walt, you cannot rewrite Christmas past, but you can choose to forget it. You should just concentrate on the future, which happens to be under your control. Tell me once more, what has soured you on the holiday, my friend. I hear that you are enjoying some Christmas music on your portable radio, so you must celebrate in some small way." Russell pointed towards the transistor radio sitting on the security desk.

"Nah, nah, nah. I am not really enjoying the music. For some strange reason, it is the only station that I can tune into tonight. What is there to celebrate, Russell? My kids never call me or even write anymore, I have not heard from them in forever. My wife is not too keen about me these days. She barely cooks or even acknowledges my existence. I have one lung, have trouble breathing, and to be perfectly honest, I have not received a Christmas present, or even a card in at least ten years or more. That is, unless you could count that leftover candy on the receptionist desk over there, which Judy told me I could eat." Walter pointed to the dish on the front reception desk and Russell turned to look at what Walter had pointed out.

"Well, Walter, I guess you could count the candy. What is there for your wife to cook? All you ever eat are those sandwiches! Why do your kids not contact you? Did you have a falling out? If I remember, you have a boy and a girl. . .." Walter stared back at Russell as Russell's voice trailed off.

He usually never spoke of anything this personal, but since it was Russell and he was the closest person to being a friend to Walter P. Thrump, then Walter decided to answer him.

"Yes, a boy and girl. They are both married, for many years now and both of them now have children too. I have only seen the grandchildren once. My son is in Saint Paul in Minnesota, and my daughter lives in Atlanta, Georgia. No, I never had a cross word for either of them. I worked thirty years for them. My wife never worked, except of course, the hardest job of all, which is being a homemaker. In fact, I still am working after all of these years. I paid for schools, colleges, and went into debt for them. They always had a nice house, food, and a roof over their heads. Only the Lord knows what I did wrong." Walter turned his head away from Russell a bit so that he could hide his eyes. The pain he felt was deep, and he did not want his friend to see any weakness.

Russell sensed the difficulty of the situation, and he decided to shift the conversation and not spoil the mood of their meal together. He knew that Walter P. Thrump must have had a bit of a rough time of it now and then. He also knew deep down, he was an exceptionally good man, and that Walter could not alter whatever happened, or the perception of what had happened. However, he still felt that you could not deny Walter's record of dedication. Russell had no reason not to think that he was as dedicated to his family at one point, or he still is, just as he is to his work. Russell could sense the hurt and he could not help but feel sorry for the little man, who seemed so alone on such a special night.

"So, what would an old dog like you are, want for a Christmas present anyway, Walt? I bet that you would just take another bag of those Big Bob's Famous Cheese Puffed snacks!"

Without the slightest hesitation, Walter answered, "I would like to receive a wristwatch. That would be the one present that I would like to receive."

Walter's response startled Russell. At first, he did not know how to respond, or what to say.

"A watch? For the man who is never late! What reason would you have for wanting a wristwatch?"

"To prove my point, Russell, that, of course, I am never late," the confident Walter P. Thrump answered with a smile. Russell shook his head and smiled back.

To continue the lighter mood, Russell then asked, "Tell

me that story again of why you still have so much hair there, Walter. It is a good one, which I like to hear every once in a while."

Walter chuckled and spoke, "It sure is a good one! If I were smart, I should have told the world and made a million dollars. You see, I was painting the first apartment we ever had when we were first married, and I had this big bucket of oil paint up on the top rung of the ladder. I was cutting in the baseboard of the wall when my wife went by the ladder and accidentally bumped it. The paint fell down from the ladder and it landed right on top of my head!"

Walter sat back in his chair and laughed loudly, as did Russell. You could see the one or two little teeth left in Walter's mouth when he laughed.

"Right on top of my head, oil paint running down all over me. Well, to get it all out without shaving my head, my wife scrubbed my hair and scalp with turpentine, and ever since then, this is what happened to my hair!"

He tilted his head forward for Russell to check it out and then added once more, "Not a grey hair in there, Russell T, Hall, or my name is not, Walter P. Thrump!"

Russell rubbed his thin white head of hair with his hand while studying Walter's hair and simply said, "Amazing."

The two men finished their meal in relative silence, as they actually had spoken more than they usually did, and the time for the meal break had dwindled away.

"Well, I had better get back over to the one hundred building. I need to relieve Officer Mendez so that he can eat. Anyway, it is almost midnight now. Soon, it will be Christmas Day, Walter, and another year will be leaving us soon after that. It will be New Year's Day, before you know it," Russell said as he stood up and packed the last remaining items of his lunch into his pail. He poured a little coffee from his thermos into his cup and a little into Walter's cup that was sitting on the security desk.

Russell lifted the cup up and held it out to Walter to

make a toast, "To a wonderful Christmas, Walter, and I hope that someday you get that watch."

Walter lifted his cup and touched Russell's cup in the air, and he smiled.

Walter did not say a word; he only smiled.

Russell and Walter drank the last of the coffee, and they each put away their cups. The two men shook hands and exchanged Christmas greetings once more. Russell waved, put on his coat and hat, picked up his pail, and out the front door, he went.

"I will radio you when I am back on duty and covering the buildings," Russell reported.

Walter P. Thrump waved back and nodded while he put his gear away and went back to staring at his security system monitoring screens.

A few minutes later, the radio silence broke once more with Officer Hall's voice. "Officer Hall reporting to one hundred thirty-three building. All clear here and at one hundred. With your permission, I will now relieve Officer Mendez for his dinner break."

"Roger, please proceed. Out." Walter answered.

Walter turned the volume back up on the radio, still playing on his desk. He sighed as he heard another Christmas tune playing merrily away. Walter checked all of his security system screens and ran the alarm panel through the paces. He could not help but stare at the lights in the lobby now, as well as the Christmas tree, and he now was finding it hard to concentrate on his duties and keep his mind off Christmas.

Everything was calm, all was quiet at the corporate headquarters, and Christmas Day was now upon them all. It was an eerie parallel to some lyrics to one of the more famous of the Christmas carols.

High up in the corner office of the sales executive suite, Mr. Lathrop glanced at his watch and realized how much trouble he was now in with his family. He had been distracted for an instant, and he had looked up from his work for just a second. He thought for just a brief moment that someone had darted into his office, or that it was Walter coming back to check on him.

He realized that it was just his mind playing tricks on him, and that he had lost all track of time.

It had been a long day. It was now nearly midnight, and Christmas Eve had spun away from him. He just had to finish this paperwork; his wife would understand, he told himself repeatedly. He gathered up his papers and sorted out his desk to make some kind of order about it.

He nearly jumped out of his skin, and he knew he was in major trouble when the telephone on his desk rang loudly. He knew it would be his wife. Picking up the telephone, Mr. Lathrop held it away from his ear as his wife blasted him for working so late on Christmas Eve.

After much apologizing, Mr. Lathrop assured his wife that he would be home very shortly, and that he was leaving right now.

Mr. Lathrop tried hard to state his case with his wife. "After all, honey, I am a key executive. A big shot of sales here. I am an important man, and I needed to finish this work, before I left for the holiday break."

Mr. Lathrop pleaded his case, and he received very little, to no sympathy from his wife, despite his making note of his high and important stature within Substantial Industries.

"Well, you are just my husband to me, so get home now! It is Christmas, so you need to leave that job where it belongs! Right there on your desk!" Mrs. Lathrop angrily hung up and the phone line went dead.

Oh boy, I am in trouble, Mr. Lathrop thought. His high and lofty position did not mean a thing to Mrs. Lathrop!

As he gathered up his papers, and his coat and hat, he rushed to turn off his lights and leave his office, when his eye caught two little boxes wrapped in Christmas gift-wrap, sitting on his credenza close to his doorway.

Hmmm, that is very strange, he thought, because he did not remember them being there before. He surmised that he had missed them, or that his assistant had left them there. He picked them up, checked them out, and saw that they were sales gifts that had somehow gone unrewarded. Specifically, these gifts were for employees of his sales team for Christmas bonus incentives. He thought that these must be leftovers, and that for some unknown reason, no one on his team had earned these particular gifts. He had given out all the other gifts to high performers of his team, but these two gifts were still here.

"I wonder why these gifts have not been distributed to someone on my staff," Mr. Lathrop spoke aloud to no one. He was puzzled as to what the reason was that caused the gifts to be in his office on this Christmas Eve.

"They are too expensive to just leave here," Mr. Lathrop said as he continued the conversation with no one. He thought about how he should give them to someone who deserved them; he picked them up and placed them both in his briefcase.

Out the door he went, turning off the light, and closing the door behind him.

Mr. Lathrop was going to slip out the side exit and down to his car parked in the executive parking lot, but he thought about how he wanted to advise Walter that he was leaving and to wish him a merry Christmas. He liked the little, serious man, and thought how he was such an interesting and unique character. He had grown quite fond of him over the years. Therefore, instead of the executive exit way, Mr. Lathrop made his way to the main passenger elevators and hustled his way to make it home to face the wrath of his wife.

"BRIINNNGGG! BRINNNGGG! BRIINNNGGG!"

The sounding of the alarm startled Walter P. Thrump out of his Christmas-induced dazes and he quickly moved into action mode. He immediately pushed the buttons on the alarm panel. He identified, and then found, the cause of the alarm to be one of the vibration sensors on the rooftop of the north tower of the building. He checked the television cameras for that location and did not see anything there. He panned the tilt and zoom of the camera in and out, but the camera did not pick up anything except a little drizzle of snow and an eerily quiet picture of the rooftop.

Walter knew that he would have to go to the location to check it out in person.

He lived for this kind of action!

In earnest, he logged the incident in his security logbook and glanced at the clock on his desk so that he could accurately log the time.

This was one of the times that he wished he owned a watch.

Walter keyed the microphone on his two-way radio and called out, "Come in Officer Hall, this is Sergeant Walter P. Thrump."

"Go ahead, Sergeant Thrump."

"I have an alarm on the north tower rooftop vibration sensor. I am going to check it out in person. The camera is negative on any activity."

"Do you want me to come over and go with you? I can pull Officer Mendez out of his break if you need me."

"Negative, I suspect it is just the wind since the camera shows no activity."

"Roger the info, Sergeant Thrump, but please be careful. There is a strong wind tonight. Keep me posted via the radio."

Walter was in his glory. There was no way that he required any backup officers. He lived for these types of moments, when there might be some type of action! God help, the criminal who decided to run afoul of the fearless and brave Sergeant Walter P. Thrump!

"Roger. I will stay in radio contact, and I will call you as soon as I check the situation. Sergeant Walter P. Thrump is out."

Walter strapped the two-way radio to his belt. He then put the "out on rounds" sign up on the security desk, grabbed his hat and coat from the security closet, and pulled the long, high powered flashlight from the tour kit. He was ready, and he confidently strode to the service stairs for the north tower. A diligent security officer never used the elevator! Only the stairs! Becoming stuck in an elevator was a potential when using the elevators and a stuck security officer is an ineffective officer.

He began the long climb to the north tower rooftop. One lung, sixty-five years old, no teeth, but tough as nails. That was Sergeant Walter P. Thrump.

Mr. Lathrop came out of the lobby elevator and expected to greet Walter at the security desk, but he was surprised to see the "out on rounds" sign posted on the desk. He looked at his watch and he noted that it was five minutes to one in the morning on Christmas Day. He shuddered at the thought of how badly Mrs. Lathrop was going to let him have it. He was slightly disappointed at missing the little security officer, but made his way to the front door when he suddenly remembered the gifts that he had placed into his briefcase.

Mr. Lathrop stopped for a moment, thought about it, and then set his case down on the lobby floor. Who better, then Walter P. Thrump and Mrs. Thrump to receive a surprise gift? He thought he had mentioned a wife to him once or twice, so these two gifts would work out perfectly! Two were better than just one, that was for sure!

Mr. Lathrop opened his case, pulled the two gifts out, walked over to the large Christmas tree in the lobby, and carefully placed them under the tree. He then went over to the front desk; he picked up a pad of paper and tore off one piece. Taking a pen, he wrote on the paper, "Walter, look under the Christmas tree for two gifts for you and Mrs. Thrump. Have a happy Christmas." He signed it, "a visitor, and admirer from the rooftop."

Mr. Lathrop smiled, laughed at his witty signature, and placed the paper on the security desk, right next to the logbook that Walter had just filled out. He then decided that the front walks could be filled with snow and ice and he should go back out the covered executive exit way. He turned, and he walked back in that direction and he went bravely to face the wrath of his wife.

Meanwhile, Walter P. Thrump, one lung and all, had finally climbed the long staircase leading to the north tower rooftop door. Gasping for breath, Walter grabbed his chest and deeply sucked in some air. He took out his flashlight, turned it on, and checked it for intensity. As he reached for the rooftop door, he gulped some extra air, pulled his radio off his belt, and keyed the microphone, "Come in, Officer Hall, this is, Sergeant Walter P. Thrump."

"Go ahead, Sergeant Thrump. This is, Officer Hall."

"I am on the rooftop and about to head out onto the roof to check out the alarm. I will keep you posted."

"Roger."

"Sergeant Thrump out."

Walter P. Thrump followed the security protocol exactly. His radio procedures were by the book and he took this all very seriously. He was a former United States Navy radioman and a ham radio operator, and he knew his radio pro-words and pro-signs! As he went to open the door and head out on the rooftop, there was not any fear or apprehension at all about what he may or may not find.

Sergeant Thrump was fearless and one tough little cookie.

He put his hand on the door, turned the knob, and stepped out on the roof, thirty-three stories up in the cold, Christmas air.

Chapter Five

That Glorious Song of Thrump

Now, you would think it to be strange that there would be alarms and sensors thirty-three stories in the air, on the rooftop of the sprawling Substantial Industries Worldwide LLC headquarters, but this was Substantial Industries! Everything they manufactured, produced, or sold was the best and without question, the top of the line, and was always over the top.

There is no room for halfway or middle of the road for Substantial; it was not acceptable.

Therefore, having roof sensors for vibration sensing, thirty-three stories in the air would be the normal thing to do. After all, even the coffee makers on the floors in the employee break rooms were made of a solid cast iron, and the coffee cups were solid stainless steel. No room for cheap, flimsy, foam, or paper cups, at Substantial Industries Worldwide, LLC!

It all fit the famous theme of the company slogan, "When the wimpy stuff just will not do the job, then go Substantial!"

No matter whom it was that decided to break into the headquarters building by landing on the rooftop, thirty-three stories in the air, then Substantial Industries would be ready for them, and so would be the faithful, dedicated, and fearless, Sergeant Walter P. Thrump.

Walter walked out on the rooftop, and the cold air stung him in the face. Little wisps of snow whipped around his long, pointed nose. He peered with his beady little eyes in the darkness and studied the rooftop from directly outside the doorway. He held his flashlight out in front of him and scanned the rooftop with the light beam. It was not a very large roof; this was actually the north tower above a smaller section of the facility. Besides some mechanical equipment and some blinking airplane warning lights, there was no large array of equipment mounted upon the rooftop.

Walter shuffled out on the snow-covered roof that the passing snow shower had covered with just a slight dusting of snow upon the roof surface. He wanted to be careful as not to tumble down on the slippery roof, so he shuffled his feet until he was able to gauge the conditions. Once he adjusted to the darkness and the roof surface, Walter moved confidently across the rooftop. He flashed his light and scanned every inch ahead of him.

It did not matter that the odds were that no one could be on the roof this high in the air, and that it was most likely the wind, or a sensor malfunction; all that mattered was that Walter P. Thrump was on duty.

He tugged at his hat, pulled up the waistband of his uniform pants, and puffed out his little chest. Walter tapped his large flashlight in his hand to test if it was worthy as a weapon if it were needed to be one, and he was ready. He thought how if this sensor was located down on the ground levels, and that the odds were higher that it was an actual criminal act on his beloved building that he would act just the same! He would take out the criminal or trespasser, no matter who they were!

Around and around, he went, checking every inch of the building and missing nothing. The slightest detail would not escape the eagle-eyed Sergeant Walter P. Thrump.

He walked back around to the opposite edge of the doorway and stopped. He then spotted that the snow along this side of the roof had long, track-like lines created in the middle of the open area. He flashed his light on the snow and walked over to it. Standing above it, Walter tilted his head, studying it for a long time. It must have been the wind, and the way it blew the snow along the roof, in and around the walls and obstacles, he thought.

Walter bent down and rubbed his bare hand over the top of the snowy ridge. It was just a pile of snow, but it surely gave the appearance that something had passed through the snow along the roof surface.

"Very strange," Walter spoke aloud.

He smiled, as the tracks were almost as if two sleigh runners had slid across the rooftop here, some thirty-three stories in the air. Given what night it was—Walter found that to be quite an amusing thought.

"Just the way the wind blew the snow, that is all," Walter spoke to convince his own mind.

"That is all it is."

He stood up and flashed his light on the area once more, and with his flashlight, he followed the path in the snow. The little tracks in the snow continued and then stopped a few feet away from the edge of the roof.

He felt a cold shudder down his back, and he pulled his coat around him tight and his hat down over his ears.

The two-way radio broke the squelch with a loud blast.

"Come in, Sergeant Thrump, this is, Officer Hall and Officer Mendez. We are standing by. Do you require any assistance?"

Walter grabbed his radio off his belt and keyed the microphone. "Sergeant Walter P. Thrump here. All clear here, Officer Hall. It is all clear. It must have been a false alarm. I am heading back down to the security desk."

"Roger, the info. We will resume our normal posts."

"Roger, Officer Hall, this is, Sergeant Thrump securing the roof and heading down now. Sergeant Walter P. Thrump out."

Walter took one last look around, shook his head at the strange snow track, walked through the door to the staircase, and closed it behind him. Down the long descent of the stairs he went, it sure was a lot easier on his lung with gravity behind him!

When Walter finally returned to the lobby security desk, he hung his hat and coat back up in the closet, and immediately wrote in his security logbook all the details of his investigation. He wrote in his typical big, blocky letters, and carefully noted every detail.

Once more, the fact that he did not own a watch caused him some lament, since he guessed at the times, and thought how he really needed a watch to be on top of every detail, during an incident like this. He logged and noted the facts of the incident carefully.

Well, in fact, to be perfectly honest, he skipped the part of the mysterious tracks in the snow. He did not want his superior to read about that strange evidence, think that Walter was playing a prank, and drift from his usual "by the book" professional security procedures.

Walter radioed to report to Officer Russell Hall, and then Officer Mendez. He checked his cameras, then his alarm panel. He also noted how the strange rooftop sensor had cleared three minutes after it came in.

Very strange, he thought, very strange.

He then glanced at the clock and he realized that he needed to perform another building tour. How the night had stolen away from him this evening!

Walter had not immediately noticed the note that Mr. Lathrop had left on his desk, and he grabbed his watchman's clock, moved some papers around on the desk, and then spotted the note as it fluttered in the air, and fell softly to the floor.

The eagle-eyed, Walter P. Thrump knew right away that this paper was not previously there, as he watched it float and land on the floor in front of him.

"Hm, what is that?" Walter bent down and picked it up from the floor.

He read the note, and a cold shiver went up and down his spine.

"Gifts! What gifts? Who could have visited me from the roof?" Walter shouted out in the lobby. He did not hesitate at his loud reaction, since he now was all alone in the giant building.

On the other hand, was he?

He turned around and around, as now Walter was not quite sure what was going on and who could have placed this strange note on his desk. He tugged at his belt, straightened out his badge and uniform, fumbled for his flashlight, checked his brass whistle, and puffed out his little chest. Once more, just to be sure, he looked around the lobby, just to make sure that he was indeed alone. This was turning into a strange and unusual evening, that was for sure.

It seemed as though he was alone. . ..

He looked over at the tree and made his way slowly over to it. Peering around the corner of the lobby, the eagle-eyed Walter P. Thrump focused his eyes under the Christmas tree. Sure enough, there under the huge, sparkling Christmas tree, Walter could see two gaily wrapped Christmas presents!

Walter stopped and smiled; he grabbed his radio and keyed the microphone, thinking that he knew the source of these little presents.

"Come in, Officer Hall, this is, Sergeant Thrump calling."

"Officer Hall here, go ahead," Officer Russell Hall, answered right away.

Walter confidently asked over the radio, "Did you come over here to the one hundred and one building, while I was on the roof, and stand at the front post?"

"Negative. Officer Mendez and I stood by together, here in the lobby of the one hundred building waiting for your orders during the alarm situation."

The radio squelch broke, and the radio went silent. Walter did not know what to say, since he knew that Russell would not fib or fudge an official request, even if he was playing a little Christmas prank.

Walter keyed the radio once more and asked another question. "Did you see anyone leave the front of the one hundred one building or a car pull up in front?"

"Negative, we did not. We thought we saw a car, but it left the executive parking lot. I suppose that was Mr. Lathrop. We may have missed something in the falling snow, but we did try to watch the front door as best we could from here. I am sure the door locked behind me when I left there, Sergeant Thrump. Are you all right over there, do you need me to come over?"

"No, no, no. I mean negative. Everything is fine. I was just checking. Thank you, it is all good here. Sergeant Walter P. Thrump out."

The radio went silent and Walter stood there, not really knowing what to make of the entire situation.

Walking over to the tree, he bent down and picked up the two little gifts. He saw that one gift was marked on the tag in large, block letters, "WOMENS" and the other gift was marked in the same type of letters, but was marked "MENS."

He held the two gifts in his hands, weighed them, and studied them as he made his way back over towards his security desk. The professionally wrapped gifts were almost identical in size and weight. He turned and walked the rest of the way back to the main security desk. When he reached his post, he pulled out his chair and sat down. He then picked up the note and read it once more to be sure of what it had said. He put the note in his uniform pocket and studied the two gifts sitting in front of him on the desk.

Walter reached over and turned the transistor radio back on. It was very strange, but he recognized that the same song, that same version of "It Came upon the Midnight

Clear," was once more playing on the radio.

Walter glanced at the clock on the desk and he made note that it was now almost two in the morning and technically, it was Christmas Day. Walter studied the gifts for a long time, with the song playing away in the background.

"Oh my, the note does say that the presents are for my wife, and for me, and after all, it is Christmas . . . so here goes."

Walter took the gift that was marked, "MENS," grabbed the wrapping paper, pulled at the little red bow on top, and pulled it apart.

There in the darkness of the lobby, surrounded by glowing, fantastic Christmas lights, on this special early morning in the lobby of the headquarters of Substantial Industries Worldwide LLC, Walter P. Thrump opened the first Christmas present that he had received in a long time.

In his haste to see what the present was, Walter tore at the package and allowed the wrapping paper to fall aside. Inside, Walter saw a little black box with a solid, sturdy, wooden lid.

"What could this be? Oh my, what could be inside of this box?" Walter was now very excited, and he was like a little boy, beside himself with excitement as to what could be inside. He pulled the lid off and peered into the small box.

Sergeant Walter P. Thrump, solid, steady, and reliable. He never was late, nor drifted from the proper security procedures as outlined in his systematic security training and procedure manual, no matter what the situation. In his mind, and others, he was a professional, dedicated, and highly trained; he never wavered, without exception.

Well, he was about to drift, just this once!

Upon seeing what was inside, Walter lifted it in the air and gave out a loud, happy cry of Christmas joy.

He lifted from the box, mounted on a small, little stand,

a perfect men's wristwatch!

Not any old watch.

This watch was special. It was a Substantial Industries, Super Deluxe, Whiz Bang, model 2-4X12 wristwatch! Top of the line, with an alarm clock feature, stopwatch, the hour and minute timers, 24 or 12-hour option, digital glow in the dark numbers, a compass, a grid square identifier, a solid, titanium wristband that could deflect bullets, and a top of the hour, voice announcement feature! It was waterproof, nuclear radiation proof, and explosion proof!

A watch, oh my, a watch!

Walter's eyes filled with tears and he could not hold back on the release of many years of missing and bypassed Christmas joy.

All the memories, all the happiness of Christmas in the past, came back to him in a mad rush. He proudly slipped the watch on his wrist and then, alone in the darkness of the lobby, he sang aloud to the words of the song playing on the radio.

He paused just a moment when the song mentioned something about a "Glorious song of. . .." He forgot the words for just a moment or two, and then he suddenly shouted, "Old!"

Chapter Six

A Thrump Family Christmas

Walter dried his eyes, and he recovered from the opening of the gift, and the brief interlude of non-approved or authorized security procedures. He then tried hard to shift back to being the highly trained security officer that he was. He glanced at the remaining box and surmised that it was a women's watch. He felt that it must be a version of the same watch that he received. He knew that he was going to give Mrs. Thrump a thrill, because it would be the first time that he had given her a gift or surprise in many, many years!

This was going to be a Christmas to remember, and he giggled as if he was a little boy at the thought of seeing his wife's face when he gave her this gift and she opened it. He could hardly wait; the excitement was a little more than he could stand!

It was Christmas, and it had shaken him to his very bones, and rattled the cobwebs of lost memories, and happy times out of his very soul.

However, for now, he needed to get back to work. He would need to explain to his supervisor the lapse in his rounds on the watchman's clock, but the alarm investigation would help with that. The rest of the time, as he sat in the lobby, well, he would just tell his supervisor the truth. He was celebrating Christmas once more!

Walter P. Thrump always reported it as he saw it.

Walter performed his rounds with his new watch proudly displayed on his wrist, and he marveled at how his built-in time clock in his head matched his new timepiece.

He could not explain any of this Christmas morning's events, and as he double-checked Mr. Lathrop's office door in the executive suite, he decided not to try to figure out where or whom the presents had come from. He also vowed never to try to explain the strange alarm or tracks on the roof. He was just going to accept that, even for an old, worn out goat, like Walter P. Thrump was, the Christmas spirit descends upon us all, once in a while for whatever reason. He was very content to leave it all at that.

Soon, it was a bright clear, Christmas morning. Joy was all around, and it echoed down upon mankind, and even upon lonely, and special souls such as Walter P. Thrump.

The security radio crackled with the voice of Officer Russell T. Hall, "Come in, Sergeant Thrump, this is, Officer Hall." Walter checked his new watch and spotted that it was seven o'clock in the morning right on the button.

"Go ahead, Officer Hall."

"Sergeant, Officer Martin is here to relieve me, so I have signed off on the logs, and I am asking for permission to hand the duty shift over to Officer Martin."

"Permission granted, thank you and have a very merry Christmas, Russell. Please wish your wife and family a merry Christmas for me as well."

Officer Hall paused for just a fleeting moment, startled and surprised by the happy response and slight drift of "official" radio procedures from Walter.

"You sound happy there, Walt. Maybe, Christmas came to you after all. Well then, I wish a very merry Christmas to you and to Mrs. Thrump too. I will see you on New Year's Eve. I guess you will be working a triple once more?"

Walter smiled and keyed the microphone and spoke. "I do not think so, just a single shift, Russell. I think that I will spend New Year's Day with my wife."

"Roger the info and the radical change of attitude there,

Sergeant Thrump. God bless you, Sergeant Walter P. Thrump. Officer Hall is out."

"Officer Mendez is reporting in for a shift change."

"Go ahead, Officer Mendez. Permission is granted as long as Officer Reilly is there for relief."

"Roger, Officer Reilly is here, and my log is signed out for the shift change. Hey, there . . . Sarge . . . Feliz Navidad there, Sergeant Walter P. Thrump.

"The same to you, Officer Mendez. The same to you!"

Walter sat back in his chair, completed his logbook, and checked all his screens. Just a few more hours, and he would be relieved from his shift, and he could start his Christmas celebration. He looked at his watch and noted the time with a smile. He checked his pocket and felt the gift for his wife safely tucked in there. He reached for the telephone on the desk and dialed his home number.

"Hello."

Walter heard the voice of his wife as she answered the phone.

"Hello honey, merry Christmas."

"Merry Christmas? Are you drunk, Walter? It is not like you to call me while you are working or for you to drink on the job!"

Walter chuckled and said, "No, I am not drunk. I just missed you and wanted to say that I will be home soon. I was hoping we could have a little Christmas celebration together this year. I—I—I—have a gift for you."

The astounded Mrs. Thrump fumbled and stumbled over her words. "You do? You did? Why? I still think you are drunk! What is going on that you missed me? You are acting very strangely, Walter P. Thrump. What have you done?"

To say that Mrs. Thrump was alarmed as to the change in her husband's behavior was . . . a slight understatement.

"I do not have any gifts for you. We have not given each other gifts or celebrated Christmas in years now!"

"I know that, honey. I do not need any gifts, just you. This Christmas is just different. It has been a strange and long shift. Please, you know that I would never drink on the job. Hey, I will see you at exactly three seventeen this afternoon. Time me, and if I am one minute late, then my name is not Walter P. Thrump. Okay? I love you."

Mrs. Thrump did not know how to answer him, so she just blurted out, "Sure, sure, Walter, sure," and she hung up the telephone.

She stood there for a long time while not really knowing what to make of the strange phone call or situation. Gifts, love, Christmas! He sounded so happy. What has gotten into her husband to have him act so strangely?

As Mrs. Thrump stood there, she suddenly felt different. She felt a Christmas warmth come over her, and for some reason, for which she could not explain, she could not help but smile. She also felt more than just a little pang of guilt at her recent behavior. Perhaps she had not been as kind to her husband as she could have been for a very long time, but they were still together after all of these years. She had to admit that although he had his little quirks, he was a good man, a good provider, and an honest, kind soul. She felt guilty at some treatment that she had subjected him to as of late.

In her heart, she had to admit that she still loved Walter P. Thrump. In fact, he was a wonderful man, a good father, and a good husband.

She suddenly remembered an old box in the basement of their home. Mrs. Thrump hoped that it was still there in the dark corner near the furnace. She hustled down the stairs, hoping that she had not tossed the box out in one of their clean up missions of recent years to reduce clutter. Once she was down the stairs, she looked in the dark corner. She was thrilled as there it was! It was still there, the box with her writing on the side that proudly reported the inside of the box contained "X-MAS DECORATIONS."

Mrs. Thrump pulled out the box, opened it up, and removed the contents. She took out the little Christmas tree and some old homemade ornaments that their children had made so many years ago.

Oh, the memories!

Oh, the good times that they had so long ago!

She took out the lights and the snowmen that the children made out of plaster molds. She took out the plastic holly and the candles for the windows. She took it all out of the box and then carried it upstairs. Mrs. Thrump put up the little tree and decorated it with the lights and the ornaments. She carefully set aside the little star for the top of the tree.

Speaking as if Walter stood next to her, she proudly said, "You always put the star on top, Walter. That is your job."

A little tear came to her eye and rolled down her cheek while she remembered all the stars that he had put on trees of so many Christmases of the past.

She put up the holly, and then she put the candles in all the windows. She took out all the old Christmas records from under the stereo system and put a Harvey Crooner Christmas record on the turntable. She selected Walter's favorite album, which was *A Happy, Happy Christmas.*

The hours rolled by, and Mrs. Thrump had not noticed the time. She suddenly realized that Walter would be home very shortly.

In a matter of just a few short hours, she had transformed the little house at 164 Maple Lane in Jersey City, New Jersey into a Christmas wonderland. She felt a thrill as she sat back and admired how it all looked.

Walter will be so surprised!

Mrs. Thrump went to the kitchen, and she carefully set a place at the table for her husband. He will be hungry after working three shifts, she thought. She took out his beer mug and set it right next to the table setting. He deserved a few extra beers for such a special day! Then she checked the bologna supply, and this time she took out four slices, and set them aside in the refrigerator for his sandwich.

In her haste, and wonder to prepare a special Christmas setting for her and her husband, she had not heard or noticed that the telephone had rung.

In fact, it had rung twice.

She may have been in the basement or in another room, but for one reason or another, she did not hear it. The little light on the answering tape machine blinked a happy message indicator. What Mrs. Walter P. Thrump will shortly find out, when she notices the light and listens to the messages, that the first call came in from an area code in Minnesota, and the other call came in from Atlanta, Georgia.

Back at the huge, giant, Substantial Industries, LLC Worldwide Headquarters, Walter P. Thrump had been relieved of his shift. He signed his logbook, and shifted command over to his relief for the rest of the day. His relief for the upcoming shift was, Officer Bert Johnson.

"Nothing to report, just a usual, quiet night and day here, Officer Johnson." Walter gave him the rundown of events.

Officer Johnson was glancing over the logbook and reading the entries from the last few shifts.

He looked up as Walter was putting his coat and hat on.

"You had a rooftop alarm on Christmas Eve, Sergeant Thrump? What was it, Santa Claus up there or what?" Officer Johnson chuckled as he pointed to the alarm entry in the logbook.

Walter stood there for a moment or two and did not answer Officer Johnson right away. He then smiled and said, "No, Johnson, just a little Christmas spirit up there, but no Santa Claus. Have a merry Christmas, Johnson."

"Thanks. Sure. The same to you Sergeant Thrump, the same to you."

Walter P. Thrump stepped out the front door and walked to his old station wagon. He checked his pocket for his wife's gift once more; he put his bags inside the car, along with his lunch pail and his trusty thermos, and dusted the snow off from the vehicle. Walter climbed into the old wreck of a vehicle.

He checked his wristwatch, smiled, and said, "Now, I am really a watchman. I really am."

He knew that he would-be-right-on schedule as he always was, or his name was not Walter P. Thrump. He turned the key, and the old engine sputtered to life, and coughed up a large bomb of blue smoke. Walter let it warm up a little and he put it in gear.

As he rolled away, he thought for just a moment that maybe he would buy a brand new, Substantial Industries Rhino 400 automobile, and finally get rid of this old bomb of a station wagon.

"I bet that Mr. Lathrop could get me a discount. Well, maybe next Christmas. Yes, next Christmas. That sure would set Mrs. Thrump's hair on fire, now, wouldn't it?" Walter said as he turned on the radio.

Of course, the radio would not come on. Walter gave the dashboard a hard bash on top of it, and the radio sprang to life. He tuned it to the same A.M. radio station that he had been listening to all night and all day.

He laughed as the same version and same exact verse of; "It Came upon the Midnight Clear," was playing once more on the radio.

"It seems as if that is the only record that they have," Walter proclaimed with a laugh and a smile.

Walter pushed the gas pedal a little, and he slowly pulled out of the parking lot. Up the road he went, the blue shadow of smoke following behind him, until he disappeared from view.

Many stories in the air, high upon top of the rooftop of the north tower of the Substantial Industries Worldwide,

LLC headquarters building, a little ridge of snow blew in the wind. The wind swirled and chased across the rooftop, and the two long tracks that were clearly visible in the snow now disappeared. The wind had covered those mysterious tracks, along with the footprints made by the boots of Sergeant Walter P. Thrump last evening.

However, what the eagle-eyed, Walter P. Thrump had not noticed in the darkness, was that there were actually two sets of footprints up there, one made by Walter's boots, and one set made by another pair of a man's boots. This set was clearly larger than the small footprints made by Walter's tiny feet. These boots were, in fact, much larger. They began over by the tracks that were in the snow and led near the vertical air shaft for one of the exhaust fan outlets.

Perhaps, the other set of footprints were from the boots of a maintenance mechanic, who had been on the roof, and forgot to check in with Walter at the security desk, before he went up to the rooftop to perform some type of emergency service work.

Then again, perhaps they were not.

The wind blew the snow, and covered up those tracks too, and they were gone forever more.

Merry Christmas, Sergeant Walter P. Thrump.

A very merry Christmas to you and yours.

THE END

Cats Do Not Have Calendars

It was early morning on Christmas Eve, and the weather had turned cold and harsh. Wind-driven ice pellets rained down upon the frozen roads and sidewalks of Haledon, New Jersey. The trees creaked and cracked under the weight of ice-accumulated branches that waved in the wind, and they threatened to break away from the trunks and crash down to the ground.

Christmas lights faintly glowed upon porches and railings, covered in ice and snow, as they struggled to display their colors through frosty coatings. The precipitation changed from ice to rain, to snow, and it was not the kind of day for anyone or anything to be out in, unless they had good cause.

Only the bravest and hardiest of souls ventured out in such terrible weather, and the city was in a shutdown, until the storm decided to pass.

To the old man, this was all part of the game. You see, he was one of those brave and hardy souls. The old man was a true northern New Jersey tough guy, a man who was not going to allow such a frivolous thing as a little wind-driven sleet, ice, snow, or frozen rain stop him. Snow-covered roads, treacherous pavement, and cars spinning as if they were tops out on the roadways was not a deterrent.

The old man had to go to work.

He was outside working in his driveway at four in the morning, scraping the walkways in front of his house at 182 Belmont Avenue in Haledon, New Jersey, and pushing the icy accumulation off to the sides of his driveway. All the time, the old man was warming up and struggling to keep his 1964 Putter Classic model 200 car idling in the driveway.

The Putter was a car that had seen as many miles as if it had been to the moon and back about three times and a little more. Every few minutes, he would drop his snow shovel, and run over to fiddle with the choke control on the dashboard, when he heard the engine sputter and almost stall out. The old car was an adventure to keep running on days such as this.

Once more, some minor obstacles, such as cars that had over three hundred thousand miles on them, never stopped men such as the old man; they trudged on through snow, ice, and cold.

It was a simple time, when families, friends, and neighbors all stuck together whenever times were tough. A time, when people took personal responsibilities and duties to heart, and never said excuses such as, "The roads are too bad out, it is Christmas Eve, and I cannot make it to work."

You see, the old man worked in a production shop for thirty years as a machinist, and he knew if he slipped up, there were many folks lined up behind him to take over his position. The old man had a wife and two children to feed, and a household to maintain.

He knew his role.

A car horn beeped at the old man, and the driver waved as tire chains mounted on the tires of the car rattled and echoed in the cold, morning air. The old man looked up from his shoveling duties to wave back to a neighbor, as he passed by in his old wreck of a vehicle. It was Mr. Redmond driving past, on his way to his shop. Mr. Redmond was the father of his son's best friend, and another northern New Jersey tough guy.

In this old, gritty neighborhood, these folks all came from the same background and mindset. They were gutsy, hardened, and determined. Looking around at folks these days, it appeared as if the mold had not only been broken, but the pieces were lost forever more.

The car warmed up, the windshield was clear, and the driveway was good to go. The old man put his shovel away in his garden shed, and in his haste to head out on the roads, he did not notice that he left a small crack between the two front doors of the shed, just a small crack, only about six inches or so apart.

He made a last-minute check of the back door to the house and he was good to go. He climbed in the 1964 Putter Classic model 200, put the push button transmission in reverse, backed out of his driveway, and out onto the main road, and he was on his way onto the ice-covered roads.

The old man had to go to work.

A city block or two away, an old, stray tomcat trudged on through the pelting snow, freezing rain, and ice mixture. The icy precipitation covered his matted fur in icy runoff that had actually frozen onto the fur under his belly. His paws were frozen, his face was frozen, and he was shivering from lack of food and warmth. He was an orange tabby, or at least at one time, he was. His head looked as if it was three sizes too big for his body. His tail was almost gone from numerous fights and battles with other cats and dogs as well as near misses with cars as he darted through the roadways and side streets on the outskirts of the city. The cat's one eye was scarred and torn-up from a battle with another territorial tomcat, and his face had additional scars and tears from numerous face-offs with fierce city sewer rats in dark corners.

The truth was that he was one ugly old cat.

The cat was a domestic and not a feral cat. He had been part of a family once, a long time ago, and for whatever reason, he was now free for years and years to fend on his own and wander for the rest of his days. Perhaps he had escaped on purpose, or he ran out the door when his master was not looking, never again to return. Possibly, the cat wandered away by accident, and the heartbroken family searched for him in vain.

No one would ever know how the old cat ended up where he was now.

He had faint memories of his human owners, a small child, a family of some sort, and he remembered that it was warm, he had food, and he received love. The old cat loved humans; he was not vicious, nor was he not approachable, and this was in spite of the cruelness of his fate. Somehow, he did not equate his situation with a family of humans who no longer cared about him, or an accident of responsibility. Now, for reasons that no one really knew or cared about, he was lost in this world, a homeless example of how cruel life can be for stray animals.

The only thing that the old cat could find to eat in the last few days or so were some old, frozen chicken bones he found in a trash can. He chomped, ground, and chewed them up the best he could and swallowed them up. His teeth were not the best. Now that the weather had turned so fierce, it was getting a bit difficult for the cat.

Still, he trudged on, another example of a northern New Jersey tough guy. All he was in search of now was a spot to try to keep warm while he rested, and another meal of some kind.

It was Christmas Eve, but cats do not have calendars.

He knew that the weather was rough and handouts were hard to come by. In fact, he could not even find any humans around in his old haunts, who would usually feed him some food scraps when he begged at their doors. In his desperation, he wandered far from his usual circles in search of his goal.

The cat limped on; he was a survivor, a true New Jersey tomcat, who had seen blazing hot summer days and long, cold winters.

This day, however, may be just a little too difficult for the old cat to handle; he may have finally come to the end of the road.

He was not going to go easy, though, not this old cat.

The cat was smart; his street senses were almost frozen, but he was still sharp. Just a few short minutes after the old man had left in his car, the old cat spotted the driveway of 182 Belmont Ave, and seeing the area where there was no snow in the driveway, he turned off the sidewalk, and headed in that direction. The cat's frozen body sensed the warmth on the ground of the driveway from the spot where the old man had warmed up his 1964 Putter Classic model 200. He was desperate for warmth now, and the old cat laid his frozen body upon the spot where the old man had parked the car, in an attempt to gather what little residual heat from the surface that he could.

It was not too much, but it was something. The ground gave up the heat all too quickly, and the cat picked his frozen, tired body up and staggered towards the backyard of the same house. There he spotted the shed door open a crack, and if he knew one thing in his nearly frozen mind, it was that inside meant warmth, and that he would not be pelted with this icy mix coming out of the sky.

He was freezing to death slowly, and the cat had not consumed enough food to generate enough body heat to survive much longer. The old cat squeezed his body through the crack that the old man had left between the doors, and he slipped inside the garden shed. Once inside the shed, the old cat spotted some mechanic's rags mounded in a heap in the corner of the shed. The rags were work rags that the old man used when working on his car. Knowing that the rags offered some kind of bed, the cat staggered into the pile of cloth and collapsed. He was not going to make it much longer if he could not warm up, and these rags were not much, but it was a lot better than any options he had come across in a long time.

On this one special day; Christmas Eve, when the light that shines so brightly came into this world, the old cat was in a very roundabout way, a sad reminder of why the joy of Christmas is something that this tired, old world needs in order to refresh itself once a year.

There he drifted off to sleep in the cold stillness of the shed, but at least he was out of the weather. The rags did produce a little warmth. The old cat stopped shivering, and his body warmth slowly returned to some extent.

The old cat slept, and he slept, while his stiff body thawed.

The snow, rain, and icy mixture stopped in the early afternoon, and slowly, the city recovered. Plow trucks and salt trucks clinked and clanked up and down the city streets. People began milling about, more cars were on the roadways, and the Christmas Eve activities ramped up. The storm clouds moved away and even a peek of sun tried to break through the heavy skies.

The shop where the old man worked closed early for the holiday, and the old man was eager to return home to join his family to start his long holiday season. As did many factories and production shops of this era, the businesses closed from Christmas to New Year's Day, and the shop where the old man worked was no exception. He was excited; this was a season that he very much looked forward to every year.

He stood in a long line of his fellow workers to pick up a Christmas turkey, in which the shop gave to all the workers as a gift every year, and the old man picked up a good one. He had been lucky and a twenty-five-pound turkey was still available! This Christmas season was starting out on the right foot, as the old man shook hands with the general foreman, and he eagerly selected the prized turkey.

"Merry Christmas," the old man wished his boss and many others.

He was in high spirits, and he chuckled at all the other workers who decided that the weather was too difficult for them this morning. They had missed an opportunity to receive a prize turkey such as the old man was fortunate enough to receive.

What a shame that companies do not give out turkeys to employees at Christmas time anymore.

After extending season greetings to his co-workers, and warming up his 1964 Putter Classic model 200, the old man scraped his windshield and glass. He then jumped in the old wreck of a car, and off he began the journey down the road towards his home. The roads were clear now, since the precipitation had stopped, and the holiday traffic was now building with last-minute shoppers and folks preparing for the big day. He stopped for a last-minute gift for his wife at a local shop, picked up a bottle of extra Christmas cheer from the corner liquor store, and he was back on the roads.

The old man crawled his way through the traffic, took some side streets and shortcuts in and around the city, and soon he found himself pulling into his driveway at 182 Belmont Avenue.

He shut off the engine and grabbed his prize turkey, the booze, and the gift from the car. He could not wait to show his family their mutual good fortune with the selection of the fantastic turkey. It was a joyous moment, and the holiday had begun! Once he was in the house, and showed his family the turkey, the old man chatted with them over a hot cup of coffee about the holiday plans and the excitement that was building for them all.

His wife explained that she was preparing a warm beef stew for a Christmas Eve feast, and the old man knew how good that would taste after such a long, cold day. The young children were eager to celebrate, and they were beside themselves with excitement, as all children are on Christmas Eve.

The family had a young fox terrier named Skippy for a pet, and the old man hitched him up for a walk in the backyard after he had finished drinking his coffee. Out in the backyard, the old man noticed how the young hunting terrier sniffed and paid an extra amount of attention to the shed entrance and the walkway leading to the front door of the shed. The dog sniffed and sniffed as though he were tracking something.

It was then that the old man noticed he had left the front doors to the shed slightly ajar, so he reached over and slid the two doors tightly closed.

While walking the terrier, the old man noticed an ice and snow accumulation had gathered on the front sidewalk since he had shoveled it early this morning. He knew that he needed to shovel the snow off of the sidewalk before it was suppertime, and before it froze solidly in the pending nighttime air. He brought the dog back into the house and headed for the shed to grab his shovel.

When the old man opened the doors to the shed, he received quite a surprise as he jumped in his own skin at the sight of the old cat. The cat had stood up and stared at the old man when he opened the doors.

"GEEZ! Ya old Pussface! Ya scared me out of my wits! What are you doing in my shed?" The old man stared at the cat.

The feline meowed very weakly and softly and staggered close to the old man. The cat knew that humans had food, and he had not frozen to death, but he was close to starving to death now. This human was his last hope now, and somehow, the cat found the strength to make it close to the old man. He then teetered, tottered, and collapsed over on his side on the floor of the shed at the feet of the old man.

The old man bent down and examined the cat, as he said, "Man, you poor, old thing. You must have been why ole Skippy had been sniffing around the door so much. Boy, you are one ugly cat. I think you are in bad shape there, Pussface. You must have crawled in here to get warm or to die. Now, that I look at you, it could be both. Cats should not die in my garden shed on Christmas Eve, but then again, cats do not have calendars."

The old man had pity on the old cat.

He scooped him up in his arms and carried him to the back-porch door of his house. He opened the door and carried the old cat into the back porch, and he gently tapped on the inside door.

The old man yelled, "Hey, Joan, make sure Skippy is tied up or with the kids, and come out here, will you!"

The old man's wife came to the door, opened it, and spotted what her husband had in her hands.

"Oh my," she said as she examined the old cat and shook her head in sympathy.

"Skippy is with the children in the living room. Where did you find the poor thing? Somewhere in our yard?" The old man's wife closed the door and stepped out on the porch.

"Yeah, yeah, yeah, I found him in the shed. I went to get my snow shovel, and I found him inside. He must have crawled in the shed. I left the doors open just a little this morning when I went to work. I think he crawled inside to get out of the storm and try to get warm. I don't think he will make it. He is very weak, and he is almost frozen. Hey, please get me some old blankets, and fill those old water bottles we have in the closet with warm water. Maybe he will eat. Could you bring out some milk and maybe a little dish of beef stew? I would hate for this old Pussface to croak right here on Christmas Eve!"

The old man's wife nodded, and she disappeared into the house. She returned with the requested items and the two young children came along. They both had heard and seen their mother scurrying about, and wondered what was going on. After safely occupying and securing Skippy the terrier, the young family gathered around the old cat.

"Please Daddy please. . .. I know that you will not let him die," the old man's daughter said with tears in her eyes. Her younger brother nodded his head in agreement with his older sister's pleas.

"Not on Christmas Eve, Daddy!" The little girl was upset as she watched her father gently place the old cat on the blankets and surround him with the hot water bottles.

The old man looked up as he knelt next to the cat and said, "Cats do not have calendars, Dorothy. We will do what we can, but I am afraid this one is out of my hands. It will be up to God, my dear, little girl."

They watched as the old cat stirred and curled in the warmth of the blankets. They placed the food and milk in a dish on the floor of the porch next to him and watched. The cat looked at them with his sad eyes and he struggled to lift his head as his nose caught a whiff of the beef stew in front of him.

The old cat's will to live was strong.

The old man's wife grabbed a spoon from the kitchen and she knelt down next to the cat, dished out a blob of beef stew, and placed the spoon in front of the cat's mouth. The old cat struggled to open his mouth. His tongue came out, and he licked feebly at the food. It tasted so good.

This old cat was not going down without a fight!

"Look! He is eating! God will not let him die, dear Mum. Not on Christmas Eve!" The young boy shouted because he was very excited to see the old cat eat.

His mother smiled and spoon-fed the old cat until most

of the stew was gone. The old man then held up the dish of milk, while the old cat did his best to lap up the milk until his strength gave out, and he laid his head down on the blankets, and drifted off to sleep.

The young boy leaned over the old cat, and bowed his head as he prayed, "Please God, let this old cat live, let him enjoy Christmas Day and many more to come."

The young boy had great faith, and even at his young age, he had a deep feeling of when he needed to pray.

"C'mon let him sleep now. He needs rest. We will see what tomorrow brings. We have done what we could. Goodnight there, ya old Pussface," the old man said as he led his family away and closed off the light on the back porch. The old man was being optimistic to his family, but the truth was that he really did not want them to see the cat pass on, and upset them all on such a special night. The family acknowledged that they had done all they could, and it was now time to eat and enjoy their Christmas Eve.

Time would tell.

Christmas Day arrived, and it was clear, bright, and a little warmer than Christmas Eve and the previous days had been. It was a glorious morning for a glorious day. The church bells pealed in the distance at daybreak, and the joy of the day shone around.

The old man and the young family had enjoyed a wonderful celebration the night before, and in between festivities, the old man had snuck away from his family and checked on the old cat sleeping on the back porch. It appeared as if the old cat had hung in there, and every time he checked on the cat, he was sleeping soundly. The old man would stare and watch to see his chest move in and out to make sure he was still breathing.

Now that daybreak was here, the old man jumped out of bed and hurried to check on the status of the old cat. He feared the worst and did not want the children to experience the horror and sadness of seeing the poor old cat if he had died during the night.

It would obviously ruin the joy of Christmas Day.

When he opened the door, he spotted a grand Christmas Day surprise! The old cat was up walking around and upon seeing the old man he sat, looked at the old man, and he meowed loudly.

"Well, I'll be! Ya old Pussface, ya made it! You made it, you, cool, old cat . . . merry Christmas there, Pussface."

The cat walked over, raised his back, and rubbed up on the old man's leg as the old man reached down to scratch the top of his head.

The old cat flopped down and purred loudly. The old man then noticed that a bag of empty beer bottles that he had set on the porch the day before, and was slated to be tossed out with the next day's trash, were tipped over and it appeared that the cat had been in them.

The old man stood up. He put his hands on his hips and laughed.

"Now, Pussface, do you have a taste for beer, or are you just thirsty?"

The old man realized that he had not set out any water for the old cat, and he thought that perhaps he was thirsty. He closed the door and headed for the kitchen. As he ran some water in a dish, he thought about it for a second. On a whim, he went to the refrigerator, grabbed a Big Boulder beer, (the old man almost grabbed a Dingleberry Beer, but they are way too sweet) and cracked it open. He poured a little beer in another dish and carried it out to the back porch. The cat once more meowed loudly when the old man opened the door and he spotted the dish. The old man set the beer down and the cat eagerly lapped it all up.

"Well, I'll be, Pussface. You are nothing but a beer loving, old hobo!"

After the beer was gone, the old cat stirred, and he stirred, and the old man could tell that the old cat wanted to leave the porch.

"Wait one minute, Pussface."

The old man went and woke up his wife, and then his children, and he told them all the happy news that Pussface the cat was fine. He even told them how the old cat loved beer! They forgot all about Christmas for just a moment and the entire family (except for Skippy) rushed to see the old cat.

The old man led them all to the porch, where they marveled and rejoiced at his restored health.

What a wonderful Christmas present!

The old man reached down and scratched his head once more and he said, "Merry Christmas there, Pussface. Now, remember we have a deal. I saved your old ass, so you come back in April, and catch some of those mice that get in my garden, and eat my corn before I can even pick it, then they get in my tomatoes, and then they eat all of Mum's birdseed in the shed. Then, we will be even."

The old cat meowed at the old man and rubbed up on his leg as if to say it was a deal.

"Man, you are one ugly, old, cat," the old man said as he opened the back door, and the entire family watched the old cat scoot out the door and disappear into the bright Christmas morning.

The old man watched him run away, and he mumbled, "Goodbye, Pussface. See you in April, but cats do not have calendars, so good luck there, old friend."

The old man recognized a fellow New Jersey tough guy, and he admired his spirit. Gutsy, hardened, and determined; that was Pussface, the cat.

It was the first Saturday in April, and spring had finally arrived in Haledon, New Jersey.

The long, difficult winter had finally come to a close. It had been a cold, snowy, and hard season, and it was wonderful to feel the warmth of the spring finally arrive. The old man was in his backyard working in his garden, eager to till his soil and prepare his small, urban garden for what he could plant.

It was not much; a small garden tucked in the corners of a city backyard, but it was his passion.

He stood next to the soil, wishing it were a lot warmer than it was as he ran his work boot on top of the soil to test the moisture content of the soil for tilling. The soil was still too wet; the old man could see that his boot mark came back too moist to till today.

Disappointed, the old man stood there and dreamt of his garden's potential for summer glory. As he visualized and planned where the tomatoes would go, where he would plant his corn, and where the peppers would sprout, he was startled to hear a loud meow of a cat behind him.

The old man spun around and looked down to see Pussface, the cat sitting there next to him! To say that the old man was shocked at the sight of the old cat was an understatement!

The old man stared in amazement as he watched the old cat pick up and then drop the body of a mouse that he had caught at the feet of the old man. The cat then rubbed up on the old man's leg and purred loudly.

The old man smiled and laughed as he bent down to scratch the top of his head. "Well, I'll be, there, Pussface. I see you kept your end of the deal. Hey, you old hobo, since I cannot till the garden today, what are you doing later? How about we share a beer together?"

You see, cats do not have calendars.

Well, most cats that is. . ..

THE END

A Simple Gift

"Do you, by chance, know a person named Mr. Franklin T. Sterling, twenty-seven?"

I stopped short as I walked through our living room, turned around, and saw that my wife was sorting through what appeared to be the daily mail.

I thought for a moment.

"No, Binky. I am afraid that the name does not ring any bells. Franklin T. Sterling, eh?"

"Yes, well, he knows you. It appears to be a Christmas card that he has sent to you. I would assume that this is a person who knew you from your old, hockey playing days, since his return address shows that he is from Norfolk, Virginia. In addition, he addressed it to Reverend Paul Twenty-Seven Henson. Therefore, this person does indeed know you from your hockey career, but they do not know you well enough to realize that you dislike being called by the title of reverend."

Binky then leaned in for one of her patented stares, looking at me deeply, until I looked up from reading the card, and acknowledged her correct analysis of the situation.

My lovely wife analyzed everything, even Christmas card addresses. She was similar to some of the world's greatest detectives in her quest to seek out clues around every corner. It was part of what I loved about her!

"Yeah, yeah, yeah, I think you are correct, dear Binky. As always, you are correct."

My wife handed me the envelope, and I had to agree that it seemed to be a Christmas card. She fluffed her hair and winked at me because she was satisfied with her correct analysis of the situation.

"Thank you," I said as I stared at the return address.

"You are very welcome, dear twenty-seven. I need to go and check on dinner and my Christmas cookies. I can hear that our children are not paying attention to them. I had left them in charge for just a moment to watch the cookies bake and I fear they have drifted from their duties. I can hear them both singing the theme song from Dinky the Orange Teddy Bear interlaced with Silver Bells from here. My poor cookies may be burning up in the oven as we speak."

"Yeah, yeah, yeah, I guess you better check on them, dear."

My mind wandered back in time to Norfolk, Virginia, as I tried to remember if I knew anyone with the name of Franklin Sterling. I did know a little kid there whose name was Frankie. Hm, I wonder. . ..

The afternoon was cold, and I pulled my old wreck of a jeep behind the small apartment complex, which I now called my home. It was cold; at least for Norfolk, Virginia, it was cold. To the locals, they would call this a cold December day, but I surely wished that it were a lot colder. It was only two weeks or so before Christmas, and I was longing to see a few snowflakes dancing in the air. Then again, I needed to be thankful for any day that the temperature was down below forty degrees or thereabouts.

I disliked Virginia, and here in Norfolk, it was very seldom less than a million degrees with stifling humidity. For sure, it was not my cup of tea.

I was a cold weather guy.

Nonetheless, we do what we have to do in our quest to make a living or earn some sort of perceived success. I had moved up the professional hockey ranks, so I should not have complained. After a season and a hairpin more in Albany, New York, playing for the Albany Flying Dutchman hockey club, the parent team that actually owned my contract made the big call. The scouts wanted me to be a step closer to a call up to the big time. The owners of my contract were the Boston Bears, and they paid me a large sum of money and moved me to a team here in Norfolk, Virginia. I was playing well in the net, certainly holding my own, and waiting for the call to the big time.

For now, I endured Norfolk and made do with the situation.

I climbed out of my jeep, reached in the backseat, and pulled my equipment bag out. I slung it over my back and made my way towards the back door of the apartment.

"Twenty-seven, twenty-seven! Did you win?" I looked up and spotted the little boy who lived about four apartments away from me, running towards me shouting.

"Hey, Frankie!" I smiled at the little boy. I grabbed him as he plowed into me. Frankie was not an athlete, and he was a little uncoordinated.

"Whoa, slow down there, kid. No, we did not play today. It was just a practice. We have a game tomorrow down in North Carolina."

The little guy looked up at me and smiled a wide, broad, toothless smile. I would guess him to be about eight or nine years old, but I never asked him his age. He lived a few doors away, and from what I could tell, it was just him and his mother alone in the apartment. He apparently had no father who lived with them. He was a nice kid, he did not follow sports, but he asked me a million questions about technical things, or other subjects. He seemed to be a very intelligent and studious young boy. I could tell that he loved school, and most likely achieved high grades in his studies.

He was also very curious.

I put my equipment bag down and sat on the back steps of the apartment. I could tell that he was going to ask me a few questions. I did not want to disappoint the little kid. He was always alone, and seemed so lonely.

Sure enough, he followed me over to the steps.

"North Carolina? Is that near where you are from?"

"No, I am from New Jersey. It is not really near North Carolina."

"Wow! I heard of that place. My mother says that is why you talk so funny, cuz you are from there."

You can always count on children to tell you a tidbit of a truthful conversation, not intentionally meant for anyone else to hear. They soak words and comments up like little sponges.

Frankie leaned on the railing and looked at me.

"Well, I do not talk that funny." I tried to defend my New Jersey accent.

The little boy shook his head and said, "A little funny, twenty-seven. You have long hair and a beard, too. You speak funny when you say dog or coffee. It sounds weird. My mom says that you are very handsome, and she would love to spend time with you, but you are stuck on some girl somewhere, because you do not speak to many people. How do you stick to a girl? I never see you with a girl stuck on you. You are always playing hockey."

I laughed, as I am sure his poor mother would be more than just a little embarrassed to hear him relaying this private conversation!

"It is just an expression, Frankie. It is the same as saying that you are in love with someone, or that you care about them."

Frankie nodded and then asked, "How many places have you been to twenty-seven? Tell me all the places!" It was almost always the same conversation with this little boy. He had a fascination with the description or mention of places, cities, countries, and states.

He was a budding geography buff for sure!

I patiently listed once more the names of all the places that I had played hockey in and visited. I told him that my mother and her family were from other countries, called England and Wales. He asked a ton of endless questions about each one. Where were they? Do the people talk funny, like I did? Is it north, south, east, or west? I had made the mistake of telling him that I spoke a little of the Welsh language, and he made me say a few words in Welsh to him and teach him what they all meant.

I was patient with him because I knew that he was lonely.

It was a feeling the two of us shared and had in common.

I think he escaped in his little mind to these places that I would describe to him and imagined what they were like.

When I told him that I had visited and played hockey in another country called Canada, he stared and his eyes became wide.

"Is that the country you told me that is north of here?"

"Yes, it is, Frankie. This time of the year, it is already cold and snowy."

"Is that where Santa Claus lives?"

"Well, I think it is near there, but Santa Claus is even farther north of Canada. He lives way up north in the North Pole."

"Have you ever been to the North Pole, twenty-seven?"

"No, Frankie, I have not."

"I bet you would like it, cuz it would have lots of ice for

you to skate on. The only ice we have here is in my frigiderator."

I smiled because the kid was correct, mispronunciation and all, so I told him, "I bet that I would enjoy a visit there, Frankie. I think you are correct."

"My mother says that Santa Claus does not come to us poor kids. I only get a new coat for Christmas, cuz my mother says that is what I need. I don't have a daddy, and we have no money. We do have a little Christmas tree this year, twenty-seven. Last year, we did not have a tree, but my mother was raised up at her job, so we can have one now. What does raised up mean, twenty-seven?"

"Well, I think you mean that. . .."

Frankie cut me off, as his little mind jumped from subject to subject. "Why do you wear the number, twenty-seven? Why not another number?"

I smiled and told the little boy the truth. "Because, when I first started to play hockey, when I was just a little older than you are right now, my father had a dream about me playing hockey. The number that he saw me wearing in his dream was the number twenty-seven. After he told me that, I took a black marker and wrote the number twenty-seven on the back of my sweatshirt that I played street hockey in, and I have worn it ever since."

"Wow! That's a cool story! I have two dreams, twenty-seven. One is that I had a daddy, and the other is that Santa Claus came to all kids, both poor and rich."

Sometimes, life is not very fair, and Christmas, with all the joy it can bring, also indirectly brings sorrow to an awful lot of people. I felt bad for the little boy, I really did. I searched for some words to answer and comfort him.

They did not come easily.

I stood up from the steps, walked over to Frankie, and then I knelt down next to the little guy. I pushed my long hair away from the front of me, and draped it over my shoulders as I put my arm around him and said, "Well, when I was your age, I had a dream too. I wanted to play professional hockey. I set my mind to it both day and night, and here I am playing out my dream. Do you know the best thing about dreams, Frankie?"

The little boy shook his head to show that he did not.

"Dreams, especially at Christmas time, do not cost anything. So, dream as big as you can, for as long as you want, whenever you want." His face broke into a wide smile, and he jumped up and down in glee.

"Dreams are for free, twenty-seven. I am rich!"

I stood up, smiled at him, and said, "You sure are, kid. You sure are."

"Frankie! Please come inside the house for dinner! Where are you, Frankie?" Frankie's mother appeared on the backstairs of their apartment, as she called for her son.

"I am here, Mom, talking to twenty-seven. He is going to caro somewhere tomorrow." Frankie turned to me and said, "Bye, twenty-seven."

"Goodbye, Frankie."

The little boy ran off towards his mother and I could hear him say to her, "He does talk funny, Mom. I like him. He is a nice guy. I think you are right, he is stuck on a girl, but he is my friend."

"Shh, please, Frankie, you do not want to hurt his feelings now."

I made out as though I could not hear them, picked up my equipment bag, and walked up the back steps. Frankie's mother waved to me as I unlocked the back door, and I waved back.

Our team was on the road, first for a game in Charlotte, North Carolina, and then a stop for our next game in Nashville, Tennessee. I did not enjoy the southeast road circuit. It was hard for me to get used to bugs still flying around in the air at Christmas time. We picked up two highly coveted road wins, so the team was in good spirits. While I was killing time in Nashville, I glanced at the upcoming schedule and saw that we had Christmas as well as Boxing Day off, but we had a game on December, twenty-seventh.

There was that number again!

I realized that I would not be able to get home to New Jersey for Christmas or Boxing Day this year. I slipped out of the hotel room and walked to some local stores that were along the main street and close to the hotel. I needed to pick up some gifts for my mum, my sister, and the old man, as well as Rose, Ronzo, and my other family and friends back home.

I went into a variety of stores, bought a number of gifts, and arranged with a shipping store to send them all back home to New Jersey in time for the holiday.

For some reason, I wandered into a bookstore that was on the same street. As I browsed around the merchandise, I spotted a large book on the shelf titled *Maps of the World, Geography of Far-Off Lands, and Places.* I picked it up, and it was fascinating. It had full-color maps and details of the United States, Africa, and Asia, in fact, the entire world. My eyes stopped when I landed on a chapter all about Canada. I knew a certain little boy who would love this book. I plunked down the cash, had the clerk gift-wrap it for me, and I was off.

When I returned to Norfolk, it was late on Christmas Eve afternoon. I had a quiet night planned. After sharing dinner with some teammates and sipping a few beers, I returned to my little apartment.

These were the lonely times. Spending Christmas alone while on the road is a bit rough.

After dark, when Christmas Eve settled upon all the land, I picked up the gift of the book, and placed it inside of a larger box. I also had picked up three magnets, which were the kind of magnets that you stick on metal surfaces to hold up notes. One was a magnet depicting North Carolina, one was a New Jersey magnet, and the last one depicted the state of Tennessee. I placed them in the box along with the book, wrote out a label, and stuck it on the box.

The label said, "To Frankie, from the North Pole." I walked over to the back door of Frankie's apartment and placed the box next to the back door.

A few days after Christmas, I pulled my old jeep into my parking space behind the apartment complex, and I spotted out of the corner of my eye, Frankie running towards me shouting, "Twenty-seven! Twenty-seven! Look!"

Sure enough, he held the book in his one hand and the magnets in the other. The smile on his face was worth more than a million dollars. A ten dollar and twenty-five cent book and a few dollar store magnets, in exchange for a million-dollar smile, on a small boy's face at Christmas time. Not a bad trade-off at all.

"Santa does come to poor kids. Look, he brought me a book about the world, and some magnets of faraway places. Even one that is from where you come from! They are cool, they stick on metal."

"No kidding! Well, I guess those dreams were for free there, kid. Please sit and show me."

We sat on the back steps for a few hours, as Frankie once again made me point out in his book and tell him about every place I had ever traveled to or visited.

A simple gift is sometimes the best. Be it a gift of time, or a gift of hope, or in some cases, a gift of direction.

I came back from an extended road trip one day in February and found a note in my mailbox at my apartment. I opened it and read the words:

"Thank you, number twenty-seven, for spending time with my son Frankie. Due to unfortunate circumstances, we had to move out suddenly, and I regret that you were not home for us to say goodbye. I wish that you could know how much you touched his life with that book, the magnets, and with your time. I wish that we all could have become closer friends."

It was signed, Frankie's mom.

I never saw them again.

I opened the Christmas card, while I stood in the living room, and began to read a note inside of the cover of the card aloud:

"Dear Reverend Henson,

It took me a long time to track you down, but it was easier when I discovered that after you retired from playing professional hockey, you became a Lutheran minister.

I must tell you that I am not at all surprised by your choice of professions. I do not know if you will even remember me, but I surely do remember you. What I did not remember, my mother was able to fill in for me.

I have a long, overdue thank you that I wanted to convey to you. I want to thank you for the Christmas gift that you gave me so long ago of that book of maps and geography. It is a treasure that I still have to this very day.

What you may enjoy knowing is that your simple gift set me off on a lifelong adventure, of not only visiting all the places of the world but also teaching about them. I also want to thank you for those magnets of the states. They still hold up notes on my refrigerator to this day. Whenever I look at them or pick up that book and glance through it, I think of you.

This past year, I received a promotion to the position of Director of Geographic Studies in my career as a professor at the University at Virginia Highlands. It was your simple Christmas gift of so long ago that inspired me to dream. Because, I know that the best thing about dreams, especially at Christmas time, is that they do not cost anything. So, dream as big as you can, for as long as you want, whenever you want.

Thank you, number twenty-seven for the most important gift of all.

Thank you for teaching me to dream.

Merry Christmas to you and your family, and thank you again for your gifts of the book, dreams, magnets, and most importantly, the gift of yourself.

Respectfully,

Professor Franklin T. Sterling,
Director of Geographic Research,
The University at Virginia Highlands."

I closed the card and smiled.

I never knew that his real name was Franklin.

THE END

Epilogue

Christmas, glorious Christmas. It is that magnificent time of the year that steals our hearts with the captivation and the lure of happy times, twinkling lights, magical sleigh rides, and gifts of hope, joy, and peace. The days after Christmas inevitably bring that deflated feeling. That sad feeling that after all the planning, all those songs, all that food, all those shopping trips, all those horrible, rude, jokes told by our drunken Uncle Joe, all that preparation, and in many cases, all the money that was spent—it all went by in a flash.

Now it is over, and we have to wait an entire year for the glorious Christmas to return.

On the other hand, do we?

As the jingle bells no longer jingle, the twinkling lights dim and fade, the music no longer sings happily to us of sleigh rides in the snow, and the wrapping paper ends up in a trash can. What do we have left?

It is simple; we still have hope, joy, and peace.

"It was Christmas, and it had shaken him to his very bones, and rattled the cobwebs of lost memories, and happy times out of his very soul."

Paul John Hausleben

24 December 2012

About Steven Michael McMillan

Steven Michael McMillan was born and raised in Elgin, Illinois outside of Chicago. There as a young boy, he knew right away that his dream was to be a musician, when he had an epiphany while listening to Pink Floyd's Dark Side of the Moon recording. He relocated as a young man to Charlotte, North Carolina, and pursued his musical career playing in various bands, and writing and performing music. An accomplished bass guitar player and incredibly talented multi-instrumentalist, Steve also can play acoustic and electric guitar, some piano, and many other instruments. Seeking fame and fortune, he packed up his instruments and along with some musical friends, he moved to Atlanta, Georgia to expand his musical opportunities. There he met the gal of his dreams, who became a vocalist in their band! Together, they began making all kinds of wonderful music, from progressive rock to atmospheric rock and many genres in between. The rest is, of course, history. Steve also works for a construction company restoring historical properties in Atlanta in between strumming his collection of guitars. He is an avid fan of the Chicago Cubs and the Carolina Panthers, and painfully admits under extreme duress and multiple injections of truth serum that he knows the author of this book. Mr. McMillan, along with his lovely wife, Lydia, and their two dogs, currently make their home in Atlanta, Georgia.

ABOUT THE AUTHOR

If you ask Paul John Hausleben, he will tell you that he is not an author, he is just a storyteller. His mission is to continue to write and tell stories to warm your heart, make you laugh, and sometimes make you cry, just a little. Most of all, he deals in memories, and helps you to remember the good times of your own life, and the special people who touched you along the way. Paul was born and raised in Paterson, and then nearby Haledon, New Jersey, and began writing at an early age. He revisited a writing career later in his life, and he now is the author of a number of novels, compilations, short stories and audio and video works. Most of his work touches upon nostalgic remembrances of simpler times, and tells the stories of heartfelt, humorous, and special human relationships. Other than writing, among many careers both paid and unpaid, he is a former semi-professional hockey goaltender, a music fan and music reviewer, an avid sports fan, photographer and amateur radio operator. He now resides in Somewhere, U.S.A., but his heart always remains along Belmont Avenue in good old Paterson, and Haledon, New Jersey.

Other books by Mr. Hausleben that you also will enjoy

The Time Bomb in The Cupboard and Other Adventures of Harry and Paul.

The Night Always Comes, Another story from the Adventures of Harry and Paul.

Reunion, A sequel to the Night Always Comes and Another story from the Adventures of Harry and Paul

The Autumn Collection

Crows on a High Wire

The Miracle Tree, Another story from the Adventures of Harry and Paul

The Summer Collection

And many others

Coming soon?

You may contact us via email at ctte27@gmail.com

www.ingramcontent.com/pod-product-compliance
Lightning Source LLC
LaVergne TN
LVHW020708110826
845149LV00012B/2156

* 9 7 8 0 9 8 8 6 3 3 6 4 3 *